KALEIDOSCOPE
Endorsements

This book will keep you up until 2:00 a.m. reading it. It's that good. The story pulls you in from the moment you read the first chapter, and you will want all of your friends to read it so you can process what just happened together. Do yourself a favor and put this on your "must-read" list.

SARA HEY

"Sandy Clements takes readers on a roller coaster of a ride in her debut suspense novel! From the moment you begin reading, there is constant action taking you from page to page. I found *Kaleidoscope of Secrets* kept me on my toes and kept me reading all the way until the end! Now, I need more! "

BIANCA BINGOCHEA

In *Kaleidoscope of Secrets* by Sandy Clements, art appraiser Mia Graham discovers a web of crime beneath her family's antiquities-import company. Her accomplished and beloved grandmother is not who she thought she was. To shield the lives of her loved ones, Mia must join a murderous criminal enterprise.

I enjoyed the surreal contrast between a high-society art auction gala and a ruthless crime operation, as well as the intriguing, accelerating developments.

JENNIFER EVANS

I just finished reading *Kaleidoscope of Secrets* and have to say I thoroughly enjoyed it! Loved the characters and the story line so much that I had a hard time putting it down and couldn't wait to find out what would happen next. The characters, places and events all came to life on the pages of this wonderful novel. Looking forward to reading more by this new author! Bravo – well done!

LINDA MYERS

Kaleidoscope of Secrets is A stimulating suspense story with creative and captivating characters. I'm looking forward to reading future novels written by this new author, Sandy Clements

PEGGY NANCE

After the death of her parents, Mia and her abuela take different paths to dealing with the aftermath. Their secrets thrust Mia into a life-or-death battle for the truth. This family thriller pits two accomplished and ambitious women against each other: one who has earned her influence and one who will kill to keep hers. I was hooked on the mystery and battles until the riveting end.

Sandy Clements writes with the accessibility of Lisa Wingate and the punch of Stieg Larsson. This debut novel introduces a new and powerful story teller, and I will definitely be reading *Kaleidoscope of Secrets* again.

SHELLY HAFERNIK

Pull up a chair and make yourself comfortable. Ms. Clements will carry you through A tale of sparkling discovery that includes mystery, family secrets, and dangerous choices. Put your eye to the kaleidoscope's lens and the journey that emerges will captivate you.

MARJORIE BRODY, Author of the award-winning psychological suspense, *Twisted*

Great suspense novel, with a clever heroine who carries herself with integrity. You're cheering her on all the way to the surprise ending. Sandy Clements has a gift of concrete imagery, making the story come to life.

CINDY LINK

KALEIDOSCOPE OF SECRETS

A NOVEL

Sandy Clements

To Judith,
Enjoy the adventure!
Sandy

StoryTell

Copyright © 2023 by Sandra K. Clements

First Printing, October 2023

All rights reserved. No part of this book may be reproduced in any form or by any electronic or mechanical means, including information storage and retrieval systems, without permission in writing from the publisher, except by a reviewer who may quote brief passages in a review.

This is a work of fiction. Names, characters, places, and incidents either are the product of the author's imagination or are used fictitiously. Any resemblance to actual events, locales, or persons, living or dead, is entirely coincidental.

Published by StoryTell, Chicago, IL

First Printing, October 2023

Printed in the United States of America

TO MRS. JACKSON,

My fourth-grade teacher whose encouragement

has brought me to this moment

With no warning, life pivots,

exposing weakness and tempting strength to show itself.

—Anonymous

CHAPTER 1

Wednesday, September 12
Present Day
Chicago, Illinois

WHILE IT HELD NO REAL VALUE, it was her ritual. Mia walked away from the adjoining gravesites of her parents, now brightened by hibiscus flowers, feeling no less torment than when she arrived.

She zipped her jacket, hoping to stop the bite of the Illinois fall morning. Her jeans clung to her legs, damp from the wet grass. Goosebumps traveled the length of her body as a sharp gust of wind ushered in a mist of rain. It seemed too early for the change of temperature. She raised the hood on her jacket and picked up her pace, making her way toward the pretentious iron gates that guarded the serene grounds.

Her phone buzzed. It was 7:00 a.m. sharp.

"Hello, Grandma."

"*Buenos días, Mia. ¿Cómo estás?*"

"I'm fine. Just leaving the cemetery." Mia worked to sound cheerful.

"How are you, really?"

"I'm fine," Mia repeated. "Focusing on the future. Isn't that what you always say?"

"Fair enough. Are you still coming by?"

"Yes, at eight."

"Perfect. I have an appointment with the new director of Homeland, Damien St. Clair. It shouldn't take long. Oh, I see him now. Got to go."

Mia smiled and slid her phone back in her pocket. The traffic on Clark had picked up and cabs dotted the street, but none seemed to notice her. Any other day, Mia would simply walk the two miles to her apartment, but with her packed schedule, taking a taxi made more sense. A half block down, a cab's light illuminated. If she hurried, she could get there in time. She watched a passenger exit the vehicle. Mia jogged up the sidewalk, glad she had opted for tennis shoes this morning. She saw the cabbie eye her in his rear-view mirror. He waited. She slid into the warm car as the driver turned and flashed his crooked teeth in an unreserved smile.

"Good morning, miss." His heavy accent nearly camouflaged the words. "Where to?"

"One East Delaware Place, please."

He turned the car in the direction of her downtown apartment. Her neck and shoulders ached, perhaps from the cold or, more likely, from the weight of her secret. For more than a decade she had carried the guilt. Carried the regret. And it had cost her.

She'd refused to talk with a pastor or a counselor, despite opportunities to do so. They didn't need to know. But she did want to confess to her grandmother. But the time never seemed right.

For nearly fifteen years, the time never seemed right. The thought sounded absurd in her head.

She considered the outcome of her confession. Would her grandmother look at her with hate or forgiveness? No matter how many times she played out the scenario in her head, she never could be sure what her grandmother's reaction would be. But, regardless, this Sunday, at dinner she would broach the subject with her grandmother. It was a risk. A huge risk. All the same, she would bring up the subject and see where it went.

She settled into the warmth of the car. Her tension lightened as the distance grew between her and the cemetery. She was glad the cabbie wasn't in a talkative mood, and she allowed the scenery to distract her. Joggers and bikers dotted the lake's shoreline, a group she knew well. She'd be joining the sweat clad runners tomorrow before the sun rose. Her prep for the Chicago marathon required regimented commitment. And besides, it was only thirty days away.

Sunlight bounced against the building's glass façade as the cabbie put the car in park. Mia was glad to be home. She dug for cash and noticed her faded jeans were not just wet, they were stained. What happened to the kid who didn't care about stains on her clothes? She shook her head, knowing no one would notice, and certainly no one would care, but she couldn't resist the urge to remedy the situation as quickly as possible. She paid the driver, and Jerome, the doorman, swung open the cab door.

"Welcome back, Miss Mia. Trusting your trip this morning went well?" He offered his bear-sized hand and walked her through the gold-plated glass doors. At the bank of elevators, he pressed the up button before returning to his post. The elevator opened and a handful of people poured out, all heading toward the tasks of the day. She had the elevator to herself and headed to her penthouse apartment.

The sun warmed the apartment and illuminated the eclectic collection of sculptures and framed art surrounding her fireplace. A sculpture of *The Seated Woman with a Shawl* sat to the right. Handcrafted by Francisco Zuniga, a Costa Rican–born Mexican artist and a friend of her grandparents, his style was honest, and she loved the authenticity of the woman in black marble. On the left hung *The Girl in Front of Mirror*. The girl sat alone dressed in a cotton slip. Her makeup covered the table beside her. Mia wondered if the girl was getting ready for an event or simply daydreaming but had nowhere to go at all. Mia smiled at the girl and hoped for her.

Above the fireplace hung her most treasured, but clearly not the most expensive, painting.

A young couple.

An inviting veranda.

The woman lounged in an oversized wicker rocker. Beautiful fern-filled planters lined the decking. A man leaned in, engulfing the woman with his chocolate eyes and captivating smile. The woman's olive skin glowed as she responded to his affection. Mia paused to take in the essence of her parents. Even if it wasn't a full truth, she'd made a personal vow to always remember them this way. Happy. Alive. It was a lie she could live with.

Mia headed to the bedroom, undressing as she went, and put on a fresh pair of dark jeans, a tight-fitting sweater, and riding boots. She pulled her hair back and applied a light foundation, pale rose lipstick and touch of blush.

Her stomach growled, reminding her that she had worked through dinner last night. *Better eat something,* she thought. She grabbed the cream cheese from the fridge and slathered it over a bagel as she hit brew on her Keurig. She checked her watch, wrapped the bagel in a paper towel, and slid it into her coat pocket. Just enough time to make the thirteen-minute walk to the North Shore.

She took the familiar route down Astor Avenue, a historic neighborhood lined with perfectly proportioned ginkgo biloba trees whose leaves were just beginning to take on brilliant hues of yellow. The homes were nestled close together, each with a private gate and foreboding front doors. The colors and shapes reminded her of a monochromatic Lego village, with each brownish-colored building connected but somehow still maintaining its uniqueness. She passed the home of the Murphys and then the Turners and the Strouds. She knew most every person on the avenue from her years of walking to and from school, and to the local bodega to pick up items for grandma. She reached 1246 Astor Avenue, the place she used to call home. The deep brown mahogany bricks across the three-story expanse spoke to its history and grandeur. Mia ascended the welcoming steps to the wide stoop and rang the bell. She glanced again at the time. 7:58. Two minutes early.

No answer. Mia waited a moment and rang again. *Strange. Maybe she's running late from the meeting.* But she couldn't think of a time that had ever happened. She considered letting herself in. Instead, she took a seat on the top stair and pulled her breakfast from her pocket, and her cell phone from her purse. She used the time to review her day's schedule.

From below, Eagles music played, and she knew it was Charlie. She looked toward the basement apartment and remembered the first day they'd met. She'd answered the door and found an attractive, 20-something, man standing next to a sizeable pile of moving boxes. His tan khakis were wrinkled, and his white button-down shirt clung to his chest. A backpack weighted one of his shoulders, and a large duffle sat next to him.

"Hello? Who are you? I mean, can I help you?" She found herself tongue-tied.

His face turned red as he responded. "I'm...um...um..." He pulled a crumpled piece of paper from his pocket and scanned it. "Charlie? I mean, my name is Charlie. Charlie Baker. You're not Louisa." He pushed up his aviator sunglasses and looked directly at her and cleared his throat. "I'm the new tenant for the garden apartment. I'm looking for Louisa Graham."

Over the next couple of years, Mia enjoyed meeting Charlie for coffee dates, Sunday brunches, or filling in as his plus one when his work as a photojournalist required him to attend receptions, and black-tie events. She found his assignments at the *Tribune* exciting, but it was his freelance work and his obsession with cars, motorcycles, bikes, boats that always surprised her. Just last week, he'd given her a sneak peak of his recent photos which included the governor of Illinois with his '65 convertible Ford Mustang, and Otto Friedli, one of the supposed founders of Hell's Angels, on his Harley. As she thought of Charlie now, a warm smile spread across her face. She hoped their paths would cross today.

By 8:05, her grandmother still hadn't arrived. As much as Mia enjoyed visiting with her grandmother, she would have to make today's visit short. Mia drank the last of her coffee, wrapped up the remainder of her bagel, and dialed her grandmother.

On the fourth ring, she answered.

"Hola, Mia. I'm sorry I'm running late."

"You sound out of breath. Is everything okay?"

"Just rushing a little. My meeting ran long, and I took a slight detour coming back."

"How did the meeting go?"

"Oh, St. Clair, he was nice enough. He tends to ramble on a bit, but we should get along just fine. I shouldn't...um."

"Grandma, what is it?"

"The sun is in my eyes. I need to cross the street. Hold on a second. That's odd."

"Grandma?" A tingle ran the course of Mia's spine as she sensed a change in her grandmother's tone. "Are you sure everything is okay? Maybe you should grab a taxi or call Sebastian. I can call him for you if you'd like."

"Oh, it's nothing. I shouldn't be long. Now tell me all about... hold on a minute. What is he doing? Well for heaven's sake."

"What?"

"He's coming awfully fast. Surely, he's..."

"Grandma, what's going on?" The sound of her grandmother's shoes against the pavement intensified. It reminded her of the clacking of horse hooves in a parade. Louisa was breathing hard. Mia stood and could feel the hair on her neck do the same.

Louisa didn't respond. Mia heard a dense thwack. It sounded like a prize fighter landing a knockout punch. A hollow cry was followed by the sound of air escaping from Louisa's lungs. Time seemed to stand still. Mia heard a second impact and the groans that joined it.

"Grandma. What happened? Are you all right?"

"Mia," she said in a shallow whisper. "Mia." Her voice barely audible.

"Grandma, talk to me. Where are you? Grandma?"

"Help me," Louisa said in a gravelly voice. "Help me, please." She groaned.

"Oh God, where are you, Grandma? Someone help her." She screamed the words to no one and anyone. She could hear Louisa's labored breathing and possibly footsteps. She shoved the phone tighter to her ear. Yes, she could hear crunching. Possibly heavy boots grinding against loose pebbles on the pavement. The steps grew louder. "Is anyone there? Can you hear me?"

"Louisa Hernandez-Graham," the stranger's voice was low and determined. "You've been warned. My boss expects your cooperation. Do you understand?"

Mia plugged her left ear to try and drown out any noise from the street. What she heard on the other end sounded like the moan of a ghost in a Halloween movie.

"Grandma." She screamed. Nothing. "Is anyone there? Can you help her? Please, please pick up the phone."

A loud cracking sound caused her to pull her cell from her ear and stare directly at it as if it would give her answers. When she put the phone back to her ear, there was only silence. She stood frozen on the stoop, tears streaming from her eyes.

CHAPTER 2

MIA STRUGGLED TO BREATHE. She pressed the phone tightly against her ear, but there was only silence. She redialed and begged her grandmother to answer. Nothing. Another attempt. Still nothing.

Mia stood paralyzed as Charlie came flying from his basement apartment, his hair disheveled and his glasses hanging tepidly from the top of his head. "Mia. Mia, what is it?" he shouted as he took the last three steps all at once.

She looked directly at him but did not speak. Barely breathing, she strained her mind to make sense of the last ninety seconds.

"Mia. Look at me. What is wrong?" Charlie frantically looked around. First at her, then the street, and then the brownstone. "What is it?" His hands waved in question.

Mia looked to the ground as if trying to remember how to formulate a sentence. "It's Grandma. Something happened." The sound of her voice was flat and eerily calm. Then, without warning, her knees buckled, and gravity pulled her to the ground as if the crust of the earth was shattering below her.

"What happened? What happened to Louisa?" He sat next to her and slid his arm around her shoulders. "Look at me, Mia," he said in a gentler tone, turning her face to his.

"I...I...think she was hit by a car." The words spilled like silent staccatos, and tears trickled down the curves of her face. He pulled her close. The passing seconds gave them time to absorb the gravity of what she was saying. Charlie pulled away and made her look into his eyes.

"Where is she, Mia? Do you know where she is?"

She shook her head. "We were supposed to meet. Here. We were talking and someone, something hit her." Her eyes shifted to the ground, and she focused with great intensity as if trying to find a lost speck of dirt.

"Mia, are you sure? Hit by a car? Mia, look at me." She met his gaze and nodded.

Mia was breathing more steadily now. "Yes, I'm sure. We were on the phone and it sounded as if she was hit by a car. I heard her groan. She's hurt, Charlie." The reality of her words began to sink in. "Oh, dear God. She's hurt."

She stood and looked at a now bewildered Charlie. "Get me a taxi," she told him. "I need to find her."

They headed down the stairs and Charlie whistled loudly for a cab. A nearby driver in need of a fare heard the shrill summons, giving Charlie a wave out his window as he pulled a sharp U-turn. While the cab made its way to them, Charlie ran to grab his wallet and phone and returned as the cab pulled up to the curb.

"Where to?"

Mia and Charlie looked at each other. "I don't know where she is," Mia said. "She was walking home from a meeting."

"Where was the meeting?"

"I don't know. I don't know where she is. She has to be close, right?"

"Just drive south, slowly," Charlie instructed. "We are looking for someone who might have been injured." The cabbie followed Charlie's instructions driving up and down the adjoining streets for fifteen minutes, their necks straining for any sign of Louisa. They searched the streets and alleys. With windows down, they listened for sounds of sirens and watched for unusual traffic, or any sign of Louisa, but eventually found themselves back on Astor Street.

"Do you want me to keep going?" The cabbie pointed toward the meter.

"Let's just go to the hospital. Northwestern," Charlie suggested. Mia nodded.

"Make it fast!" he added.

Now heading south along Astor, Charlie grabbed Mia's hand and turned to look directly at her. "Okay, Mia, start from the beginning. Tell me again, exactly, what happened or at least what you think happened." She gave him a look. *Did he think I was making this up?* She let it go and recounted everything that had happened.

Mia's throat felt like sandpaper, and tears pooled in her eyes. "She has to be okay."

"We'll find her," he said as he pulled her close. She could see he had questions and was thankful he withheld them. She looked out the window, comforted by his being there, and watched the city pass by.

Kaleidoscope of Secrets

The cabbie jutted in and out of lanes, working to get them to the hospital as quickly as Chicago traffic would allow. At this time of day, the ride would take at least another ten minutes. On any other day, she would have praised his efforts. But today, she needed his cab to produce wings and fly.

The line of cars at the corner of Michigan and Chicago Avenues, a busy intersection at any time of the day, was at a dead stop. No one was moving. *Come on, come on.* Mia willed them to move with no result.

"What's the holdup?" Charlie asked. They were five cars back from the light and there was no movement. The cabbie put the car in park, opened his door, and stepped out. Mia and Charlie did the same. Gazing down the row, she could see white steam rising from two vehicles. There had been a major crash. Mia searched the scene for Louisa, but quickly concluded this couldn't have involved her. This gnarled mess had only just happened. There were no rescue units on the scene.

Using the inside of the cab door as a step stool, Mia could see a crumpled, late-model SUV. It had collided head-on into the side of an eighteen-wheeler. The truck's trailer lay on its side, next to the cab forming the shape of a V. A few other cars sustained minor damage, but the SUV got the worst of it. Mia could see the couple inside. They were not moving. The marshmallow-shaped airbags were deflating and spattered with fresh blood. The semi driver, now out of his rig, stumbled toward the silvery tangle of metal.

"Oh my God," said Charlie, momentarily frozen as he took in the scene. The cabbie muttered something in his native language and made the sign of the cross. Looking over the top of the cab, he told Mia and Charlie he was going to go and try to help.

"No, wait!" demanded Mia. "We…we…I have to get to the hospital." The cabbie looked at her and then back at the crash site. He grabbed his keys and headed toward the lifeless couple.

Mia pressed her hand tightly against her mouth fighting the urge to vomit. She stepped down and leaned against the cab, struggling to remove the scene from her mind. Shaking her head, she could still see the blond woman, probably close to her own age, who appeared to have taken the worst of the impact. "I can't help her," she said aloud trying to convince herself. Her mind raced. *I can't help any of them. I can't.* "We can't help them," she said again, louder this time and with a resolute tone. Then, looking over the car directly at Charlie, she added, "I'm going to the hospital." She reached into the backseat, grabbed her purse, and began on foot toward the hospital.

"Wait, Mia. I'm coming with you."

Charlie caught up with her as they passed the smoking truck that covered half the sidewalk. People were gathering, most simply gawking, but a few came to offer help. She pushed ahead, Charlie in tow, tears wetting her face. She could feel strange looks from the growing crowd as she and Charlie jogged from the scene and toward the hospital. Less than half a mile. Desperate, she prayed she would find Louisa.

The emergency room doors opened, and for the first time they slowed their pace. The woman behind the desk began to speak when Mia beat her to it. "There was an accident involving a sixty-seven-year-old woman—about thirty minutes ago. Louisa

Hernandez-Graham." Mia's gaze pierced through the woman's wire-framed spectacles. "Do you know where I can find her?"

The receptionist raised her finger as if to say, *give me a minute.* She scanned the computer screen and methodically thumbed through the folders on her desk, before looking back up. "I'm sorry, ma'am. There's been no one brought in this morning matching your description."

"Are you sure? Please check again. She has to be here."

The woman gave a fake smile accompanied by a glare and with her brightly pink manicured nails, clicked a few keys on her computer and thumbed through a second pile of papers stacked neatly in file organizers. "No accident victims this morning," she said dismissively. "I'm sorry I can't help you, miss."

Firmly grabbing Mia by the shoulders, Charlie urged her toward the doors. "Come on, Mia. Maybe Louisa wasn't hurt badly or not at all. Try to call her again."

Mia nodded and reached for her phone. As she waited for the call to connect, sirens of an approaching ambulance permeated the room. The doors opened and a flurry of movement caused everyone in the waiting room to pause and look. Two paramedics, pushing a gurney, were met by a three-person medical team. The paramedics shouted information to the medical staff and moved at a brisk pace. They all joined to push the patient down the hallway to the ER.

"BP one hundred over sixty and dropping. Breathing shallow."

"Get OR three prepped. We need to get an X-ray and CAT scan, and someone page Dr. Cheung, stat!"

Without even seeing her, Mia knew it was Louisa. She nearly took flight as she headed toward them. Moving into the mix of people, she landed right next to her grandmother with Charlie a few feet behind.

"Abuela," she called. "Abuela, can you hear me?"

An assisting nurse grabbed Mia's arm and pulled her back as the gurney slipped from Mia's left hand and continued down the hall.

"Ma'am, do you know this patient? Ma'am?" The nurse moved in front of her like a seasoned linebacker and slowed her to a near stop. The staff rolled Louisa through the large, secured doors that were already closing Mia out.

"Ma'am, can you tell me the patient's name and how you know her?" The nurse worked to get her attention.

"Yes, yes, I know her. Her name is Louisa Hernandez-Graham. She is my grandmother. What happened? Is she going to be alright?"

"Your grandmother was in an accident, and we will know more after the doctor examines her. You can help us by providing some information about your grandmother. Let's start with your name."

"Mia Graham. I need to know if she is going to be okay." She couldn't hide the desperation in her voice, but knew there was no way this woman, who could have easily had a second career as a bouncer, was going to let Mia see her grandmother. Not yet anyway.

"I will find out and let you know. My name is Sylvia Patton. I'm an RN and will be helping with your grandmother's care." She led the stunned pair toward the receptionist desk.

Sylvia handed Mia a clipboard with admittance papers. A ballpoint pen dangled from the long, metal chain. "Mia, I need you to fill out as much of this paperwork as you can. Any information you can provide us about your grandmother will help us. Please come with me."

The nurse led them to a semi-private area in the back corner of the waiting room. It was a small enclave with four vinyl chairs and a side table, but still within view of the doors to the ER. Sylvia left them and promised to report back soon. Mia, with one eye on the ER doors, worked to answer the questions. It surprised her, as she agonized over the seemingly endless form, all she didn't know about her grandmother's medical history. Regardless, she answered as thoroughly and quickly as possible, determined to get it done so she could get an update or, even better, go see her grandmother.

She dropped off the paperwork at reception and asked that they get it to Nurse Patton right away. Then, without asking for permission, Mia headed straight toward the large double doors.

AUTHORIZED PERSONNEL ONLY the sign read and then repeated itself in Spanish, *SOLAMENTE PERSONAL AUTORIZADO*. Mia leaned up onto her tiptoes and peered through the small square window. Feeling like she was twelve years old again, she longed for Louisa to be alright.

CHAPTER 3

THE PACE OF THE ER HAD CALMED, but Mia's nerves had not. She paced the tiled floor, working to convince herself that Louisa was in good hands and would be fine. Charlie watched her and urged her to sit. She shook her head and continued pacing. She wondered how he could sit there, so calm. She envied that.

Mia walked to the ER doors, still locked tight. How long would they have to wait? When her path circled in Charlie's direction, he volunteered to get coffee.

"Mia, please have a seat." He pointed toward the chairs. "You're making me nervous."

She folded her arms across her chest and settled into the out-of-the way enclave.

The TV mounted in the corner was set on CHB 5. The morning anchor, Abby Harrison, new to the Chicago market, was the definition of a stereotype, at least to Mia. She couldn't be more than twenty-five years old, had perfect teeth, a slim hour-glass figure, and, of course, perkiness. Mia exhaled. The phoniness of the news media and the people who were flashed in front of the viewers had turned her off to almost everything on TV. Yet, today, Abby provided a tolerable distraction as she chirped about the stock market, the Cubs, and the latest city government scandal. Abby turned to Clint Busby for the weather. "Clint, I sure felt a chill in the air this morning. Please tell us that cold weather isn't already in the forecast!" she said with a high-pitched giggle.

"Well, sorry to say, Abby, there is a cold front moving in and we are going to feel a strong wind coming from the north and cold temperatures. The kids are going to have to bundle up at the bus stop over the next few days," Clint said in a serious voice as he clicked to a live feed of the wind blowing the flags in front of the Marriott.

Mia looked around the drab waiting room and felt alone, even with Charlie there, who was battling to get the coffee dispenser to spew out two cups of strong and most likely overheated brew.

She stood and returned to circling the chairs that sat empty in the center, and watched the secured doors, praying Louisa would appear any minute. *Please God, let her come through those doors, walking, smiling, and just a little bruised.* She rounded the chairs again.

With each circle, a question formed. *What was the future without Abuela?* She used the inside of her sleeve to dab the beads of perspiration from her forehead. Another lap. *What if Abuela doesn't walk out of here? What will I be? A family of one? Whoever heard of such a thing?* Her head pounded from the swirling scenarios. *Stop. Stop it now.* She retook her chair, her thumb scraping against her fingernails, and fought with herself to keep the worst-case scenario from gaining residence in her mind.

She looked at the people who also waited and tried to gauge their concern. No one seemed on edge, like her, and most were lost in their phone screen or silently shuffled about. It was like watching a movie in slow motion inside a stuffy theater. How could they sit so stoically? She gripped the chair handles and tapped her finger to the point of pain. She needed to see Louisa. Maybe, if the ER doors opened, she could blend in with the group and make it down the hall. As long as Nurse Linebacker wasn't there to stop her. She almost smiled at the thought of being tackled in the hallway. While she labeled the plan as a bad one and discarded it, the imaginary scenario reinforced her resolve. A resolve she decided to hold on to.

The shriek of sirens cut into the quiet and triggered nurses to appear from nowhere. The glass doors whooshed open and EMTs wheeled in a patient.

A woman.

Mid-thirties.

Secured with orange straps. Her neck in a brace.

"Prep the OR," someone said.

"BP is dropping."

"Let's move, everyone," Mia heard Nurse Linebacker shout.

Bright red stained the temporary wrap around the woman's head. As the gurney turned toward the ER doors, Mia saw her face. Mia recognized her. The woman from the SUV.

Mia's skin crawled and her body bristled. A deep sense of guilt rose from her gut along with the bitter taste of bile. She worked to hold back a sob. *How could she have just left and not tried to do something?* She watched the doctor as he half jogged next to the woman and shouted to the team to prep the OR, just as they had done earlier with Louisa. It was clear, for this victim, time was a precious commodity.

A second gurney followed carrying a man, presumably the second victim from the accident. He was alert and responding to the nurse. In an instant, the space had been electrified, as if lightning had shot straight from the clouds into the room. For the people in the waiting room, the entry of the victims had created a temporary paralysis, each person suspending all activity to watch the action. And then, as quickly as it came, individual worry settled back in, and they all resumed their positions.

Charlie slipped in beside her and handed her a Styrofoam cup. The heat of the liquid quickly reached her hand, and she nearly dropped it. He offered to hold it for her, but she declined. She moved the steaming sludge to the other hand and gingerly balanced it on her right knee.

Mia looked at him and wondered if she looked as worn as he did. His brow was creased with worry, probably as much for her as Louisa. She found his concerned look comforting and allowed herself to lean against his welcoming shoulder. She breathed in his musky scent and enjoyed the strength of his arm.

"How much longer?" she asked, her question half directed to Charlie and half to herself. "Surely someone can tell us what is going on." She scraped at her nails. "I think I'm going to ask for an update."

"I asked before I came over with the coffee. The receptionist said she'd call when you can go back."

Mia glared in response, but quickly softened. He was only trying to help, and even though she felt desperate, she knew she would have to wait.

His eyes surveyed her, and offered a compromise. "How about we give it ten minutes and then I'll go ask again. Or you can. Fair enough?" His tone was soft.

She took a breath and nodded, appreciating his initiative and ability to find middle ground. His face was beginning to show stubble. He was naturally handsome with just the right amount of wave in his hair. Louisa had always told her that she and Charlie had a natural connection. "He is a good man," she would say when Mia resisted taking the relationship to the next level. "And he is clearly interested in you. Why do you resist, mi bella?"

"I don't need anyone in my life, Abuela." Mia's standard response. "Plus, he is too opinionated," referring to the ongoing feuds that could brew for weeks at a time. Once they had a month-long debate over the ethics of diamond mining. Charlie believed mining of precious stones and gems left the landscape eroded and the ecosystems destroyed. Plus, he took the stance that people in third-world countries were being taken advantage of and forced to work in terrible conditions for subpar pay.

Mia did not back down. "Responsible mining is not only possible, but actively taking place in many regions of the world." She would know. Her father, like his father before him, sold derocking equipment to mining companies in remote regions that not only improved the efficiencies of mining, but significantly reduced damage to the environment. And their company, Graham Mining and Supply, had always implemented fair working conditions for the laborers. She was always happy to remind Charlie that without the mining jobs, many of the people in these areas would have no work at all, and the pay from mining often more than doubled the national average standard of living.

Over time, they agreed to disagree and move on, but she appreciated his desire to find the truth and always do the right thing. He was a good, honest person. And that was the real problem. Good did not mix with the darkness of her past. Her actions had caused the death of two people. How could he, or any man, love someone who hid such a despicable secret?

She drummed her fingers on the arm of the chair. A soft rhythm she found soothing. She didn't know how long she had been repeating the pattern but stopped when Charlie gave her a look and then shifted his eyes to her bouncing fingers. She raised her hand in apology and reached for the flower-shaped pendant around her neck. It had been a gift from Louisa for her thirteenth birthday. She held the keepsake lightly, letting the weight of the diamonds and emerald permeate her fingers. She thought of Louisa and silently prayed, *Please let her be alright.*

CHAPTER 4

MIA SCANNED THE ROOM, anxious for a distraction. Two men in wrinkled trench coats stood visiting with the receptionist. *When did they come in?* She watched the three of them talk, and then the receptionist pointed in Mia's direction. The trench coats turned and headed toward them. Gold CPD shields hung around their necks. Did they know something about the accident? Without warning, she bolted from the uncomfortable chair. Charlie jumped and was barely able to hang on to his now lukewarm coffee. Before he could recover, she was seven paces ahead and nearly to the two cops.

"Are you Mia Graham?" the older man asked.

"Yes."

"I'm Detective Taylor of the Chicago Police Department, and this is Detective Ramirez." He leaned forward and shook her hand. "We'd like to ask you a few questions."

"Questions? Are you here about my grandmother's accident?" Charlie stepped next to her, wiping drips of coffee from his hand onto his faded jeans. Ramirez looked up and gave him a nod.

Taylor continued. "We are investigating the incident today. For the record, you are Mia Graham, Louisa Hernandez-Graham's granddaughter?" Mia nodded.

"Yes. What can you tell me?"

"This morning, at approximately 8:05 a.m.," he read from his notes, "Mrs. Graham was illegally crossing East Scott Street, heading north." Taylor paused to collect his thoughts. "She appeared to be moving toward an alley in the middle of the nine hundred block. Before she could cross and reach the sidewalk on the north side of the street, she was struck by an oncoming vehicle." He concluded as if finalizing a report at a press conference.

"Illegally? What do you mean she was crossing illegally?" Mia looked him square in the eye. "Are you saying this accident was her fault?"

"Well, no ma'am." He cleared his throat. "Well, to clarify, she was crossing illegally, however I do not think that was the leading cause of the accident."

The muscles in Mia's neck tightened and she tilted her head while giving Taylor a glare that asked the next question without her saying a word. He took a half step back and cleared his throat again.

"Ms. Graham, we have reason to believe that this may not have been a random accident. We believe it was a hit-and-run." He let the information sit in the air. She did not respond and mulled the words "hit-and-run" through her mind. Detective Taylor waited and then continued. "I need to ask. Do you know of anyone who might have wanted to harm your grandmother? Had she received any threats lately? Maybe she mentioned something out of the ordinary?" The questions spilled out in a steady cadence. She looked up at him and then Ramirez, who was touching the end of the pen to his tongue, ready to scratch out her comments on his note pad.

"Harm her? No one would want to harm her. Everyone loves my grandmother." Mia paused and worked to understand what the detectives were getting at. "Are you saying she was hit intentionally?"

Taylor and Ramirez both gave a subtle nod. "Can you tell us where she was coming from?" Taylor continued.

Ignoring his questions, she continued. "Do you know who hit her? Have you arrested someone?" Her mind raced. She needed answers.

"No current suspects, I'm afraid. Which is why we are talking with you. We only know that the driver who hit your grandmother fled the scene. We have officers looking for witnesses in order to determine if this was a premeditated hit-and-run or perhaps a drunk driver or someone who simply fled the scene after realizing what had happened."

"So, you don't know anything? You have no witnesses? No traffic cameras? Listen, Detective, what are you doing to find out who did this?" Her olive skin was now a deep scarlet. She looked at them in disbelief, then at Charlie. *Why are they here wasting time? They need to find out who did this.*

"Can you tell us when you last spoke to your grandmother?" Taylor continued undeterred by her tirade of questions.

"This morning," she said.

"Did she seem concerned? Say anything that may have, now looking back, seemed out of the ordinary?"

Mia recalled her grandmother's panicked state and the man's voice she'd heard. Before she could respond to Taylor, there was a solid tap on her shoulder.

"Excuse me. Mia Graham?" The interruption caught her off guard. "What?" she said a bit more harshly than she had intended. She turned to face a gray-haired doctor with thick glasses.

"Miss. Graham, I'm the attending physician, Dr. Cheung, and am treating your grandmother." He extended his thin hand to curtly greet her.

"How is she? Can I see her?"

Dr. Cheung turned to the two detectives. "Would you excuse us?"

"I don't mind if they are here," she said. "How is my grandmother?"

"We'll step away for a moment and let you talk." The senior detective glanced down at Ramirez and nodded him toward the windows. Ramirez flipped the black cover over his note pad, and they headed toward an empty row of seats.

"Your grandmother is currently unconscious." The doctor's voice was dull, and he kept his eyes glued to the folder in front of him, only occasionally peaking over the black frame of his glasses. "Currently, we are running tests, and we are working to stabilize and determine the extent of her injuries outside of the obvious contusions, fractures, and broken bones. We are monitoring her neural activity and will be taking her back for additional tests to assure there is no internal bleeding. That's all the information I have. As soon as we know more, we'll be in touch." He closed the folder and pushed his glasses back to the bridge of his nose and turned toward the emergency room.

"No, no, no, wait. I want to see her." She gripped his white coat as he turned.

The doctor bristled and faced her as he pulled his arm away. "Miss Graham, I will have a nurse come and get you as soon as you are able to see your grandmother." Then, he turned and moved briskly down the hall.

She felt the room spin, the square linoleum tiles seeming to dance under her feet. Charlie turned toward her. He said something but she did not respond. Words evaded her. Fear, frustration, and anger boiled inside of her. He pulled her close and they stood together, not moving except for the trembling of her body. After a moment, he gently pushed her back and looked her in the eyes.

"Are you okay? Do you want to sit down?"

"I'll be fine," she said as she reset herself. "What we need are some answers."

"I agree," he said.

She looked into his eyes for direction and watched as Charlie's forehead tightened as he began a shift into full-on journalist mode. Usually this was her forte. Research, facts, answers, but her brain had taken a momentary sabbatical and she needed his help to find direction.

"While you wait to see Louisa, why don't I see what I can find out about the accident?" he offered.

"That sounds good. What are you thinking?" she said.

"I'll start by calling the city desk and see if there are updates coming across the blotter. I'll also check with the uptown beat reporter. Let's see what we can learn while we wait."

"I appreciate your doing this, Charlie. And for being here," she said reaching for his elbow as he turned to go. "But I would understand if you had other commitments." Her I-have-to-face-the-world-alone instinct was kicking in. It was as natural to her as the sunrise is to the day. "Don't you need to get to work? Surely someone somewhere needs you out there snapping pictures for the evening edition?" she said.

She watched his face tighten, showing the slight sting of her words, but he was not deterred.

"I want to be here, with you. Work can wait. I'll be back in a few minutes." He turned to go and then stopped, turning back toward her with a slight smile. "And don't you go anywhere." He waited for her to agree.

It only took a slight nod and Charlie punched in a number and walked toward the front doors to make the call.

⇒ ⦀ ⇐

After only five minutes of sitting in the stiff chair and thinking about the lowlife who had ran her grandmother down, Mia stood and began her musical chairs routine again, circling the perimeter of the waiting room with no music, going nowhere in particular. Keeping her body in motion calmed her nerves and cooled the anger that rumbled inside her. She wanted to find out who had hit Louisa. The coward needed to be caught and held accountable. Until she could talk to Louisa, see her, this would be her focus.

Detective Taylor was leaning against the wall near the windows, chewing the end of a stir stick with his phone held to his ear. The sun illuminated his weathered face, and Mia guessed he was probably near retirement. Ramirez, on the other hand, was young, especially for a detective, and Mia surmised he still had a couple more decades before he'd collect his pension. The newbie had nestled into an armless chair, his brow furrowed. He held his black book and scanned his notes while sipping some steaming coffee. Mia composed herself, strode over, and slid in beside him. When he looked up, she gave him a warm smile and turned slightly in toward him.

"Excuse me, Detective. You don't mind if I sit here, do you?" She had his attention. He worked to straighten himself, nearly dropping his coffee and notebook. The black fluff of hair fell across his forehead as he looked up at her. His face a bright pink.

"Sure, Ms. Graham." He cleared his throat. "Did you need to talk to Detective Taylor?" pointing in the tall man's direction.

"It looks like he's busy. I'm glad to speak with you," she said a bit more softly.

"Sure. What can I do for you?" he said leaning in ready to help.

"Well, I been thinking about the information Detective Taylor shared with me. The question is, who would want to do this? What do you know so far about who might be responsible? Was there any evidence at the accident site?"

"Well, Miss Graham—"

"Call me Mia."

"Well, Mia," he said taking on a more authoritative voice, "we are still investigating, but you need to know that these types of hit-and-run are often never solved. There were no tire marks present at the scene indicating the driver did not try to stop or avoid an accident."

"I was on the phone with my grandmother, at the time of the accident. I got the impression that she was…rattled and a bit winded. I felt like something was off."

Detective Taylor sat his coffee on the ground and began taking notes.

"Did she say anything that might help us?"

"No. But after the accident, I heard a man's voice," Mia said, unable to control the quiver that joined her words. "He said her name and then he said, 'You've been warned.' Then the line went dead."

"What time was that?"

Mia checked her phone for the exact time of the call. "Have you found any witnesses? Someone had to have seen something."

"We have officers canvassing, but, no, so far, no witnesses. We will need you to come down to the station and make a statement."

"I'll be glad to, once I'm able to see my grandmother."

He fumbled inside his coat pocket and retrieved a business card. "Call me if you think of anything else and when you're available to come to the precinct. We can send a car to drive you."

"Thank you," she said as she held the card by its smooth edges and turned it over. DETECTIVE PAUL RAMIREZ, CHICAGO POLICE DEPARTMENT 9TH PRECINCT. It also had his direct cell phone number and other contact information. She slid it into the small pocket of her Louis Vuitton bag and stood to go. "Detective Ramirez, may I ask you one more question?" He nodded. "Who called to report the accident?"

"It was an anonymous call. We're attempting a trace, but it is unlikely we will find out who called it in."

With that, Mia headed back to the open area to find Charlie. She spotted him outside the doors still on a call. She glanced at the table where she had left her coffee cup. It was gone and her seat taken by a man who looked to be in his eighties. As she reflected on the news of the anonymous caller, she headed to the dilapidated coffee machine wondering if she should trust it. She hit the button labeled "Dark Roast" knowing it wouldn't compare with the Costa Rican coffee her grandmother had taught her to appreciate. The heat seared through the flimsy Styrofoam. As she blew on it, the receptionist waved her over.

"Miss Graham, I received a call from the nurse. She has an update for you if you'd like to go back." No response was needed. Mia set the coffee cup on the counter. The receptionist nodded letting her know she would take care of it and pointed her brightly painted nail toward the doors. As Mia approached, she heard a buzz and the doors opened wide. Her heart beat so loudly she barely heard the nurse call her name.

CHAPTER 5

"Miss Graham? I'm Sylvia Patton, the nurse on duty. We met earlier." The double doors clicked shut behind them.

"How is she?" interrupted Mia, surprised by her own rudeness. Sylvia offered a patient smile and reached toward the hand sanitizer on the far wall. Mia did the same.

"She is stable, but unconscious." Sylvia glanced at the file. "Your grandmother sustained significant injury when she was hit. Broken bones, including her femur, collar bone, and pelvis, five ribs, and a hip fracture. We are watching her liver and kidney function closely." Nurse Patton walked at a steady pace. "We are testing for trauma to her brain and spinal column. Right now, she is breathing on her own, and that is a good sign. We will know more once she wakes up." Mia wanted Sylvia to move quicker. She also wanted to turn back. They rounded the corner and passed four enclosed patient units. Nurse Patton opened the large glass door. "As I mentioned, your grandmother is unconscious. She won't be able to respond." Mia nodded, but hesitated. "We'll be moving her to a private room in the intensive care unit shortly. You can stay until then." Nurse Patton slid the heavy blue privacy curtain aside and Mia stepped inside.

Louisa lay silent as if she were in a light sleep. Only the cadence of the machines interrupted the stillness of the room. Mia's heartbeat echoed loudly inside her, outpacing the monitor attached to her grandmother.

She scanned the scene as if looking through a telescope, starting from the top of Louisa's head and moving to her feet. The color gray permeated everything. Her face, her hair, and the flimsy gown that covered her. The overhead lights, while dimmed, accentuated the somber color one sees just before dark. Gray.

Mia fought to regulate her breathing. How could this be her grandmother? Louisa was full of life. Tough. Kind. Smart. She had seen Louisa glitter like gold confetti dropped on New Year's Eve, but never a dull gray. This. This gray. It dominated the room, and Mia did not recognize the woman who lay six feet in front of her.

She stayed in place, using the sterile counter for balance. Like a puppeteer with a marionette, she willed her legs to move, step by step, until she made it to the side of the bed. She had never seen anyone in the hospital and never imagined seeing her grandmother here. Mia glanced at the door, momentarily thinking of escaping. No. She could do this. Steadying herself, she inched forward, gripping the side of the bed and holding tight for balance. She scanned Louisa from her head to her feet and then back again, stopping at her hand. Slow tears rolled down her cheeks. One and then another. Mia covered her mouth and wiped away the moisture.

Louisa's blue-gray veins bulged against her thin skin, an IV tube taped securely to it. Mia reached down and gently picked up her grandmother's cool hand. Bandages ran the length of her arms and legs, and a cast stretched from her hip to her knee. A long seam of stitches zigzagged across her forehead and down her cheek. Around her eyes, neck, and arms, gray bruises threatened to burst into deep shades of purple as if to offer a challenge to the gray.

The stillness of her grandmother's body unsettled her. She watched for the rise and fall of Louisa's chest, for any sign of life. Nothing. Mia glanced at the square blue monitor next to the bed. It echoed Louisa's heartbeat and reassured her. Mia concentrated on the steady rhythm. *Louisa is alive and she is tough. She will survive this. She has to.*

The constant beat pierced the quiet and reminded her of the metronome that sat on her grandmother's piano. She listened and allowed it to calm her. Mia opened her mouth to speak but could only produce a strong whisper. "Abuela, it's me, Mia," she said in beat with the monitor's cadence. Mia cleared her throat so she could speak audibly. "I'm here. Can you hear me?" The words evaporated into the air. She waited for the silence to be broken by Louisa. "Please don't leave me," she said as she caressed Louisa's hand. Tears returned and fell like a soft summer rain and landed on the stiff blanket.

Who did this to you? "Abuela, I need you to wake up." She carefully observed the woman who, for more than half her life, had raised her and loved her.

It felt like only a minute had passed when Nurse Patton returned.

"Miss Graham, it's time for us to move your grandmother to ICU."

"I want to stay with her."

"I'm sorry, but I can't allow that. We'll take good care of her and will call if there is any change. You can visit again this afternoon after two thirty. In the meantime, why don't you go home? Try to get some rest. It may be a long couple of days."

Mia stayed seated. Sylvia gently but firmly took Mia by the elbow and led her to the door. "Come on. I'll walk you out." Mia briefly considered arguing with Nurse Patton, and then reconsidered. The woman carried her linebacker build with a confidence that telegraphed her authority. Mia turned toward Louisa and whispered. "I'll be back, Abuela, this afternoon. I love you." Sylvia shut the door and led her down the hallway in the same steady pace they had entered.

"She will be moved to the fourth floor, room 442. I'll tell the nurse on duty to expect you this afternoon. Also, we need to get your grandmother's updated insurance information. Can you bring it when you come back?" Mia nodded and confirmed that Sylvia had her contact information.

"You'll take good care of her? And call me the minute she wakes up?" She locked eyes with her grandmother's caretaker, sizing her up, looking for commitment in her words.

"Of course."

Mia walked, ghostlike, through the double doors and into the waiting room before she remembered—Charlie. There he was. Pacing. His brow furrowed. *He would understand, wouldn't he?* She had told him he didn't need to stay.

"Charlie! Over here!" He turned. Her eyes locked onto his clenched jaw. He was a step past frustration.

"Mia, I've been calling you. Where have you…" She watched him evaluate her, the situation, realizing where she had been. "Is everything okay? What happened?"

"I got to see her," she said simply, avoiding a discussion of why she didn't tell him where she was going.

"How is she? I mean, is she okay? Are you okay?"

"She looks awful. Really awful. And she's unconscious, but for the moment, stable. They are going to move her to another floor. They wouldn't let me stay but said I can see her again in a few hours." The tears returned.

She updated him on everything she had learned, and when there was nothing more to say, she worked to refocus her attention. "Did you find out anything from the *Tribune*?"

"Not much yet. I do know that they are tracking the story and will probably do a full workup. The buzz is that MacKenzie Miller will get the assignment. They expect her back in the office anytime. I thought I'd go see if I can catch her. Will you be okay for a while?"

"Yeah. I'll be fine."

"Listen, if you feel like getting some fresh air, why don't we meet at Ozzie's in about thirty minutes or so? Get something cold to drink?"

She considered his suggestion. Fresh air would be a nice change.

Mia nodded. "Okay. I just have to be back here by two thirty."

"Sounds good. I'll see you there."

He gave her a light hug and kiss on the cheek. They exited the ER and headed in opposite directions.

CHAPTER 6

EVERY STEP AWAY FROM THE HOSPITAL felt like a betrayal, but the wait would be more tolerable at Ozzie's. The smell of beer and fried food met her at the door, and the two men at the bar turned to acknowledge her before returning to nursing their draft beers, both acting as if the baseball games on the screens were of real interest to them.

Mia chose a booth near the back. She settled in and allowed the coolness of the aged wood to absorb some of her stress. A bleached-blond musician casually set up her equipment on the postage-stamp-sized stage housed next to an equally small dance floor. Her crimped hair, half pulled up into a bun, worked for her. She looked like a seasoned performer with knee-high boots and a flowy top but perhaps out of place in a downtown Chicago bar and grill. Mia guessed at her age. Maybe twenty-one? Not much younger than her, although much more youthful.

The woman smiled at her.

Mia wondered what her life might have been if there had been no fire. No loss of her parents. She knew she would not have been a singer. Mia auditioned for fourth-grade honors choir. Mrs. Kline, the director, did not hesitate when she recommended that Mia join the after-school art club. "A much better placement of your talents," she had said. Turned out, Mrs. Kline was right.

"Test, test, test." The words, accompanied by high-pitched feedback, popped loudly through the speakers. After an adjustment to the system and one more test, the bartender gave her a thumbs-up.

"Hey, everyone," she said to the meager crowd. "I'm Julia Moore and I'm gonna share a few songs with you. If you have any requests, just let me know. Going to start out with a classic. I hope you enjoy it." The two guys at the bar turned to check her out, then went back to their beers and the muted TV screens. The lunch crowd filtering into the bar seemed unaware, but it did not phase Julia. Grabbing her weathered guitar, she settled in on a bar stool and music flowed from the instrument. "Desperado." *A good choice for a Wednesday morning*, Mia thought.

The bartender sauntered to Mia's table. "What can I get you?" he said over the bluesy voice of the singer.

"How about two sweet, iced teas and a large order of wings? Actually, let's change that," she said, not sure if Charlie would appreciate the mess that came with wings. "Just give me two of today's special."

"You got it."

Mia watched Julia. Her voice danced with the chorus. The song told of a fading youth and a personal prison of loneliness, and it seemed directed straight at Mia. She thought she knew what being alone felt like. But the thought of being in the world without Louisa, well, that sounded like a whole new level of hell.

Mia's phone vibrated. A quick scan told her none of the calls were from the hospital. She took that as a positive sign. The nurse had assured her they would call with updates or if any changes to her grandmother's condition occurred, so no need to panic. Slightly relieved, she sifted through the other messages. Two were from clients wanting estimates on their collections, one from her boss, Lionel, and one was listed as UNKNOWN CALLER. She sent a text to Rebekah, the wonder woman of an assistant who served the DaVinci Auction House with great enthusiasm and asked her to reschedule her appointments, only sharing that there was a family emergency, and she would touch base later. As Mia was about to play the voicemails, Charlie slid into the booth. Everything else could wait.

"That was quick," she said. "What'd you find out?"

"They gave Mac the assignment."

"MacKenzie Miller. Isn't she the one who uncovered the governor scandal awhile back?"

"She's the one. My contact told me that they are going all in—a full workup on Louisa—her career, philanthropy, her Chicago roots," he paused, "and her family. Front-page story."

Mia recoiled. She took a deep breath and gritted her teeth. "I don't have time for this, and I won't talk to them."

"I know. I already told them you were off limits." She should have known Charlie would take care of this. She needed to trust him.

"Do they have any leads on the driver?"

"The story running through the mill is basically what we heard from that detective we talked to at the hospital. Taylor. Wasn't that his name?

She nodded.

"The CPD said the accident is officially hit-and-run. They identified the vehicle as a newer-model sedan, dark blue or black, based on a small piece of headlight that was left at the scene."

She grimaced at the thought of Louisa being hit so hard it damaged the car and found herself in an angry stare down with the ketchup bottle on the table. Charlie said nothing. When she forced her eyes back to his face, she could see his concern. "Go on."

"No leads. No witnesses. Mac is trying to track down anyone with information. She has a meeting set up with someone from the State Department," he said glancing at his notes, "but that's about it. Mia, you have to know, it's a long shot, finding out who did this." She looked back toward the ketchup, as if checking to be sure it hadn't moved, and massaged her face hoping to relieve the tension in her jaw and forehead.

"Here you go." The bartender set the iced teas and straws on the table. "Your order will be up in a couple of minutes."

Mia grabbed her straw and Charlie reached for her hand. "Mia. Talk to me."

She pulled away and unwrapped the paper. She took a long drink and looked up at Charlie with a controlled determination. "I'm going to find out who did this. I need answers. Someone has to pay. Who hits a sixty-seven-year-old woman and leaves her lying in the street? Even for Chicago, this is just crazy." Her voiced quivered despite her attempt at bravado.

"Okay, we won't give up. We'll figure this out together." He reached for her hand again. This time, she did not resist.

Charlie looked relieved. The lines above his brow softened as he met her gaze. She could hear his words, even though they weren't said aloud. He would do anything for her and Louisa. But she needed to be careful. The people she cared for ended up dying, leaving, or getting hurt. And, she needed to stay in control. Exercise caution. It's how she protected herself and those she cared for, and she did care for Charlie. More reason to keep him at a safe distance. Her heart could not take any more loss.

The bartender placed two Italian beef sandwiches with sweet peppers and fries on the table along with their bill. "Let me know if you need anything else," he said as he headed to the next table.

Halfway through his sandwich, Charlie's phone chirped. "It's my boss. Guessing he has an assignment for me. I'll call him back."

"Go ahead and take it."

"You sure?" He waited for her nod. "I'll only be a minute. Try not to disappear on me."

She couldn't help smiling. Charlie wiped his face and walked toward the front doors past the two guys at the bar who were getting a fresh draft.

After nibbling on a few fries, she pushed her plate to the side and worked on a plan to get answers. She could start with the detectives. That seemed the logical choice, but they didn't seem motivated. They probably had a dozen cases on their desks at any one time. She would follow up with them but would need to do her own digging. But where?

A crew of construction workers passed the booth for a seat near the pool table, and the Sheryl Crow wannabe started another oldie, "Bad, Bad Leroy Brown." The song reverberated off the forest green walls and dated light fixtures. Everyone in the bar involuntarily moved in response to the beat. The song made her think of Pete. He was a bit like old Leroy Brown.

As she doused a fry with ketchup, she realized it had been nearly four months since she and Pete had last talked. Well, since she had talked to him. Pete had finished his tour of duty and had returned to Chicago in the spring. They'd met at Wrigley Field for the home opener. It was their tradition, and they hadn't missed the opening game for over a decade.

It had been May and people packed into the ballpark as she headed to general admission, and to their regular seats. She'd waved to Pete, and as he turned, she realized he was not alone.

"Ellie," he said to her, "I'd like you to meet a friend of mine. Courtney, this is Ellie. But everyone else calls her Mia." Mia nearly dropped her hotdog and beer. Courtney was bubbly and all girl and intruding on Mia and Pete's baseball game. She didn't know what part of the scenario made her the maddest. It wasn't like Mia and Pete were a thing, but they were best friends. And this wasn't something a friend blindsides a friend with, was it? She wasn't sure because she didn't have many real friends, well none besides Pete.

It was the longest game she had ever sat through. Baseball would never be the same. After the game, while Courtney headed to the restroom, Mia and Pete took the opportunity to say what had been brewing for two and a half long hours.

"Mia Eleanor Graham," he said, "what's wrong with you? I didn't realize you could be so rude to another person."

She did not respond.

"You're mad 'cause I brought Courtney?"

"Well, it would have been nice to know beforehand, that you were bringing a date." He looked flabbergasted. "Actually," Mia continued, "I'm not really sure why you brought her or anyone for that matter. I can't believe you."

"I can't believe you," Pete said back to her. "You are acting like I shouldn't be dating anyone."

"And you're acting like opening day isn't our thing. I mean, how many years have we been coming here together, just you and me? Maybe fourteen? Clearly it doesn't mean as much to you as it does, correct that, *did* to me."

"Oh, come on, Ellie," Pete said. His tone was a bit softer with a hint of defeat. "Are we not both here, you and me, on opening day, together? I can't believe you're mad because I invited a friend."

He clearly did not understand, and that turned her frown into a scowl. "It's not that." She struggled with what not to say. How could he be such an idiot?

The object of their contention emerged from the ladies room. "Hey, you two," the perky brunette waved and headed in their direction.

"Oh, look, here comes your date." Pete glared at her. He clearly didn't like her tone. She continued in a flat, matter-of-fact tone. "I need to get going."

"We need to finish this conversation."

"Sure thing. But don't bother calling me. I'll call you," she said as she turned. Mia wondered if actual smoke was emanating from her head as she headed toward the exit. She scolded herself on not controlling her temper. Anger was not her friend, and it only brought trouble. She took a deep breath and worked to reign in the emotion. Even with the slight adjustment in her attitude, Mia never looked back. She didn't want Pete to see her tears. It wouldn't be fair. Besides, they had always been just friends. The way she wanted it. Why was she sending him mixed messages? Surely, a grown woman of her age knew better, didn't she?

Pete called her despite her telling him not to. He left messages, sent a letter, and even showed up at Louisa's. But Mia wouldn't budge. She wasn't sure why, but the incident had really struck a deep nerve. So, she didn't return his calls, write him back, or come to the door. Radio silence.

Four months. Now it seemed silly. They had never gone this long without speaking since the day they'd met as kids in her backyard. But now, with Louisa in the hospital, her hurt feelings didn't matter. She knew Pete would want to hear from her, especially about Louisa, and he would help her if he could.

She expected the call to be awkward, but only for a moment. She'd considered calling right then, while she had the nerve, but what if Charlie came back? She'd call him after lunch.

She leaned out of the booth. Charlie stood with his back against the front window of the bar, engaged in a conversation. She decided to check her vibrating phone. The caller ID said UNKNOWN CALLER. Again? Her instinct was to ignore it. *Let it go to voice mail.* But what if it's someone from the hospital? She debated and then hit ACCEPT.

CHAPTER 7

THE LEAR JET CRUISED AT AN ALTITUDE of thirty-seven thousand feet and would land in Chicago by 2:15. Anxious to arrive and check every detail of the upcoming event, Nikki's nerves were frayed. She had a lot at stake. The anticipation of her mission coursed through her sculpted body. She would not fail.

The plane smelled of new leather and imported wood. She'd sparred with her parents for six long months over its purchase, but knew appearances were important, especially with her clientele. Besides, she had an image to maintain, and the need to impress was important. In the end, she was right.

Taking the opportunity to stretch her legs, she stacked her laptop and notes on the mahogany desk that sat between the four captain-style chairs and headed toward the lavatory. The cabinet held her toiletries and nausea medication, which she hadn't had to take since leaving Costa Rica, a relief, as the trip had been noneventful. Her full lips patted the freshly applied wine-colored lipstick that coordinated perfectly with the mustard-colored turtleneck, one of the few winter clothing items she had retrieved from storage for this trip. She smoothed her jet-black hair into a leather ponytail. As she headed out, her mind turned to details of the day, both personal and business.

To start, she wondered if Miguel had confirmed the hair and makeup teams she would use while in Chicago. She might also need to see about a new assistant, one she wouldn't have to ask about such things.

She'd grown accustomed to a staff that were always one step ahead. The people her parents employed had mastered the art of seamlessness, an ability to orchestrate each day, regardless of its events. As her family's company transitioned from one generation to the next, employees of the Santos estate entered retirement and were envied by the locals of Escazu. Most people of the region worked their entire lives, never dreaming of such a luxury. These designated few received modest accommodations on the outskirts of the family compound and a generous annual distribution, until their death, as reward for their unwavering devotion. Now, it was her turn to rebuild her house staff and company minions, ones she hoped would be as loyal and competent as the previous ones had been to her parents.

The senior flight attendant, whose name she couldn't remember, greeted her as she walked to her workspace. "May I get you anything, Miss Santos? Perhaps a snack or a beverage?"

"Sparkling water with lime."

"Right away, Miss Santos."

Nikki read through client backgrounds. She glanced up from the document and let her eyes stop at the window. She saw her reflection. Creased brow, squinted eyes, and her mouth clenching the pen between her teeth. Nerves. She hated showing weakness. She considered returning to the lavatory to take something to calm herself. The pressure to make the event go off seamlessly, with everyone happy and wealthier, caused tightness throughout her entire body. It wasn't Saturday's event that unsettled her. She felt prepared and had spent the last few weeks and most of the flight reviewing auction comps against the items on the gala's docket. It was the one critical transaction that gnawed at her.

She checked the time. Should have heard something by now. She stared out the oval window. Thick white clouds that looked like a baby's blanket surrounded the plane. She tapped her closed fist against her mouth. What could be taking so long? Her phone buzzed.

"It's about time," she said. "Were you successful?"

The man cleared his throat. "Well, Miss Santos, things didn't go quite like we had planned. Our target suffered some injuries. She was taken to the hospital."

"She what? What happened?" Everyone on the plane, the crew and her staff, stopped momentarily and then quickly looked away as if they hadn't noticed the outburst.

"We were following her this morning, just like you asked, and, well, our driver didn't think a lady that age could, well, quite frankly, move that fast. The plan was to only give her a scare, like we discussed, and right as he went to swerve so as to miss her, she...well...she bolted. Head-on collision. The old lady really took a hit. Even did damage to the car."

"*Dios mío, ¿qué has hecho?*" she said, her words nearly biting him. "What have you done? And where is the driver now?"

"He made it to the rendezvous point. He wasn't followed. Listen, Miss Santos, we're monitoring the police blotters, in touch with our contacts. From what we hear, there are no leads. No witnesses."

"You be sure it stays that way. Dispose of the car and make sure your driver is out of the country before sunset, understood?" she said, her voice lower but steady. "Now, what about Louisa? What is her condition?"

"I overheard a few conversations at the hospital. The word is that she is unconscious and in serious condition."

Nikki gasped as she rolled the news around in her head. "This is unbelievable. I need her alive, Marco, and at the gala this Saturday. Do you understand? Do you?"

"I know what you need, but I would say that is unlikely, Miss Santos."

His tone was even. Calm. And that infuriated her. She moved the phone to her side, closed her eyes, and took a deep breath as she composed herself.

"Miss Santos? Anything else?" Marco said, interrupting the silence.

"You are sure she isn't going to walk out of the hospital in three days?"

"Like I said, ma'am, that seems highly unlikely."

"Meet me in the lounge at the LeBlanc. Four o'clock. I will expect a full update."

"Four o'clock."

She slammed the phone down on the desk and reached for her laptop. The flight attendant carefully placed the glass of imported sparkling water next to her, gave a slight nod, and moved toward the back of the plane.

Nikki searched local news feeds for any reports on Louisa. There it was. The third listing on the page.

Police respond to a hit and run in North Chicago. A woman, approximate age 65, was struck around 8:00 a.m. The victim was transported to Northwestern Hospital. Authorities do not have any suspects in custody at this time and are waiting to release the name of the victim until family is notified.

She shook her head in disbelief. The stakes of the next few days had just been amplified. Her clients would not care if Louisa was in or out of the picture, only that they received their merchandise. Making sure that promise was kept became her only priority.

It wouldn't be long until the State Department would be involved. That was the double-edged sword in working with Louisa. Her thirty years' worth of connections inside the agency, as well as her prominent position with the gala gave her clout and clearance. But, because the accident victim was also former ambassador Louisa Graham and chairman of the board for Graham Mining and Supply, this incident would not go uninvestigated. She drummed her fingers on the arm of the chair and stared at the mass of clouds, now a dark gray that reflected her mood. An investigation would bring unwanted attention. She needed to move fast to be sure the job was completed and erase any trace of her involvement.

She considered the possibility that Louisa couldn't make the gala or orchestrate the exchange. The next most logical option was Louisa's granddaughter, Mia. That may be the best bet. Certainly not ideal, but she knew how to make a person complete a job.

Nikki had not worked with Mia before and recalled only meeting her once, at a charity dinner in Madrid. She knew of Mia's reputation in the antiquities industry, but that was about it. How much did Mia know about the Graham family's involvement in black-market trades? Had she been read in? Involved or protected? Nikki made a mental note to gather additional intel. She would consider other options, but for the moment, Mia was her plan B.

Mia, as a senior employee of the DaVinci House, should have full access to the items being auctioned on Saturday. And as Louisa's granddaughter, she should have access to the merchandise, if she knew where the old lady had stashed it. Nikki would need to figure out how to leverage the younger Graham to do the job. The cost? Inconsequential. Nikki had an empire to run, clients to appease, a fortune to make, and she felt prepared for this moment, thanks mostly to her father.

She picked up her phone to call him but stopped. If her mother answered, it would only lead to a discussion Nikki didn't want to have, and she didn't want the headache. No, she'd wait to call her father. Besides, she knew what he would say. *I believe in you, Nikkole.* She smiled. He believed in her, and that is what she loved most about him. The bond they shared helped her overlook his toughness, almost ruthlessness, as he taught her, tested her, and pushed her. She hated his hard side, but had learned that it counterbalanced his kind side. Both were required in this business, a business she was prepared for.

She'd worked hard to receive his blessing. At the age of nine, after her older brother died in a car crash, Nikki decided she would run the family business, when she was old enough. Her mother, convinced that Nikki did not have what it took, began her own quest to have another child. Her attempts produced four consecutive miscarriages. The doctors told her mother that continued attempts would put her own life at risk, so she acquiesced and turned to Nikki, then twelve, and vowed to help train her to become a woman worthy of the leading role of Santos Distributing.

Nikki battled for her mother's approval knowing she might never get it. That was fine. She had won her father's trust, and that was enough. He was enough. He was everything.

They were alike, her papa and her, and had bonded over their love of adventure. They gravitated toward it like children to cotton candy. They shared a love of mountain climbing, skydiving, and sailing. Especially sailing. The solace, the conversations, and the unexpected battles with the sea. It was heaven.

The summer of her sixteenth year, just before the start of school, her father planned a three-day excursion off the coast of northern Spain. The outing pushed against the edge of the season. Despite her mother's objections, the duo jumped at the chance to go on one last voyage.

Until the third morning, the trip was uneventful. They turned south toward the shores of Spain, and, before the sun could rise, dark clouds formed in the distance.

"Looks like it could be a rough one," her father said. He tossed the last of his coffee into the lapping waves. "Start tying things down. I'll check the radar for any alerts."

Within minutes, gusts of wind pushed against the sails, and Nikki knew this wasn't an ordinary storm. The air was electric and, to some, would have felt terrifying, but Nikki loved her body's response. Adrenaline. It surged through her veins with an excitement that only a lion tamer might understand, and she welcomed the challenge.

Nikki reached inside the cabin door for a rain slicker and deck boots and headed toward the stern. She moved with purpose, stowing supplies and securing the sails. Rain fell, first in a steady mist, and then a fierce attack, soaking everything aboard. Now at an angry pitch, the wind rocked the cutter and Nikki's hair flung wildly, acting as a painful whip against her face. She slipped on the wooden floorboards but held tight to the railing as she bobbed back to the helm. For six dark hours, Nikki's dad monitored the ship's systems, and she steered the vessel and maintained communication with the mainland. She battled the fierce waves until the sun finally broke through the dense clouds and the rain returned to a friendly mist.

Seagulls appeared, hungry for food, and Nikki and Papa shared a triumphant smile, a smile that said that no storm could take them down. Not now. Not ever. They were Santos after all.

"You did well today, mi Bella," he said as she navigated toward Bilboa. He filled two speckled enamel coffee mugs with warm wine. "Cheers." He handed her a cup and they watched the sky melt into a canvas of pastels.

"Miss Santos?"

"Yes Miguel?"

"A note from the captain. We will be landing in thirty minutes."

"Bring me an updated guest list and itinerary before we arrive. Also, find out what the temperature is," she said, still hoping she had enough warm clothes packed for the stay. "I also need Mia Graham's phone number."

"Yes, ma'am."

A light mist spotted the window and she shivered. The news of Louisa's accident would travel fast. She needed to get ahead of it and provide reassurance to her clients. They had confidence in her family, but now that she was in charge, she had to build trust with them herself, and she knew that that meant no mistakes. She pulled out her note pad and took inventory of her resources.

People. With Marco's connections, she could put a few more bodies on the ground if needed.

Time. She had just over three days, plenty of time to execute a plan.

Motivation. She had that in spades. She smiled. Whatever was necessary to see it through. Yes, she could do that.

Best case scenario, Louisa recovers, attends the auction, even if on crutches, and holds up her end of the bargain. A more likely scenario was that Louisa would not be able to attend. In that case, Nikki would either need to get the merchandise herself and assure its transfer, or find someone else who can take Louisa's place, most likely Mia. Her first three objectives were clear. Get an update on Louisa's condition, find out where the merchandise was stashed, and get a read on Mia.

Nikki hit redial.

"Yes, Miss Santos?"

"Marco, get three of your best men lined up. I may have a job for them tomorrow."

"What skills are you looking for?"

"Search and rescue of inanimate objects. I need a team that is skilled and fast. Security systems, locks, safes. That kind of thing."

"A team like that, and such short notice, will not be cheap."

"Just get it done, Marco. And one more thing, put a twenty-four-seven tail on Mia Graham, Louisa's granddaughter."

"Sure thing. Anything specific we are looking for?"

"Routine, people she associates with, vulnerabilities. I want to know where she is at all times. I'll expect a full update this afternoon."

"Anything else?"

"Yes. Don't screw this up any more than you already have." She disconnected the call knowing full well she could count on Marco, despite the morning's mishap. He had completed several jobs for the family and, while not a staff member, had proved himself an excellent resource. The accident was most likely a fluke, but all the same she would talk with him about who he was putting on his teams and assure future mistakes were avoided.

"Miguel," she said loudly.

She looked up as her fit, thirtysomething assistant took long strides toward her. Dressed in a form-fitting charcoal-gray suit with a perfectly knotted deep-maroon tie, he clutched his executive binder that held all the need-to-know-at-this-moment information. It was clear that Miguel took his position seriously, but she found it difficult to gauge his enthusiasm. Most employees barely disguised their joy when offered a coveted spot within the Santos family empire. She pointed to the seats across from her. Miguel unbuttoned his jacket and sat in the chair closest to the aisle.

"Let's start with today's itinerary."

"Certainly." He pulled a tablet and pen from the padfolio.

"2:10 p.m.: We arrive in Chicago and your driver will take you to the hotel. We should arrive there at approximately 3:05 where we will meet with hotel security, unpack, and settle in.

"5:00: We have a meeting, in your suite, with the museum director, a Conrad Barnes, and security to review the setup and key protocols for the management and transfer of merchandise before, during, and after the auction."

"6:00: A light meal will be brought to your suite."

She raised her hand to stop him.

"Change in plans. Reserve a private table in the lounge. I've scheduled a four o'clock meeting with a colleague. Push the meeting with the museum people to four thirty. I will need you to assure all the details are in order. I will also stop by Northwestern Hospital at six o'clock. Please be sure the driver is available throughout the evening. Wait on dinner until I decide on my evening plans. Are there any reception details you need my input on?"

"Everything is in order. I've forwarded you the phone number you asked for. It should be in your inbox. Is there anything else?"

"Monitor the State Department news feed and the local news channels for any updates on the condition of Louisa Graham. She was involved in an accident this morning. Also, schedule time this afternoon to get a trim," she said pointing to his face. "I need you looking your best this evening."

"Yes, ma'am," he said as he stood. He unconsciously reached toward his Van Dyke–styled goatee that had been carefully crafted to accent his chiseled face. She could see his discomfort at the suggestion, but she expected nothing less than excellence.

The flight attendant approached, but Nikki waved her away and dialed Mia's number.

CHAPTER 8

"This is Mia Graham." Mia perched on the edge of the seat, hoping to hear Nurse Patton's voice.

"Hello, Mia. This is Nikki Santos. I'm an associate of your grandmother's and the lead acquisitions and donor liaison for the upcoming gala."

Why hadn't she let it go to voicemail? "I know who you are, Miss Santos. What can I do for you?"

"Please, call me Nikki. I hope this isn't a bad time."

It was a terrible time. "It's really not a good time," she said.

"I heard about Louisa's accident. I'm very sorry. How is she doing?"

"You heard about the accident?" Mia searched her mind. How could anyone have heard so quickly? Perhaps it was already in the news. The thought angered her.

"Well, you know, as they say, *La palabra viaja rápido*. Word travels fast. How is she doing?"

Mia remained silent. She did not want to discuss Louisa with anyone. It was none of Nikki's business. That's what she should say. "She's being treated at Northwestern and receiving excellent care. I'm sure this is not why you are calling. What can I do for you, Miss Santos?" Mia ground her teeth and closed her eyes.

A picture of Nikki formed in her mind. A trip to Spain, maybe four years ago? Nikki Santos is a woman no one would easily forget. Stunningly beautiful. A shoo-in for winning the Miss you-name-the-beauty-pageant, even on a bad day. Mia shook her head to release the image.

The call cut out. "Are you there? Did I lose you?" Mia thought she'd caught a break. Lost call? But before she could disconnect, she heard Nikki's voice.

"I'm here. In the air. I'll be landing at O'Hare in about an hour."

"You're in Chicago?"

"Of course. I'm coming in for the gala on Saturday. And I'm hosting a reception Friday evening at the LeBlanc. I know Louisa was planning on attending. Is there any way you can possibly come…many of our top collectors will be there…eight thirty or nine o'clock?"

Mia breathed in sharply. "I don't think I can make it." She glanced toward the entry. Now would be a good time for Charlie to show up.

"Of course, but perhaps Louisa will be better by then? You do think she will be well enough to attend, don't you?"

Mia said nothing. Could Louisa be well enough to attend anything in three days?

"I'm sorry, Mia." Nikki finally broke the silence. "I know this is difficult and, well, as you know, Louisa and my family go way back. I'd like to come by the hospital and see you later. Around six o'clock?"

"I'm not sure she is ready for visitors."

"I understand. I'll make it a quick stop. And while I'm there, I'd like to visit with you, just briefly, about the gala. I appreciate that you have a lot going on, but we have people coming in from around the world for this one. I may need your help, Mia." She paused. "Of course, we will pray Louisa is fully recovered and will be attending, just like we planned, but if not…" She let the statement trail unanswered.

Static from Julia's sound system interrupted the momentary silence and a new melody sifted in, taking Mia down a yellow brick road until Nikki interrupted, "Mia? Six o'clock? I'll be by for a quick visit. And know that I'll be praying for Louisa. I'm sure she will be better in no time."

Mia heard Nikki gasp and then a clatter. She waited.

"Are you still there? Is something wrong?" Another chance to end the call.

"Oh, we've hit some turbulence. I dropped my phone and need to buckle my seatbelt."

"Probably the cold front that's coming in. Hope you brought something warm to wear," Mia said with a small hint of satisfaction knowing the stark difference between fall weather in Costa Rica and Chicago. She imagined the South American beauty shivering at the thought.

Before Mia could get back to denying the hospital visit, the call disconnected.

She didn't look up when Charlie slid into the booth and dug into his sandwich. Mia couldn't shake her lingering frustration.

Charlie looked at her and stopped mid-bite. "What happened while I was gone? I was gone for what...," he glanced at his watch, "an entire ten minutes?"

"That woman is awful," Mia said. "I can't believe I took her call. I'm such an idiot."

Charlie laid his sandwich down and wiped his mouth.

Mia continued. "And what in the world does my grandmother see in her? I don't understand it."

"Back up a second. What did I miss?" His eyebrows raised at her outburst.

"Nikki Santos, you know from the infamous Santos family in Costa Rica? Louisa and my parents have worked with her family for years. I've heard of her, and actually met her once, but haven't ever had to deal with her." Mia's voice rose as she spoke. "Not only is she bossy, she has some nerve."

Charlie pushed his plate to the edge of the table and leaned back to listen.

"She called to ask about Louisa," the sarcasm dripped from her voice, "but she really is only concerned about the gala on Saturday. She wants my help and wants me to attend a ridiculous reception. Ha. Rain or shine, the show must go on. The gala is the last thing on my mind." A deep growl escaped through Mia's clinched teeth. "I hate two-faced people like her."

"Just tell her she needs to visit with your boss at least until you get Louisa home. Better yet, just tell her no. You have a lot on your plate right now. I think she would understand."

Mia took a long drink of her tea. "Oh, I plan to do just that. When she comes to the hospital this evening." She watched for his reaction.

"She's coming to the hospital?"

"Yep. Can you believe it?"

"Just tell her no, Mia."

As Charlie finished the last of his tea, Mia considered how she would handle Nikki's visit to the hospital. She needed to keep her cool. Her grandmother needed her to be strong and manage things until she was back on her feet.

Charlie leaned forward and offered an encouraging smile.

"Sorry for taking that out on you."

"Don't give it a second thought." He reached over and squeezed her hand. "Everything will work out."

"Yes, I have to believe it will.' She allowed her hand to stay under his a few seconds longer than she should have. But his strong grip felt nice.

"I've had a couple of messages from my boss," she said as she pulled her hand back and reached for her phone. "I need to return his call and head back to the hospital. But I am curious, what did Richie Rich want?" she said mustering an ornery smile.

Richard Richfield currently reigned as editor in chief at the *Tribune*. Mia had met him eight months earlier at an awards banquet she'd attended with Charlie as his plus one. The minute Mia met Richfield, she disliked his oily demeanor. The rotund man arrived in a chauffeur-driven Rolls Royce and dripped with flashy jewelry. His date looked like a real-life barbie doll. Because of the overt display of money, Mia nicknamed him Richie

Rich, not meaning any disrespect to the cartoon character. Charlie told her that Richfield had a fierce temper that shot at people like an electric current. Mia surmised that Richfield was simply an overweight egomaniac, who would keel over dead in the middle of one of his tirades one day.

"Do you have a nickname for everyone, Mia?"

"Maybe."

"Do you have a nickname for me?"

She smiled and moved her finger across her lips as if to zip them. He shot her a look.

"So, what's he needing from you?" she asked diverting the conversation.

"There's a protest at the new high-rise development down by the river. Do you know the one? It's just a block down from the Bradbury."

"A protest? That should be interesting."

"They need a few photos for tonight's edition. Shouldn't take too long. Can I meet you later?"

"Sure. I need to make a few phone calls. I need to stop by Louisa's before I head to the hospital. I'll check to see if you're back then."

Charlie placed some cash on the table next to their bill. "Do you want to take your sandwich with you? You didn't touch it."

With a flick of her eyes, she declined his suggestion as he leaned down and kissed her cheek, his unshaved face scratching lightly at hers.

"Talk to you later," he said.

Mia scooted further into the booth and leaned against the wall. Her first call was to Lionel. No answer. She left a message with Rebekah. She called the nurse on Louisa's floor for an update but had to leave a message there as well. Why wasn't anyone answering their phones?

Julia finished her set and thanked the disinterested patrons. Mia walked to the stage and dropped a twenty in the tip jar that sat on the piano. "Enjoyed your music," she offered before heading out into the mist-filled afternoon. Despite the gloom, the fresh air offered some encouragement. She took long strides toward her apartment and decided to keep an optimistic attitude. Just two hours until she could see Louisa.

CHAPTER 9

Cars dotted Rush Street and darkly clad people scurried along the crowded sidewalks. Mia liked the bustle of Chicago. It brought motion to an otherwise gray landscape.

The half-mile walk to her apartment took her by the majestic art building of Loyola University. It reminded her of a Tibetan monastery with its impressive oval stained-glass window.

The covered courtyard outside the art department sparkled with a display of prisms. Some dangled from tree limbs, and others were attached to posts or rooted into the ground. A half dozen people or so milled leisurely through the maze of hanging formations.

When she reached the stone fence that encased the courtyard, she paused. A large installation caught her eye. She walked to it and read the placard. Kaleidoscope of Sound by Asha Behran. The individual prisms were hollowed-out pieces of thick stained glass, each a different length. Strung together by thin wire and connected with a repurposed mirror, the mixture of color was breathtaking. A breeze brought the prisms together. The crisp tones reminded her of Christmas Eve service, when the handbell choir performed "Silent Night." As a bonus, a small sliver of sunlight cut through the clouds and the cylinders drank in the beam. Their reflection danced across the fabric of Mia's sweater.

Mia had seen a sparkle like this before. At last year's gala. Louisa had worn a floor-length, sequined gown, cinched at the waist, and a stunning necklace that boasted a rose-colored poudrette gemstone. The light from the chandeliers bounced against her grandmother's ensemble. The former ambassador gracefully shifted across the ballroom, and a potpourri of colors skipped across the faces and clothing of the people who watched. It reminded Mia of a kaleidoscope. Vibrant. Interesting. Full of color. Always changing. A stark comparison to Louisa's present display of gray.

Mia reached for her emerald necklace as she headed back to the sidewalk. How could someone so full of life be so lifeless? What if she doesn't get better? Mia's pessimism snuck through the backdoor of her mind. *No, don't go there.* She shook her head as if to deny entrance to negative thoughts. "She will get better. She will be okay," Mia said to the universe and, much to her own surprise, out loud.

She turned the corner onto Pearson and half collided with a young woman pushing twins in a stroller. They avoided the impact, but the woman's sack of groceries came loose. A head of lettuce, a loaf of bread, and a few canned goods hit the pavement. The woman grabbed at the bag but couldn't prevent the tear from spreading. A large can of formula rolled toward the curb and Mia rushed to stop it. She returned it and worked at gathering other stray items.

The toddlers were bundled in blankets and oblivious to the interruption in their trip. One more item on the ground, a small jar of spices. Mia reached for it, and a tall, solid man barreled around the corner and collided with her from behind. She grabbed a metal signpost, firmly cemented into the sidewalk, and avoided a full-on faceplant. The man's boot hit her leg before he banged into the stroller. Mia was on all fours, looking like a kid doing the crab walk. She looked at the man who went on his way. Unbelievable. He never looked back. Mia watched as he regained his pace, his black lined trench coat flapping behind him.

"Hey," Mia called out after him. "what's wrong with you? Watch where you are going!" Mia righted herself and turned her attention to the mom and girls. "Are you okay?" she said as the woman checked on the toddlers.

"I think everyone's okay. What's with that guy, anyway? What a jerk," she said. "Are you hurt?"

Mia felt the burn of raw skin on her knees and hands. Her lower leg, where the creep's boot connected, throbbed. Perhaps a bruise?

"I'll be fine." She rubbed the heels of her hands against her jeans, which only made them sting more.

The two in the stroller gave Mia a wave. "Well, they look unharmed." Mia handed the last jar of runaway spice to the woman. "Here you go. You have everything?"

"Yeah, we're good. Thanks for your help."

Mia smiled but refocused her attention in the direction of the man. He'd headed north. She half hoped she would catch up to him. Why did people have to be so rude? And why did people still smoke? She rubbed her nose trying to remove the pungent smell of cigarettes.

Mia regained her rhythm, still wondering where the oh-so-important man had disappeared to. She was halfway between Pearson and Chestnut when she saw him. He was inside the Happy Bean Coffee Shop, sitting at the counter that faced the window. Now she wasn't so sure she wanted another encounter. Something about him seemed off. She kept walking, temporarily not breathing, as she passed the shop. *Act normal. Keep walking.*

Goosebumps rolled down her spine. She glanced in his direction. *Try to act casual. Just a glance.* She wanted to get a good look at him. But he was intently looking away. His head was cocked to the left, and his hat covered most of his face. *Don't overreact*, she said to herself. *It's cold outside. He probably just stepped inside to get coffee and warm up.* Yet something still seemed off.

She lengthened her stride and increased her pace. As she waited for the stoplight to change at Chestnut, she took a casual glance back. Less than a half block back, she saw him. He carried a newspaper now but no coffee. The crossing light turned, and she infiltrated a group of pedestrians. Once across the street, she decided to take a detour and try and lose him.

Mia looked ahead and saw the Hunan Garden. Three storefronts away. That would work. Mia and Louisa visited the popular Chinese restaurant nearly every week and, over the years, had become friends of the owner, Mr. Kim. The bell over the door announced her entrance.

"Oh, hello, Ms. Mia," Mr. Kim said in his jagged accent. "How you doing?"

"Hello, Mr. Kim. I'm fine, thank you. I'm just heading home. Would you mind if I used your back door to get to my apartment?"

"Everything alright, Ms. Mia? I can have Malik walk with you. Malik!" He yelled for his nephew who ran the kitchen. Mia raised her hand and waved off the offer, interrupting his calls for Malik.

"I'm fine, Mr. Kim. Thank you, I'm just in a hurry. Do you mind?" she asked as she passed the restrooms and toward the kitchen door that said EMPLOYEES ONLY, briefly glancing over her shoulder.

"No problem, Ms. Mia. Come back soon. Malik will make you special batch chicken lo mein, just for you."

"I will. Thank you, Mr. Kim." The bell chimed from the front door just as she headed through the kitchen doors. She glanced back to see who'd entered. Straining, she looked through the pass-through window, but the person was out of view. She decided to keep going.

The kitchen staff nodded politely as she made her way past the long silver worktable and the double refrigerator lining the far wall. Mia gave them a quick wave and headed to the door that opened to the alley and led straight to the back side of her building.

Tall buildings flanked the alleyway and Mia could feel the drop in temperature. The air carried a damp, rotten smell. Her feet slid in the muck below her. It smelled of grease and stuck to her soles like dense mud. She tried to step out and around it, but there was no avoiding the murky substance. The bottom of her boots turned a deep shade of brown as she continued down the path that led to her apartment building. She scolded herself for overreacting.

The events of the morning had rattled her, and she vowed to get her nerves under control. *Having to clean these boots will teach you*, she said to herself. She turned the corner onto the sidewalk. Her right boot hit the pavement and she grabbed the corner of the building to keep from slipping. She came to a complete stop and hugged the brick surface. The man with the hat stood in front of her building talking to Jerome. She wasn't imagining it. What was going on?

She leaned against the cold, red brick and worked to catch her breath. She considered what she should do. She could slop right through the front door and allow Jerome to walk her to the elevator. But not only did she want to bring her muddy mess into the lobby, she wasn't sure she wanted to encounter the Marlboro man again. Not yet.

Mia retraced her steps, and gingerly slogged through the alley to the side door of the apartment building. She pulled out her key card and headed toward the service elevator doing her best to wipe her feet on the mat. She exited on the main floor and walked along the wall to the bank of mailboxes. From here she could see Jerome and the stranger. She felt confident, from this angle, they couldn't see her. A stocky gray-haired man scooted in front of her to gather his mail. He gave her a quizzical look but went about his business. Mia dug in her bag to give the impression she was searching for keys while keeping her eyes aimed at the front door.

Mia could see Jerome. He was smiling, talking, and then pointed somewhere toward the west. Jerome tipped his hat, received a tip, and the stranger headed away. Relieved, Mia headed to the main elevators, trying not to track grime across the lobby floor.

Happy to be back in her apartment, she bolted her door and carefully took off her boots. Tossing her coat on the couch, she buzzed Jerome using the apartment's intercom system and inspected her scuffed hands as she waited.

Jerome answered. "Hello, Mia. How can I help you?"

"Hi, Jerome. I wanted to ask you about the man you were just talking to outside. The one in the dark trench coat and hat? I know this might sound strange, but can you tell me what he was wanting?"

"Why yes. He said he was lost and asked for directions to the brown line. Why, is anything wrong?"

"No, um, it just looked like someone I might have known. Sorry to bother you, Jerome."

"No bother at all. Have a good day."

Don't over think it, she said to herself. Maybe he was lost. Or perhaps, simply a coincidence, although she did not believe in those. Her gut told her something was off.

She glanced at the clock. Time seemed to be moving in slow motion. She needed to distract herself. With the prospect of spending the next couple of days at the hospital, she decided to take a shower and catch up on some pressing work items. She'd still have time to swing by Louisa's and get back to the hospital by two thirty.

She checked her voicemail. Nothing from the hospital. Everything else could wait. She set her phone on the charger and headed to the shower.

The hot stream of water massaged her entire body, and the smell of the peppermint-infused soap filled the oversized shower. The steam lifted the tension from her shoulders as the pulse of the showerhead massaged her neck. She took her time washing her hair, and then her face. Relaxation washed over her and then exhaustion, an uninvited guest. Exhaustion would have to wait. She turned the faucet to cold and allowed the shock of the water to bring her abruptly back to life.

She slipped on her robe, wrapped her hair in a towel, and grabbed a soda from the kitchen before heading to her office. Her oversized Queen Anne writing desk overflowed with thick books on eighteenth-century artifacts, and stacks of documents. The upcoming gala had added several appraisals to her normal workload. Normally, the pile of work excited her, but now, with Louisa in the hospital, she would need to pass off some of her scheduled jobs. Plus, there was the looming possibility that she might have to play a heightened role in Saturday's gala, if Louisa could not attend.

Mia would do anything for Louisa, but the idea of playing her part at the gala still sounded awful. She let out an audible groan at the thought and hoped that Lionel would volunteer to step in and take the lead, giving her a pass on Louisa's duties.

She stacked the research books on the floor and sent emails to collectors letting them know when they could expect their appraisals. An hour passed. She printed the gala's auction list and reviewed her mental to-do list. One last task. Send an email to her boss.

> Lionel, I've sent the updated gala auction file to our team. I'm still waiting on 2 items but should have them by tomorrow. Once that is done, I'll do a final review, and then Rebekah should be ready to publish and print.
>
> I'm guessing that you've heard about the accident Louisa was involved in this morning. As of right now, she is in serious but stable condition. I think it is safe to assume she will not be at the gala. I know it will create some challenges, but I believe she had most everything set and ready to go. I will update you as I know more.
>
> Mia

She reread her email before hitting send, dreading the possibility she may be asked to take on the coordination of VIP guests, the giving of speeches, and the schmoozing that her grandmother managed so skillfully.

Mia stowed her computer and work files in an oversized handbag before sliding into a pair of burgundy skinny jeans, a mint-green turtleneck, and ankle boots. She tucked the flower pendant necklace inside her sweater and slipped on a pair of black onyx earrings, a Christmas gift from Louisa, and then tossed several mix-and-match clothing pieces into a duffle.

She dialed the front desk. "Hi, Jerome," she said as she grabbed her black biker jacket. "Would you call me a cab? I'll be down in a couple of minutes."

Before heading to the elevator, she stopped and looked out the window. No trace of the man who reeked of tar and nicotine. "You are not being paranoid," she said out loud as she attached her can of pepper spray to her key fob. *I'm just taking precautions.*

Even with the pepper spray, her nerves were on high alert. Louisa was in the hospital. The gala was days away, and she needed to call Pete. That would take an extra dose of courage. She knew she'd been avoiding it for too long. And time never made things easier.

Her cab pulled to the entrance as she exited the elevator. Jerome was on the phone. She waved at him and carefully scanned the lobby and then the street. She didn't see the man and wondered where he might be.

CHAPTER 10

"I'll only be five minutes," Mia told the driver as the taxi pulled in front of the brownstone.

The cabbie switched the meter to wait mode and slid his cap over his eyes. Mia hopped out and made her way up the concrete stairs to the large oak door of 1246 Astor Ave. Inside the dark entry, she deactivated the security system and reached for the lamp. Before she could turn it on, she heard something. She froze and listened as her eyes acclimated to the darkness. "Is someone here?" With her left hand on the pepper spray, she inched toward the lamp until she found the chain. As she pulled it, she felt a thud against her chest and nearly lost her balance. She screamed. Jasper. Louisa's cat. The furry feline apparently had a stealth mode and lacked social etiquette. Mia dropped her keys. The cat's claws stuck tight to her sweater and his fur covered half her face.

"Jasper. You scared the life out of me. Now get down." The cat landed softly on the hardwood and scampered toward the sunporch. Releasing a sigh, she locked the door and headed upstairs. She stowed her clothes and toiletries in the closet that adjoined the guest bathroom, and continued to the end of the hallway.

The aroma of worn leather and wood permeated the air of Louisa's office. Mia ran her finger across the bocote wood desk that had been handcrafted and flown in from Central America. The large, lace-covered windows faced the garden and invited the slices of afternoon sun to warm the wood floors. Any other day, the ambiance of the office would have coaxed her to take comfort in one of the mustard-yellow leather chairs that faced the large desk. But she was anxious to get to the hospital, and the cab was waiting.

Art and books filled the expansive bookcase. To the far right sat a sculpted elephant and a small stack of books. Mia moved them to the desk. She slid her finger along the underside of the shelf and found the small switch. In one move, she twisted and pushed in on the knob and the paneled wall popped open revealing Louisa's safe. Mia punched in her birthdate and turned the silver pull. She took the entire stack of items and sat at the desk.

After a quick sort, she opened the file labeled PERSONAL DOCUMENTS and found the medical power of attorney, copy of the insurance card and HIPPA forms. That should do it. She reassembled the remaining papers, and noticed a thin, velvet box about the size of her hand. She hesitated then carefully removed the lid. A patinaed cast-iron key lay on a soft cotton lining. The key was heavy and old. She turned it over in her hand and searched her memory. It seemed familiar. Yes, she was sure. It was a key she had held before, but where and when? The muffled honk of the taxi broke her concentration. With the unneeded documents returned to the safe, Mia slid the mysterious key into her coat pocket and made her way down the stairs to the waiting cab.

CHAPTER 11

NIKKI PULLED THE WOOL WRAP tightly around her shoulders and exited the limousine. A valet met her, umbrella open, and escorted her inside the turn-of-the-century building. The hotel was constructed of large white stones, dark metal accents, and just the right touch of gold. It dripped in elegance. Inside the glass doors, Nikki watched the staff unload her bags from the limo. She glanced at the second car, an SUV, that carried a collection of Costa Rican artifacts for the auction. She surveyed the two burly, armed men who were on loan from her family's estate. They escorted the cargo like secret service protecting the president. She could see the items were in good hands.

Nikki pivoted to find the hotel staff and guests looking her way. She loved capturing a room, especially one as grand as the lobby of the LeBlanc. She spotted Miguel, already at the registration desk with room keys in hand. There was something handsome about him. A bit short but he moved with purpose. He looked great in his Armani suit, and the back of his dark hair had just a hint of a wave. But looks aside, she still had a few doubts about Miguel. But only a few. Time would tell. Until then, she would be wary but enjoy the view.

Halfway across the polished marble floors, she was met by two of the hotel's executives. Miguel joined them.

"Good afternoon, Miss Santos," the hotel manager said. "Welcome back to Chicago. We are delighted to have you here."

"Thank you, Mr. Miller."

"We have your suite ready and have reserved a private room for you in the lounge. Mr. Smeltz is our head of security. Perhaps you remember him from your last stay?"

"Good to see you again, Mr. Smeltz." He was all business as he offered his hand. A dragon tattoo appeared just beyond his tailored shirtsleeve. He looked intimidating. All part of the job she reasoned. "May I assume you are prepared to secure our cargo and oversee safe transport to the event site?"

"Yes, ma'am." His voice was softer than his appearance. "All the arrangements have been made and I will be reviewing the itinerary with your assistant and the security team at the Bradbury Museum. They have excellent protocols in place. You also have a safe in your residence if you should require it, and the valet can provide you with any assistance you need. Is there anything else you require?" She got the sense that he would be glad to assist her. With anything.

"Not at this time." Her nod to him caught his eye. His lips spread in a thin smile.

"Then, the valet is ready to show you to your suite."

The valet, dressed in full uniform and looking like a throwback from the 1960s, stood waiting, along with a female assistant. They entered the opulent elevator; its chandelier caused the gold-trimmed paneling to glisten as they headed to the presidential suite.

This was the second year Nikki's team had been at this hotel, after more than a decade at the Waldorf. Nikki preferred the Waldorf, but when the two majority owners of the LeBlanc, William Caster and Prince Al Saud of Saudi Arabia, expressed interest in attending the annual gala, the venue was changed. And the move had proved lucrative.

"Miguel, I'd like to see the details for Friday's reception," Nikki said as they ascended the building. "And where are you on welcome gifts for our guests? Has the hotel arranged to have them distributed?"

"Yes, ma'am."

"One more thing. Send a flower arrangement to Louisa Graham at Northwestern Hospital."

"Of course."

The elevator door opened to her spacious suite. The floor-to-ceiling windows came alive with the view of Lake Michigan to the east and city views to the north. The valet gave Nikki and Miguel a tour of the suite. Almost three times the size of the average home in Chicago, the space provided the perfect backdrop for Friday evening's intimate reception of dignitaries, donors, and clients.

In her private bedroom, Nikki found the valet's assistant already unpacking her garment bag. "Any special instructions, ma'am?"

"Leave the smaller duffle to me. The rest can be hung and steamed as needed. And secure my valuables in the safe." She took her bag into the master bathroom and shut the door. She carefully unclasped her jewelry and pulled the turtleneck over her head, letting her silk slacks slide to the floor. She looked closely at herself in the mirror. She looked good for thirty-nine. Her curvy body hugged perfectly by the black lace bra and panties. *In three short days*, she said to herself, *you will run the Santos empire*. One final, small exchange and she would earn her place at the helm.

She closed her cosmetic bag and took one last look in the mirror before heading to the bedroom. Miguel was there, a file folder in hand. She watched his eyes dart to the floor. His face reflected the surprise of a twelve-year-old boy. She smiled.

"What is it, Miguel?"

"The reception information you asked for, Miss Santos," he cleared his throat. "Also, the auction items have been placed in the hotel vault and each item accounted for. They'll be transferred to the museum in the morning. Is there anything else you need before your four p.m. meeting?" He stood motionless. She walked to him and could see that her lightly clad body rattled him.

"No." She took the folder from his hand lightly brushing her forearm against his. "I will be ready in ten minutes. That's all, for now." She watched him make a quick exit and shut the bedroom doors behind him. He might be a good addition to her staff after all.

CHAPTER 12

MIA DIALED PETE'S NUMBER, and he answered on the second ring. He told Mia he was in Seattle, wrapping up a security job for a tech firm. Their conversation lasted the entire ride to the hospital, and neither of them brought up the Wrigley Field debacle.

Mia told him everything she knew about the hit-and-run, the inept police investigation, and Louisa's condition. He remained silent as she talked, and she imagined a deep shade of red move from his neck to his face. He was not taking the news well. Not just because of the callousness of the act, but because of how he cared for her, and Louisa.

They'd met on the day Donald "Pete" Haines moved in with his foster family just behind Mia's childhood home and a stone's throw from Mia's backyard fort. He called her Ellie, short for her middle name, Eleanor. The pair bonded over long afternoons collecting rocks, playing in the creek, and making plans to explore the world. But the trust Louisa placed in Pete began fourteen years earlier on the day of the funeral.

⇒ ╫ ⇐

The front pew of the church was covered in a thick, red velvet and Mia wanted to disappear into it. A long, silver casket lay directly in front of her. Its twin sat to the left. She imagined that the one closest to her held her father. She'd attempted to remain stoic, like the bronze statue of Abraham Lincoln she had seen at Chicago Park, and now her neck ached from holding the position. As people passed by, she concentrated on not reacting, not looking, and not moving. Invisibility was her goal. Unnoticed. Untouched.

The minister tapped the microphone, and everyone took their seats. The air around Mia cleared as the line of people evaporated. Her head ached from clenching her eyes, so she relaxed and opened them halfway. The instrumental music faded from the speakers. She blinked, trying to moisten her eyes, when a pair of shoes stopped directly in front of her. She sighed loudly and resumed the statue position, hoping they would not stay. Through slatted eyes, she saw the legs bend. The stranger's hand brushed her cheek. Her body bristled, but her mind told her there was something familiar in the touch. Pete. She leaned forward and hugged him, perhaps too tightly and too long. He was a buoy she could not afford to lose. She pulled him onto the pew and watched him glance at Mr. Acosta and then her grandmother. No one objected.

Mia remembered almost nothing the minister said during the service or at the cemetery. She felt like a blind person, being led from one place to another, not absorbing her surroundings, just holding tightly to Pete. When all the strangers were gone, Mia, with Abuela on one side and Pete on the other, walked down the stone path, away from the gravesite. Louisa wore dark sunglasses, perhaps to block the sun, and a tailored overcoat. Louisa's face looked pale against the black of her ensemble, but her steps were solid and resolute. Mia wanted to be strong. Instead, she felt numb and guilty. There was no room for anything else. No tears. Not even grief. Once the numbness wore off, she thought, that would leave only guilt.

She felt Pete's gaze. His being next to her provided some relief, and she hooked her arm through his as they walked.

A black Town Car waited, its back door open. Mia looked at Pete. She bit her lip and a tear rolled down her face. He took her face in his hands. "I will come see you next weekend. I promise. And we will write each other every week. Okay?"

She smiled at her only friend. "Okay."

That day, fourteen years earlier, Pete became a part of Mia and Louisa's circle. Every Sunday afternoon, he rode the train downtown for a visit. And on holidays, Louisa set a place for him at the dining table. He was family. Welcomed and trusted.

The cabbie pulled in front of the hospital's main entrance and put the car in park. Mia raised a finger to the driver asking for a minute to finish her call.

Pete's tone was resolute. "I'll wrap up my project this afternoon and catch the next flight out," he said.

"You really don't have to come," Mia said.

"Of course I'm coming, Ellie. And Ellie…," he said.

"Yeah?"

"You watch your six." Military talk.

"Aye, aye, Sarge," Mia said as she paid the driver. "You'll let me know what time your flight arrives?" She listened to his response and then continued. "Looking forward to seeing you too."

CHAPTER 13

THE HOSPITAL LOBBY SMELLED of cleaning solution. The maintenance worker mopped the endless gray square tiles to the beat of a song that seeped through his earbuds. Mia followed the signs to the elevator, the heels of her boots echoing against the floor.

She walked by a dimly lit chapel and slowed her pace as she passed the open doors. Inside, one lone man occupied the surrogate church. She pitied him. There were only two types of people who needed the services of a hospital chapel. Those who were desperate or those who were mourning. Mia refused to be in either category. The elevator ascended to the intensive care unit located on the fourth floor.

She pressed the buzzer and waited for the floor nurse to respond.

"May I help you?"

"Mia Graham. I'm here to see Louisa Graham." The door clicked twice. She entered the ICU. The sterile smell intensified as she went down the somber hall. Except for the monotonous sounds of medical equipment, it reminded her of the study section in the city library. There were visitors inside patient rooms, most sitting silently or whispering to family members.

Room 442 was in the far-right corner of the ICU. Mia turned the corner and saw a middle-aged woman in pink scrubs at the fold-down workspace outside of Louisa's room.

"Excuse me. I'm here to see Louisa. I'm Mia Graham."

"I'm Connie Miller, and the nurse on duty. I was just getting ready to return your call." The RN pushed her glasses up to rest on her mussed hair. Mia saw dark circles under her eyes.

"Nice to meet you. How is my grandmother doing? Has there been any change?"

Nurse Connie opened the file. "Her vitals remain stable, but there has been no change. We're keeping her comfortable and monitoring her condition. Would you like to go in and see her?"

They entered the private room. Louisa had been propped up with a pillow but lay motionless as the machines around her provided proof of life. Mia stared at Louisa's bruised face, which was now the shade of ripened eggplant. She forced herself to look away and saw a small bouquet of lilacs on the windowsill. The sweet aroma fought the neutralized smell that lived there. The nurse checked the monitors and connections. Mia retrieved the requested paperwork from her handbag and gave it to Connie.

"Is there anything you need? Something to drink?" Nurse Connie asked.

Mia only needed one thing—for Louisa to wake up. Connie said she'd stop back after she'd checked on her other patients.

Anger and grief battled for the emotional upper hand, both rising inside her as she considered Louisa's condition. *Who could be so evil to do this?* She wondered if Detectives Taylor and

Ramirez were up to the task to catch the driver. What if Louisa didn't regain consciousness? Mia's legs felt as if concrete blocks were attached to her feet. She moved to the left of the bed and adjusted the drab blanket that could not possibly keep her grandmother warm. She held Louisa's small hand in her own and did not restrict her tears from running their course.

"Hey, Abuela. I'm here," she whispered. "Can you hear me? I love you and I need you to get better." She half-sat on the edge of the bed, with no idea of what she could do and no additional words to say, so she simply sat, her face wet, feeling the beat of her heart outpacing her grandmother's.

Lulled by the steady sounds of the equipment, she sat motionless until she felt a hand on her shoulder. She turned to see a familiar face.

"Oh, hello, Sebastian. I didn't hear you come in."

"You were a long way away. I'm sorry if I startled you."

"I'm fine. It's good to see you." She stood to hug him, and he embraced her and held her close.

Sebastian Armani, a long-time family friend, and Louisa's personal chauffeur, looked softly at Mia, his expression acknowledging her heartbreak as well as his own.

"Charlie called me. I came right over. Hope you don't mind."

"Of course not. I'm glad you're here."

"How is she?" he asked as he walked to the side of the bed.

"Unconscious. Unresponsive."

"She really took a hit, didn't she?" he said looking down at the frail state of his friend and employer.

Mia could not muster a reply or stop herself from trembling.

"Mia," he said, slipping his strong arm around her shoulder, "Louisa is strong, and she is a fighter, just like you. If anyone can get through this, it is her. We need to be strong. For her."

Mia contemplated his words. "You're right. She would not approve of either of us standing here expecting the worst. I have to believe this is a fight she can win."

"She will." He squeezed her hand. "Who are the flowers from?"

"I don't know."

Sebastian walked to the sill and read the card. *"Praying for your speedy recovery. All our love, Henry and Ophelia."* He looked at Mia.

"You know Henry Petrakis, don't you? Louisa's handyman?"

"Yes, I've met him, though it's been a while."

There was a knock at the door. Doctor Cheung and Connie had arrived for afternoon rounds. Sebastian gave Mia a quick hug and said he'd be in the waiting room. The doctor looked at Louisa's charts and proceeded with a quick physical exam. Mia watched as her grandmother showed no response to his prodding and poking.

Dr. Cheung turned toward Mia. "Your grandmother is in serious condition. I'm concerned about brain swelling and the increase in her blood pressure. We are adjusting her medication to help deal with the blood pressure, and we have scheduled an additional CAT scan for today. Neurology will review the results and compare them with the scans from this morning. The nursing staff will continue to monitor her vitals and keep her comfortable." He handed the charts to Connie and placed his hands in the pockets of his white lab coat after adjusting his glasses. "Do you have any questions for me, Ms. Graham?"

Mia usually had a dozen questions for every situation but found herself with only one. She looked at Louisa and then met the doctor's gaze. "Will she recover?"

"It's hard to say," he said dryly. "Once she regains consciousness, we will be able to better access her prognosis and provide a timeline for recovery. Until then, we can only monitor and wait. The nurse will be back shortly to get her ready for the scan."

Mia felt her anger resurface and wanted to shout at him. *Aren't you a doctor? You're supposed to be so smart, and you say we can only wait. Surely there is something you can do besides order a test.* Instead, she stuffed her emotion away, remained silent, and turned her gaze back to Louisa. Connie and Dr. Cheung left the room. Mia pulled the chair next to the bed rail, reached for Louisa's hand, and prayed.

CHAPTER 14

Nikki could feel the eyes of everyone in the bar and she enjoyed it. The upscale lounge was peppered with business suits and tired shoppers who had spent their afternoon spreading their wealth along Michigan Avenue. Nikki drank in the attention and let it warm her. She had always craved the limelight, but it had been difficult living in the shadow of parents who were powerful and beautiful. Nikki now had her chance and did not lack confidence, one of her most appealing, and sometimes most intimidating qualities. She made direct eye contact with each man at the bar, most likely lawyers grabbing a drink after a long day in court. Her black ensemble, plunging silk blouse, and flowing wrap-around skirt moved in just the right ways pulling along the imagination of her audience. She had pulled her hair up into a French twist that highlighted her long neck and diamond drop earrings.

The maître d' led her to the reserved table tucked in a private corner. Miguel followed. The man sitting at the table stood as she approached and removed his worn hat. As he sat, he smoothed his hair back, its oily texture keeping it in place. A half drank long pour sat in front of him and he waited while the server took her order and headed back to the bar.

"Good to see you, Miss Santos. You look lovely, as always," the man offered.

"Well, you look like hell, Marco."

"It's been a long day, ma'am."

"I know you have a lot to accomplish, but you must do something about your appearance." She glanced at Miguel who nodded knowingly. She considered Miguel's presence before continuing. If she was going to trust him, bring him into the fold, now was the time. "Give me an update. Let's start with this morning's incident."

"Everything has been handled. No witnesses. No vehicle. No driver."

"Details?"

"Suffice it to say the driver will soon be in route to South America for an extended vacation, ma'am. Out of the picture."

"And the car?"

"It is being chopped as we speak. There should be no trace. Nothing for you to worry about." He paused and looked up.

"Here you go." The eager waiter smoothly placed a glass of chardonnay in front of her. "Anything else I can get you?" He flashed a hopeful smile.

"This will be all," she said while taking in his deep green eyes. "Thank you." She could see his face flush as he turned to leave.

In a near whisper, she continued. "Marco, I'm counting on you. If Louisa does not walk out of that hospital in two days, then Mia is our next best bet. Who's tracking her?"

"Antonio is covering for me while I'm here, but I've been tailing her. She is currently at the hospital and seems to maintain a simple routine. It's no problem to keep tabs on her."

"Good. I want you to up the surveillance. Get someone on her email, calls, do a deep dive and stay on top of it, understand? We may need to utilize her in the merchandise transfer, and the more information I have the better."

Marco nodded but said nothing.

"Now, if Louisa doesn't recover, thanks to you, and Mia is uncooperative, we may need to find the package ourselves. I am checking on Louisa this evening and I'll know more after that. How are you coming with the team I asked you to assemble?"

"I have a team of three coming together. Experts in security, safecracking, and burglary. I'm going to need some cash. Plus some extra for the increased surveillance. Eight large."

"I should take it out of your pay. You hired the guy who messed this up."

He shrugged.

"Miguel will see to it. Have your team ready by end of day in case Louisa is no longer in play."

"Not a problem, Miss Santos. Anything else?"

"Yes, once we have the merchandise, we will still need someone to intercede before the auction. Mia will be the one we use. And if she doesn't want to cooperate, then we will need to apply pressure, understood?"

He raised his eyebrows and gave a deep nod of understanding before tossing back a handful of mixed nuts and washing them down with a swig of his draft. She didn't appreciate his cavalier attitude.

"We need leverage, and you need to have that lined up, just in case, before the gala."

"I believe we can handle that."

"Marco, my entire family is counting on you. This is your screwup, and it must be fixed."

"Yes, ma'am."

She paused. "I will be in touch this evening. Do you have any questions?"

Marco shook his head, finished off his beer, and stood to go.

She looked toward her assistant. "Miguel, please find a place for our associate to get cleaned up. And he needs some cash. Eight thousand." Nikki watched him for a reaction. The man didn't even flinch.

"I will be back down in a few minutes, Miss Santos," Miguel said as he turned to escort Marco upstairs.

Nikki leaned back in her chair and surveyed the room. It was happy hour and people continued to fill the lounge. The piano player checked his mic, looked directly at Nikki, and winked. His fingers began to stroke the keyboard, and a soft jazzy rendition of "I Only Have Eyes for You" began to loft through the room. She watched as a suited woman walked by the baby grand and dropped a tip in the jar.

Nikki's phone vibrated. The caller ID flashed GABRIELLA.

She repositioned herself as she answered. "Hello, Mother. What a nice surprise." Nikki did not try to mask her sarcasm.

"Hello, Nikkole. How was your trip? Everything on schedule?"

"Yes. Everything is fine here. How is Papa?"

"Not having a good day, I'm afraid, and I can't get him to stop worrying about this weekend's transaction. I told him I would get an update. You are sure everything is in order?"

"He has nothing to worry about. We had a small wrinkle, but I, with Marco's help, am working through it."

"What do you mean, 'a wrinkle'? What has happened?"

"Louisa was in an accident this morning. A hit-and-run."

"What? Is she okay?"

"She is alive. At the hospital. I'm paying her a visit later this afternoon. If she can't fulfill her obligations, I already have backup plans in place. Don't worry, Mama. I can handle this. Please trust me."

"Nikkole, do I have to tell you—"

"I know what is at stake," Nikki interrupted. "I have everything taken care of. You take care of Papa, and I will make sure our clients are happy. When is his next treatment?"

"Tomorrow morning. We will get an update from the doctors at that time. Nikkole, you understand that our future, your future, is on the line. We all have much to lose. Perhaps I should come to Chicago?"

"No, Mama. I can manage this."

If you have any doubts, you will tell me, si?"

"Yes, I need to go. I will visit with you tomorrow. Send my love to Papa."

The call ended and Nikki took a long sip of her wine. Her mother was a force, and, in a way, her father's cancer battle kept her occupied. That was the only redeeming thing Nikki could find in her father's illness. He only had two more rounds of chemo to go, and then, with luck, the cancer would be gone.

She stood and turned to see Miguel visiting with Conrad Barnes, the Bradbury Museum's executive director, at the entrance of the lounge.

"Conrad, good to see you again," Nikki said joining them. "Do you and Miguel have all the details worked out for our event?"

"Everything is coming along fine, Miss Santos."

"That is great to hear. I know I can count on you and your fine staff."

"We are working closely with Lionel McMasters at the Da-Vinci Auction House, and they are doing an excellent job. We are heading to a meeting with the head of security. Would you like to join us?"

"No, I will leave you in Miguel's capable hands. If you have any questions, Miguel knows how to find me. I do appreciate all your work on behalf of the gala. I know, with your assistance, it is going to be splendid. Now, if you'll excuse me, I'm going to go freshen up before heading to my next meeting. Miguel, I will see you in the lobby at five thirty. Have a good evening, Mr. Barnes."

The elevator door opened as if on command, and she headed back to the forty-sixth floor with a growing knot in her stomach that would not be loosened until she met with Louisa.

CHAPTER 15

MIA'S LEGS TREMBLED as she walked to the waiting room. The afternoon sun had found its way through the thick clouds and yellow rays warmed the space, yet Mia shivered as if the temperature had dropped ten degrees. The drab space accommodated two middle-aged women who sat chatting by the doors, and an oversized man who sat alone, hunched in the corner engrossed in a wrinkled newspaper. By the far windows stood Sebastian. His eyes were fixed on something in the distance. Even from here, she could see the crow's feet developing around his eyes.

Sebastian and Louisa went way back, although Mia only knew bits and pieces of the story. Looking at him, he appeared to be a hard-working, middle-class man, in a nice suit. No one would guess, however, that he held a master's in finance from MIT and had worked at the largest financial investment firm in Chicago. Mia assumed that is how he and her grandparents had become acquainted. Sebastian had risen to the top and, while he apparently hated the grind of the business, he had learned how to successfully manage and grow his money. Just before he was to be named partner, he stepped away and developed a private practice that allowed him to focus on his own investments and financial growth. It had been a move that proved lucrative. That was twenty years ago, just after her grandfather had passed, and from that time on he had become a personal chauffeur to Louisa, investment advisor, and a regarded family friend. Mia suspected his change in profession may have had something to do with her grandfather and a promise made between the two men. She made a mental note to ask Louisa for the whole story once she got her home.

"Sebastian. Everything okay?"

"Yes, fine. What did the doctor say?"

"They took her for more tests—they are concerned about her blood pressure and swelling in her brain." Mia swallowed hard on the words.

Sebastian hugged her. "She's in good hands, Mia." She responded with a non-convincing nod.

"How are you doing?" he asked. "You look pale. Maybe we should grab a bite to eat?"

"Not sure I can eat, but a cup of coffee sounds good. The nurse said it would be at least an hour."

She took his arm and headed to the elevator bank. As they waited, the doors behind them opened.

"Hey you two. Where are you headed?"

She turned and smiled at Charlie. "To the cafeteria. Want to join us?"

They entered the elevator, and she watched as Sebastian took one last long look at the lone gentleman in the waiting room. The worry lines returned to his face and then joined her brow as well.

⇒ ∭ ⇐

With fresh coffee in hand, they found an out-of-the way corner table. Mia updated them on Louisa, and Charlie filled them in on his assignment. A three-way battle brewed between the locals, the developers, and the union workers. Currently it was civil, but Charlie suspected it would get heated. The trio held a light banter, attempting to distract and ignore the slow passage of time. But Mia couldn't help noticing Sebastian pulling back from the conversation, sporadically nodding as if engaged. She watched his eyes flit back and forth from the cafeteria crowd to Mia and Charlie and hoped to have an opportunity to get to the bottom of what was eating at him. Yes, perhaps worry for Louisa, but maybe there was more to that relationship than Mia knew.

After a second cup of coffee, they headed back to the slow-running bank of elevators. As they waited, she asked Charlie if he'd stop at Louisa's and feed Jasper.

"Sure, but I can stay for a while if you want," he offered.

"No, I'll be fine. I'll probably stay here tonight."

"Okay, but you'll call and update me later? Let me know if you need anything?"

"Of course."

He kissed her softly on the cheek and looked in her eyes. "Anything you need, call me, okay?"

"Yes, I said I would." Mia's face turned a bit red at his insistence, and a tension appeared between them. Mia pushed the button to the elevator again, willing the doors to open.

"Where are you off to now, Sebastian?" Charlie asked.

"I was hoping you could stay for a few minutes," Mia interjected, "if you don't mind."

"Sure thing, kid. Charlie, I'm sure I'll see you soon."

"See you soon."

The two men shook hands, and Charlie headed toward the parking garage. Mia and Sebastian boarded the elevator. Once inside, Sebastian turned to her. "When are you going to give him the time of day?"

"What are you talking about?"

"Charlie. He's crazy about you. Surely you know that. And I think you like him too."

"No, no, no. Just a friend. We are too much like oil and water. That would never work, and besides, I'm not looking for a commitment."

"Well, maybe you should be." She wondered what that meant. Had her grandmother said something to Sebastian?

The elevator stopped to pick up another rider, interrupting their conversation. Just as well. She didn't really want to have this discussion with Sebastian. The doors opened on the fourth floor, and Mia and Sebastian exited. "So, what's on your mind, Mia?"

She sat down in the first row of chairs and patted the seat beside her.

"I've been watching you, and I want to know what's worrying you, Sebastian. You seem distracted. Are you worried about Louisa, or is it something else? Please be honest with me. Is something wrong?"

He loosened his linen tie and leaned forward in his chair. "Mia, you said the detectives weren't sure if this was an accident, right?"

She nodded.

"I'm just wondering, what if Louisa is still in danger? What if you are in danger as well?"

She pulled back and let his questions ruminate. "What are you saying? You think someone might try again?"

"It's a possibility."

She let the idea simmer for a moment. "That's why you were looking out the window and checking out the people in the cafeteria. Have you seen anything suspicious?"

He shrugged. "Not necessarily. And, it's only a thought and you asked me to be honest. I think it's best to be on guard, at least somewhat."

She looked away and remembered the stranger she'd seen.

"What is it, Mia?"

"There was a man I literally ran into earlier. I just got a strange feeling that he was following me."

"What did he look like?"

Mia's phone vibrated. "Hold on a second." She read the text. "Abuela is back in her room. What do you say we go see her and I fill you in later?"

They headed through the waiting room, now only occupied by the solitary man who had been there earlier. He was asleep in the corner. Sebastian took her by the elbow, and she felt a shiver go up her spine as the doors of the ICU opened and they headed to 442.

CHAPTER 16

"Who are these people? Has something happened?" Panic permeated Mia's words as she approached Nurse Connie and the group of suited men standing in front of Louisa's room.

"These people are from the State Department," the nurse said as she gathered her files and shut the workstation a bit harder than necessary, "and they shouldn't be back here. Those two are here as security detail. And that man, St. Clair, is in charge." She pointed to a tall man with a government-style haircut leaning against the nurse's station and engrossed in a phone call.

Nurse Connie approached him from behind and rapped on his shoulder. "Excuse me?"

The gray-suited man turned as he finished his call. "Yes? What can I do for you?"

"Mia Graham is here."

"Oh yes, I've been trying to reach you," he said as pocketed his phone and pushed past Nurse Connie. "Damien St. Clair, deputy director, State Department." He took a long look at Sebastian and offered a hand to Mia.

"What are you doing here, Mr. St. Clair, and why have you been trying to reach me?" She kept her hand unavailable, and he reluctantly brought his arm back to his side.

"Let's step into this consultation room," he said as he put his hand on her elbow to lead her.

Mia pulled her arm away and held her ground. "I want to speak with the nurse about my grandmother's condition."

"I'm sure the nurse can come back in a few minutes. This won't take long."

Mia looked at Connie.

"I need to check on a patient, Mia. I should only be a few minutes and can give you a full update then."

Mia looked straight into the eyes of the bull-headed man. "You have five minutes."

"Would you like me to join you?" Sebastian offered.

"I'll be fine. I'll only be five minutes." She turned and walked past the two guards who were careful to avoid eye contact. She stood in a cramped semi-private room that held three chairs and waited for St. Clair to catch up.

"Let's sit down, Ms. Graham," he said as he unbuttoned his gray jacket and began to sit.

"I'll stand." She crossed her arms.

"As you wish. I can certainly see the resemblance between you and Louisa."

Her face tightened. "What is it you want, Mr. St. Clair? More specifically, what are you doing here?"

"I'll get to the point."

Mia waited for him to continue.

"Because of the attempt on the ambassador's life, the State Department has a responsibility to protect her and any government secrets she may possess. We have started our own investigation and are trying to determine if there is an ongoing risk. As a precaution, I have issued a security detail, just as a precaution. We will be monitoring the hospital and screening all visitors. Until we know more, we will continue to investigate. Our top priority is to assure her safety."

"Well, it seems you're a little late for that, aren't you?"

"Ms. Graham, we are following protocols."

"Fine. I do appreciate that my grandmother is receiving a security detail, however, do not overreach, Mr. St. Clair. I will not have you or your people impede my access to Louisa or her care by the staff. Is that clear?" She waited for a response.

"No argument from me," he said raising his hands in resignation.

"Fine," Mia continued, "if we are done, I am going to visit my grandmother. You don't have a problem with that, do you, Mr. St. Clair?"

"Of course not. But I must tell you that the FBI is also involved in the investigation, and both agencies would like you to come downtown to answer some questions."

Mia's face reddened.

"After you pay a visit to Louisa, of course," he added.

She reached for the door. "Not today, Mr. St. Clair," and headed to 442.

The FBI? Now that was an agency that left a bad taste in her mouth. After the fire, they'd hounded Louisa for weeks wanting to interview Mia about the "circumstances surrounding the explosion." The investigators had been cold, calculating, and expressionless, and Mia had been terrified, but Louisa had protected her from their probing. But now, she may need to shove her disdain aside. These agencies had valuable resources, and they might be of help in discovering who was behind this morning's attack. The fact that they were there, this quickly, told Mia that both her and Sebastian's instincts were right. There was more at play here, and the security provided by Homeland might very well provide some peace of mind when it came to Louisa's safety.

The two guards shifted as she and Sebastian approached the door and blocked their entry. "Mr. St. Clair," Mia said loudly as she looked back at the fortysomething career politician walking confidently in her direction. "Tell them to move. Now." Her tone of voice surprised the darkly clad men, and she saw Nurse Connie look up from the adjoining workstation and flash a smile of respect in Mia's direction.

He nodded and they shifted back toward the outskirts of the door frame.

"And Mr. St. Clair, please let them know that I am allowed unobstructed access to Louisa. Is that clear?"

St. Clair clenched his jaw and gave a slight nod. "We do need to screen visitors, Miss Graham," he said glancing in Sebastian's direction.

"He is with me."

"It's okay," Sebastian offered. "You go on in, Mia. I have some business to attend to, if you don't mind. I won't be too long and I'm just a call away."

She nodded and then turned to the redheaded guard who was the size of an oak tree. "When he returns, you let him in. And," she added her finger pointing up to his face but barely reaching his chin, "don't frisk my guests." He remained stoic as she entered the room.

Mia pulled the chair next to the bed and clasped Louisa's cool hand and willed her to wake up. As she listened to the clock tick away the minutes, she considered her next steps. How she wished for Louisa to wake up so together they could figure out who was after her and why.

"Abuela, it's me, Mia. I hope you can hear me. I love you and I need you to fight and come back to me. I know you're pretty banged up, but you're tough. I need you to get better." The resolve and desperation in Mia's voice twisted together and then dissipated as she considered what she needed to do. "And Abuela, as far as the people who want to hurt you, well, I'm not sure what kind of trouble you are in but I want you to know, I'm gonna find out what is going on, and I will keep you safe. You've always taken care of me, and now, I will take care of you. You have my word. I hope you can hear me, Abuela. I've got this."

Louisa remained silent. The monitor indicated a steady and strong heartbeat. For now, it would have to be enough. Mia pulled out a spiral notebook and jotted down the timeline of events beginning that morning. When she had listed everything, she called Charlie to see if he had any new information.

CHAPTER 17

At 5:25 p.m., Nikki, with her crimson red wool coat over her shoulders, made her way to the lobby. Her security detail, and Miguel, waited near the front doors. She strode through the plush lobby, catching glances from onlookers.

The Bannister brothers stood as she approached the sitting area just to the right of the front entrance. She tried not to react but knew her gait had hiccupped, and worked to recover. She continued toward them, inspecting their look and demeanor. Custom suits, pressed trench coats, and hats. Although they weren't twins, they clearly resembled one another, and despite their graying, well-trimmed hair and handsome smiles, they had a sordid reputation when it came to business. They played high stakes and had a lot riding on the upcoming auction.

"Well, what a surprise. Good afternoon, gentlemen." She offered her hand.

"Nikki. Good to see you," the elder brother said.

"What brings you to the LeBlanc this afternoon? You know the reception isn't until Friday evening?"

"We were in the neighborhood. Thought we would stop by to check on things. We heard about the ambassador's accident. Wanted to see if you knew how she was doing."

"I see. Well, I am on my way to the hospital to visit with her right now. I will be glad to send your regards. As to the auction, I can assure you that everything is being taken care of."

"That's good to hear. Your father assured us that we could count on you," the younger brother said. "We have no tolerance for failure. You understand?" His eyes narrowed while his smile widened.

"Gentlemen, all details are being attended to. There is no need for you to be concerned or offer reminders. I am sorry I don't have more time to visit, but my car is waiting so I must excuse myself. I look forward to seeing you both on Friday. The presidential suite at nine?"

"We will be there."

"Jonathon, Andrew, it was good of you to stop by."

They tipped their hats and she moved toward the front doors. Miguel was looking directly at her and, as if reading her face, whispered to the lead security guard. As she passed them, the guard fell in line and followed her to the car. Without a word, he climbed into the front as the driver closed her door. Inside the safety of the car, she finally looked through the tinted window at the two men who could secure or ruin her future. They stood in place, watching her, with no expression. Were they simply sending her a message or contemplating if she was capable of the task at hand? Either way, she assured herself that she could do whatever was necessary. There was no turning back.

CHAPTER 18

Nikki shoved the unspoken threat from the Bannister boys to the back of her mind. Her plan was to funnel her anxiety into action, and that meant seeing this deal through. She would know soon enough if Louisa would be able to uphold her end of the bargain, and if not, she knew what she would need to do. Convince Mia to get on board.

As she made her way to the intensive care unit, Nikki's very presence brought a vibrancy to the dull colors of the hospital. She looked out of place, and despite her outward confidence, she hated being in a hospital. She buzzed the nurse.

"May I help you?"

"I'm here to see Louisa Graham."

"Your name?"

"Nikki Santos."

"One moment." The floor-to-ceiling windows that flanked the waiting area served as a mirror, and Nikki assessed herself in the reflection but made no adjustments. "Come on through. Room 442." The door opened and Nikki made her way to Louisa's guarded room.

"Good afternoon, gentlemen," Nikki said to the stoic men outside room 442. "Aren't you a pleasant surprise?" The words hung mischievously in the air. "I'm here to visit Louisa."

"ID please," the first guard said as he reached for his clipboard. "Your name?"

She closed the space between them. "Huh, I like a professional man," she said just above a whisper as she slid her passport into his large hand, lightly caressing it as they touched. "Nikki Santos. And you are?"

"What is your relation and reason for the visit?"

"Family friend," she said meeting his gaze.

Samson ignored her flirty behavior, scanned her ID, and called in her information. In the time it took to confirm her identity, Nikki disregarded the seemingly blind bodyguard, and redirected her mind on the task at hand. Her nerves tingled with anticipation as she waited, but still managed to lean casually against the tiled wall and wait for the okay from the hulk holding her ID. He finished his muffled phone call and scratched a note on the government-issued clip board before lightly knocking on the door. "Miss Graham," he opened the door a few inches. "Would you care for a visitor?"

Nikki's hope surged. Louisa was alert and awake. This was good news.

Samson stepped back and held the door open. Nikki gave him a seductive smile. He met her eyes and then readjusted his posture.

Two steps in, Nikki stopped. She couldn't control her surprise. The guard had been speaking to Mia, not Louisa. Nikki barely recognized the woman in the bed. Her face gaunt, her hair half covered with gauze, bandages covering most of her exposed body. She looked small under the oversized hospital blanket. She would not have thought Louisa alive except for the ECG readout that displayed an active heartbeat. Nikki took a breath and turned her gaze toward Mia.

"Hello, Mia, darling. I am so sorry." She extended her hand.

Mia slid her hands into her pockets "Oh, it's you. I'm sorry. I was expecting someone else," she said as she stood.

"I do hope this isn't a bad time. I did mention I would be stopping by, remember? Tell me how you are doing. And how is Louisa?" She allowed a crack in her voice to penetrate her last question, although she already knew the answer. She listened to Mia's grim update, which only affirmed her current predicament, and turned her focus to Mia. They sat, Nikki on the vinyl love seat and Mia in the chair. The overhead light had a yellow tint, yet it did not take away from Mia's natural beauty. Despite Mia's tough exterior, she had an approachable air about her, like you'd feel with an old friend. But her eyes, they were on guard, a steely knowing look, and Nikki knew she would have to manage the next steps carefully.

Since this morning, Nikki had learned that Mia was raised by Louisa after her parents died. She'd finished her undergrad and post-graduate studies in the time it took most to receive their four-year degree. Currently, Mia worked as the senior research and appraisal consultant for the DaVinci Auction House. A respectable firm and role, but Nikki's intel indicated that Mia had passed on several high-profile positions. Why, Nikki could not quite figure out.

Nikki mentally compared herself to Mia and found them to be on equal footing when it came to intelligence, success, and wealth. But unlike Nikki, Mia had not followed her grandparents and parents into the family business. Her lack of involvement seemed peculiar to Nikki and created a future hole in the operation's supply chain. Was this a choice by Mia, or was she deliberately kept out of the loop? Either way, the time had come for Mia to get on board.

There was a knock, and a nurse's assistant poked her head in. "Excuse me. I have flowers for Mrs. Graham. May I leave them with you?" Mia stood and took off the wrapping to reveal a fresh bouquet of white lilies. They looked like something you'd send to a funeral.

"Who are they from?" Nikki asked, hoping these weren't the ones Miguel had sent.

Mia opened the card. "They're from my boss. I'm sure he is on pins and needles with worry about the gala."

"Speaking of the gala. I hate to talk business while I'm here, but I do have an item that needs to be added to the auction roster. I was working with Louisa on the arrangements. Had she mentioned it to you?"

Mia bristled and remained standing. "I thought the auction list was finalized. I am delivering the final appraisals to Lionel tomorrow. Why? What item are you referring to?"

"A set of bronze lion chenets. She assured me it would not be a problem getting them included. They were delivered about a week ago. Have they been appraised?"

"I believe I saw something on those. My grandmother was handling that and had asked Angela, one of our best appraisers, to look at them and provide the report. I've not had a chance to review it."

"I'd really like you to look at them. I know this is a terrible time, but my client is very important, and it would mean a lot if you could do this. I need them in this weekend's auction."

"That's only a few days away, plus I have Louisa to think about."

"I know Louisa shared my interest in getting this item added to the list. She was ramrodding the addition. I really need you to do this, Mia. I can count on you, can't I?"

"I'll check with Lionel and see if I can look over the item and the appraisal. Satisfied?"

"Well, there is one more thing. A private matter and one of great importance."

Another light tap on the door and Nurse Connie stepped in. "Sorry to interrupt. We will need the room. Housekeeping is here and I need to go over a few things with the charge nurse for tonight."

"How long will you be?" Mia asked her.

"Thirty minutes or so."

"That's fine," Mia said. "My guest is just leaving." Mia held the door and waited for Nikki to leave the room. They walked down the hall, saying nothing.

"Mia, let's visit in the morning. Breakfast at the Four Seasons?"

"No, I don't have time for whatever this is."

"It's very important. I can wait until Friday, but I must insist on meeting with you privately. It's a personal matter that affects an agreement I have with Louisa. What time on Friday will work for you? I can come to your grandmother's residence, if that is more convenient."

Mia sighed. "Fine, Friday at one thirty. I have a meeting at the event center after that, so we'll have to make it short."

"Yes. I'll see you on Friday."

Nikki entered the elevator and held the door, but Mia did not enter. She was a bit stronger than Nikki had expected. *That could be good*, she thought.

As soon as the doors closed, Nikki pulled out her phone and dialed Marco. Plan B was in motion. All bets were now on finding the merchandise and making sure that Mia would do her part in making the transaction happen.

"It's me. Get your team in place and meet me at the hotel in thirty minutes. I'll fill you in on the details when I see you." Her heart was racing. She recognized this feeling. It was like she was in the middle of the storm again, being tossed between exhilaration and fear. The next three days would be one for the record books if she could pull this off.

CHAPTER 19

MIA LOOKED OUT THE LARGE HOSPITAL WINDOW where the evening sky offered a parade of colors, a welcome addition to the bland room.

"Excuse me. Miss Graham?"

"Hi, Connie," Mia said.

"I thought you might be hungry, and we had an extra dinner delivered to the floor." Mia welcomed the warm gesture. If only it could brighten her dark mood that had arrived with Nikki's visit.

"Thank you. Just set it on the counter if you don't mind."

"Amanda is the night nurse, if you need anything. I'll be back in the morning."

The smell of gravy and roast beef made her stomach grumble, but she left the food untouched. She turned to Louisa who seemed to be sleeping peacefully.

Mia wished for someone to talk to, someone to be with. She thought of Sebastian, then Pete and then Charlie. All three were just a phone call away. She picked up her phone and considered calling Charlie. Since the first of the year, he'd made his interest in her clear and had considered allowing their relationship to go to the next level. Mia found him funny, smart, and sexy. But a serious relationship required honesty, and she didn't know if she would ever be willing to share what she had done.

She pulled the chair close to the bed and laid her head on the edge, her face touching Louisa's hand. The clock on the wall kept time with the monitors and set the pace of her breathing. The light outside the window faded as Mia rested next to her grandmother. A tear trickled down Mia's cheek, and she felt a finger gently wipe it away. She opened her eyes. Was someone there? She scanned the space. No one. Then she looked up. Louisa's eyes were half open and her grandmother's hand gently squeezed hers.

Mia's heart nearly stopped as she leaned forward to touch Louisa's face. "Mi abuela. Can you hear me? It's me, Mia."

Louisa mustered a small nod and tried to wet her dry lips. Mia gently gave her a small piece of ice from the cup on her dinner tray.

"I need to get someone. A doctor. And let them know you're awake."

"No, Mia." Louisa spoke just above a whisper and held tightly to Mia's hand. "We need to talk."

"Abuela, you were in a terrible accident. Do you remember?"

Louisa gave a slight nod. "No accident."

"I know. They think someone did this on purpose."

"They will come…after you. I'm sorry."

"Who will? Who is trying to hurt you?"

"The Santos family. You must," Louisa swallowed hard, trying to form her words, "cooperate." Mia gave her another piece of ice. She slowly let it dissolve before continuing. "I'm so sorry, mi Mia." Mia wiped a tear from her grandmother's face, already looking weary from the conversation.

"You have nothing to be sorry for. Just get better so I can get you home. Why don't you rest. I should get the doctor."

"Mia." Louisa's voice was barely audible, and her eyes no longer focused. "Collide...collide...scope." Her face turned ashen and her words slurred. "Co...cold...soap." She gasped for breath. For a long moment she was silent. Then her last words stuttered out in syllables "Mi, Mi, a" as she began to convulse.

The alarm jolted Mia's heart to a full sprint, and she screamed for the doctor. Medical staff pushed Mia aside and filled the room. The door remained open, and the two bodyguards looked in on the scene. Mia watched the medical team as they shouted out orders and information, everyone moving in sync to save Louisa.

A woman Mia had not met took charge and barked orders to the medical team. "She's having a seizure. Amanda, I need you to hold her head. RJ, page the doctor. Now. And someone, please clear this room."

A young nurse took Mia firmly by the arm and led her into the hall. The patient emergency alarm continued like the horn of a fire engine. Mia desperately wished someone would turn it off. She swallowed hard to keep bile from exiting her body, and nearly lost her balance. When she looked up, the guard from the hallway was by her side, and she accepted his support. What had she done? Why didn't she call for a doctor? And what was Louisa sorry for? Mia did not know how to quell the ache in her chest or withhold the sobs that erupted into the chaos as an orderly whisked Mia and the DOH security detail down the corridor toward the waiting room.

It was unclear how long Mia had been waiting outside the ICU doors. Maybe an hour. Maybe more. The entire time, she paced the hallway and held tight to her emerald necklace. She walked back and forth in front of the two bodyguards, who seemed more out of place than before and now had no one to guard. The ICU doors opened. Mia caught a glimpse of the charge nurse and sped in her direction.

"How is she? What is going on?"

"The doctor will be here in a minute to update you. I can tell you that we have been able to stabilize your grandmother."

"She's okay? You're saying she's going to be okay?"

"Here comes Doctor Cheung now. Let's visit with him."

Flanked by two white-coated residents, Dr. Cheung walked toward Mia. They talked in hushed tones as they approached.

"How is my grandmother?"

"We've been able to restabilize Mrs. Graham. Her brain had begun to swell. That is what caused the seizure. We have placed her in a medically induced coma, which will give her brain time to heal. She is in overall good heath, and I think, with time, she could very well recover."

"How long will she be in this coma?"

"No longer than necessary. We will monitor her closely, watch for a decrease in the swelling, and let you know when we think she is ready. Any other questions?"

"She woke up before this happened and talked to me. Did I cause this? Did her talking to me cause this?" Mia's face tightened in agony at the thought.

"This was not your fault." He reached out and gently touched her shoulder. "The fact that she regained consciousness, even for a minute, is a very good sign. You should be able to go back and see her in a few minutes. If you need anything else, the nurse can page me."

Mia melded into a chair, a blanket of terror now removed, and waited. Finally, the doors reopened and Mia, flanked by the two guards, headed back down the corridor. Samson opened the door to Louisa's room. If it was possible, her grandmother looked worse than before, now with a breathing tube, monitors, and wires surrounding her.

Mia prayed that Louisa would, as the doctor had said, recover.

CHAPTER 20

Thursday, September 13

The door to Louisa's hospital room opened and the nurse tech rolled in a squeaky cart. "Good morning," the young woman said. She took Louisa's vitals and hummed as she worked.

Mia wiped sleep from her eyes and stretched as she got up from the vinyl chair. She had spent most of the night trying to make sense of her grandmother's words. Why would Louisa apologize to her? And what did the Santos family have to do with this? Mostly she wrestled with the word *cooperate*. Cooperate with who? And what had she said about collide and soap? It didn't make sense. Maybe the words didn't mean anything at all. She rubbed her forehead hoping to relieve the headache that had joined her in the night.

She looked in the mirror and splashed cold water on her face. Using her fingers, she brushed through her hair and retied it in her ponytail. As she exited the bathroom, Connie entered the room.

"Morning. I heard you had a rough night. You doing okay?"

"I'm fine. Just a little tired."

"I checked with the night nurse, and your grandmother is stable. That's a good sign." Connie checked the monitors and rolled Louisa to her right side. "Why don't you go home and get some rest. There's nothing you can do here."

Mia remained in place. Her eyes shifted from Connie to Louisa and to Connie again.

"I will call you if there is any update or change. I promise. You might as well get some rest."

"I feel like I should be here. If she wakes up."

"That won't happen until the doctors decide it will happen. And you will know when they make that decision. Until then, she sleeps. You can call us anytime for an update. I will take good care of your grandmother."

"Okay, I'll go," Mia conceded. "Check in with you later?"

"Sounds good."

Mia gathered her things and kissed Louisa's purple and blue forehead, then headed to the main entrance. While she waited for a cab, she turned on her phone. It came alive with missed calls and texts—eight in the last hour. Lionel, Nikki, Charlie, and Louisa's neighbor, Mrs. Murphy. Four were from Charlie; the last text from Charlie seemed urgent, almost panicked. *Mia, where are you? I need you to come to the brownstone ASAP.*

"Where to?" the cabbie asked.

"1246 Astor Ave." Traffic was light, and within a minute they were driving north on State Street. Mia opened her voicemail and listened. Lionel left a message to confirm a couple of details for the gala. She could call him later. She moved on to the second message.

"Mia, where are you?" The urgency in Charlie's voice jumped at her. "I haven't been able to reach you and I need to know that you are safe. There's been an incident at your grandmother's house. If you get this message, call me or better yet, come to the brownstone."

CHAPTER 21

THE CAB TURNED ONTO Astor Avenue and came to an abrupt stop. A hundred yards ahead a CPD patrol car, its lights flashing, blocked the road. The officer stood in front of the angled car flagging drivers to turn around. Two police cruisers, a forensics van, and an unmarked police car filled the closed street. The vehicles were parked at angles to the tree-lined sidewalk, and people milled about in small groups.

"Looks like something is going on down here, miss," said the driver. "I'm not going to be able to go any further. Do you want me to drop you somewhere else?"

"No. I'll get out here." She handed him a twenty.

"Want your change?"

"Keep it." She pushed her way out of the car and took long strides toward Louisa's brownstone. A cop stood in the center of the road directing traffic. Mia ducked to the right and out of range before he could stop her. She sped up and scanned the crowd.

Mia stepped over a barricade when she saw Charlie. He was deep in discussion with two men. Their backs were to her. "Charlie!" she yelled. He looked up and motioned her toward him. The two trench coats turned around. Detectives Taylor and

Ramirez. She'd shortened the distance between them by half when a woman in uniform stepped up to stop her. Before the rookie cop could say anything, Detective Taylor let out a bark, "Officer Williams, let her through. She's with us." The woman took a hard look at Mia and then turned, nodded at Taylor, and stepped aside. Charlie met her halfway.

"What is going on? Why are all these people here?" Her eyes darted across the scene.

"Mia, your grandmother's home was broken into earlier today. They are all here...investigating," Charlie said.

Mia searched Charlie's eyes and then looked back at her grandmother's home. The news stole her breath and she felt Charlie take her hand.

"Sorry to see you again so soon, Miss Graham." The senior detective was cleanly shaven and all business as he approached. "I assume you told her?" he said to Charlie.

"Yes, he did," Mia snapped. "What is going on?"

"We received a call from a Mrs. Murphy who resides at 1284 Astor Ave," he said as he reviewed his notes. "Mrs. Murphy reported seeing three suspicious individuals approaching the house through the back. Turns out, she was right. It appears the house was broken in from the back door. The perps weren't in there long and we're not sure what they were after. We see that the residence has a security system, but it was not armed. Any idea why?"

Mia clenched her jaw and said nothing. She looked at the brownstone and then at Charlie for answers.

"Miss Graham? The alarm?" Taylor continued.

"No. No, I don't know why it wasn't set. What did they take?"

"Well, we're hoping you can help us with that, Ms. Graham."

"Can't you do anything without my help? And, please, call me Mia." She could no longer hold back her exasperation.

"Okay, sorry, my apologies," he cleared his throat, "Mia, I'd like to ask you a few questions." He watched her before continuing. "Can you tell me if you have recently been in your grandmother's home?"

"Yes, yesterday. I came to pick up some insurance forms. For the hospital."

"What time was that?

"Around one thirty. Two at the latest."

"And did you set the alarm when you left?"

"Yes, I think so. I was in a hurry."

The men waited for a more definitive answer from her.

"Yes, I'm sure. I set it before I left."

"How often do you come to your grandmother's residence?"

Mia narrowed her eyes in response to his question. "How often? At least once a week. I'm here on a regular basis if that's what you are asking."

"Well, in that case, we'll need your fingerprints for elimination. After forensics is done, we'd like you to do a walk-through to see if you recognize anything that might be missing. Can you do that for us Miss—um—Mia?"

"Yes. Of course." Mia scanned the greenspace and then looked to the left, past the Strouds' and then to the north. The once-peaceful sidewalks were filled with what looked like the entire Chicago Police Department, neighbors, and bystanders, all looking at her grandmother's home. Gossiping. Speculating. She wanted them to leave.

"Detective Taylor, do you always bring this many people to a break-in?"

"Well, no ma'am. But we have had interest in your grandmother's case from the feds, in light of what happened yesterday, and we need to be sure that the two incidents aren't related. Due diligence, ma'am. Ramirez, get someone over here to take Miss, um Mia's prints for elimination."

Ramirez took off to find the crime scene tech just as a young officer came by offering water bottles. Mia passed on the water and sat on the curb. Charlie joined her and they hugged. She grasped him tightly and finally released her grip. "Can you believe this? Did you see or hear anything?" she asked as she pulled her knees to her chest.

"I don't know. I've been gone most of the night. I got here as the cops were arriving."

"Did your apartment get broken into?"

"I don't think so. They haven't let me in, but Detective Taylor said it was only your grandmother's house that was ransacked."

"Ransacked?" That word sounded much worse than break-in. She dreaded going inside. And dreaded telling Louisa when she woke up. "What do you think they were looking for? I can't believe everything that is happening. This is just crazy."

"I don't know. Here comes the fingerprint lady. When she's done, let's see if we can go in. It looks like they are wrapping up."

⇒ ⫼ ⇐

Mia and Charlie wiped the ink from their fingers as they made their way toward the front door. Detective Taylor flagged them in.

"Okay, they just gave us the go-ahead. Are you ready, Mia?"

She nodded. The detective instructed her to point out anything unusual. To let him know if she noticed something missing or simply out of place. Ramirez was ready with note pad. He held his pen in his left hand and pushed back his disheveled hair as they made their way up the stairs.

The foursome crowded past a CSI photographer heading out. Louisa's three-story home was lit up like a football stadium. As if the incandescent bulbs didn't offer enough brightness, the morning sun lasered in through the upper windows. Charlie and the two detectives nudged her forward, unaware she had stopped.

"Mia," Taylor began, "we'll walk through the house, one floor at a time. Just look carefully at everything. Where would you like to start?"

Mia instinctively headed to the top floor, away from the commotion below. The curved handrail felt familiar under her hand. They walked by original artwork as they mounted the stairs. Not a single piece had been touched, not even the prominently placed Gerhard Richter painting that hung on the first landing. Mia estimated its worth at nearly a half million.

The group toured the top floor and inspected the room she had occupied as a youth. The faded pink comforter, usually warmed by the sun from the skylight, was now on the floor along with the mattress. The corner of the room housed an oversized chair, its cushion on the ground, and a small glass side table. A classic white desk sat near the oversized window, its now-empty drawers pulled out and left hanging.

Mia gripped the door frame as her legs buckled. Someone coming through your space, your things, felt like a violation. Charlie slipped his arm around her waist, and she leaned into him. After a few seconds, she regained her determination to continue.

"Thanks, Charlie," she said reading the concern on his face. "I'll be fine."

She continued to the walk-in closet. Its contents littered the floor. She squatted and picked up a collectible Holiday Barbie, valuable but clearly not what the thieves were looking for. She placed it in the mesh basket that held the rest of the Barbie accessories.

Mia's favorite records and books, all classics, along with her gemology set were strewn across the floor. The gemology set was clearly not valuable, but it had been at the top of her Christmas list when she was fourteen. Complete with a rock polisher, fake gemstones, velvet-lined viewing boards, and a microscope, she had spent hours researching and documenting rocks she'd brought home from trips abroad.

In the back corner of the closet, her teal duffle bag, her only remaining item from before the fire, lay open, its contents exposed. A sob caught in her throat as she gathered her diary, along with the clothes she had packed almost exactly fourteen years earlier. She hated that her things had been touched by strangers.

"Anything?" Detective Taylor interrupted her thoughts. "We have a lot of ground to cover."

"Let's keep going," she said. The small assemblage glanced into the bath across the hall, the guest room, and the guest bath. All were undisturbed. They headed to the second floor.

She stopped at the threshold of her grandmother's expansive bedroom. Every dresser drawer had been pulled out and their contents flung across the intricate Persian rug. The mattress lay on the floor, deep gashes opened to reveal foam and coils. The night tables were overturned. Mia's legs felt like jelly, and she imagined she looked like a newborn giraffe attempting its first steps. The three men around her didn't seem to notice. Determined to keep going, she gripped Charlie's arm for extra stability.

In the dressing room, the contents of Louisa's jewelry drawers had been dumped, in a surprisingly careful manner, across the counter. Mia fingered the rings and necklaces. It seemed the bulk of Louisa's jewelry remained.

Mia picked up the ruby necklace, the one she'd worn to the World Business Forum when she was seventeen. The necklace had highlighted her black floor-length gown and Mia's newly forming curves. The entire ballroom of the Waldorf sparkled with beautiful people and champagne fountains. Near the end of the evening, Mia wandered to the balcony that overlooked the lake to breathe in the cool evening air. A brightly lit ship drifted by, and Mia wondered what it would be like to spend her life traveling and studying foreign cultures and artifacts. *Maybe even publishing a book about it someday*, she thought.

"What are you doing outside by yourself on a night like this?" Charlie leaned in beside her, placing his warm jacket over her exposed shoulders.

Mia's stomach fluttered as her handsome neighbor, dressed in a black tuxedo, now without his jacket, focused all his attention on her. That night, she saw Charlie with fresh eyes.

As she stood in her grandmother's closet, her finger tracing the ruby necklace, Charlie's hand on her shoulders brought her back to the present.

"Mia, do you think anything is missing?" Charlie said.

She set down the necklace and wondered if he remembered that night. "No, not that I can tell," she said, "but my grandmother kept her best jewels in her safe, through here." She led them into a back section of the dressing closet to a safe tucked behind three full-length mirrors. It had been drilled open. No small feat. While it wasn't a bank vault, it was a substantial safe and would have taken an industrial tool or two to have penetrated its steel exterior. The velvet-lined drawers were on the floor, empty. Mia told the detectives that all of her grandmother's jewelry was documented and insured. She would find the paperwork and get it to them soon.

"If they wanted jewelry, why didn't they just start here? Why bother with the other rooms?" Mia asked.

"Very good question, Mia," Detective Taylor said.

Taylor mumbled something to Ramirez before they headed to her grandmother's private office. Papers and books littered the wood floor, the items scattered as though a tornado had blown through. She bent down to pick up an autographed baseball signed by Babe Ruth and returned it to its stand. Charlie picked up another baseball, this one signed by Mickey Mantle. On the ground lay the framed, original artwork from Walt Disney. Mia knelt to gather the piece and dropped the broken glass into the receptacle, reattached the frame, and returned it to the shelf. Mia inspected the mishmash of Louisa's collectibles that were strewn around the room.

"I'm sorry, Detective, I won't know what is missing until I go through everything. Even then, no guarantees until my grandmother comes home." Mia's own words stopped her. Louisa. The break-in had distracted her, and she hadn't even checked to see if there was a message from the hospital.

She reached into her pocket as they headed to the main living area, which housed the study. Four missed calls.

"Miss Graham. Mia." The detective's voice boomed startling a young officer walking by. Taylor pointed to her phone. "Just a few more minutes, Mia, and then we can wrap this up," he said more as a directive than a suggestion. Detective Taylor took her elbow and directed her toward the parlor. He was more on the ball than Mia had originally given him credit for. She returned her phone to her pocket and gave the last leg of the walk-through her full attention. She wanted to be done and check on Louisa.

"Go ahead and look around, Mia," Taylor said. "I need to sign off on this report. Ramirez." Without further instruction, the junior detective assumed the position of walking aside Mia as she examined the library.

Although she was no expert, it was clear to Mia that the burglars had expended a fair amount of effort in the room—not as extensive as the upstairs, but they had given it a good once-over. Cabinet doors were left open, contents tossed to the floor. At least a half dozen of the bookshelves had been emptied, books scattered across the sofa and the area rug. But as Mia explored the mess, she admitted there wasn't much to dig through. The highlight of the room was the baby grand piano, which filled the right corner. The large windows with their moss green window treatments pulled back allowed light to soften the chaos. Despite the invaders' attempt, the room remained inviting.

As Mia gave the room a final scan, her eyes stopped at the security monitor, neatly hidden among books on the top shelf. "Detective Taylor, what did you say happened to the security system? Why didn't the break-in alert the monitoring company?" Mia asked.

He looked inside the folder he held. "According to the preliminary report from the tech team, the power was cut this morning, temporarily disabling the system. The perpetrators probably knew exactly how long they had before the backup would kick in and send notification. This was clearly a professional job."

Despite the growing fatigue Mia felt, they continued onto the main floor, which included the dining room, kitchen, family room, a small butler's pantry, and the screened-in porch. The main level appeared to be basically intact with the exception of the rear door. Hundreds of small shards of glass covered the floor.

"This is where they came in," Taylor explained. "The intruder took a blunt-force object and broke the glass. It appears one of the perps may have cut themselves, probably their upper arm, when they reached in to disengage the lock. Forensics gathered a sample and it's been taken to the lab. There's no indication that they went to the garage or to Mr. Baker's residence, but we can do a walk-through if you would like." He looked to Mia as they paused on landing.

"No, I'd like to finish this up."

Taylor nodded and Ramirez, who had been pulling up the rear, turned and led the group back into the kitchen. Ramirez pulled out a form and asked Mia to sign it. The last few crime unit techs gave Taylor an obligatory nod as they headed out the front door.

"We'll analyze the evidence we've gathered and continue to visit with witnesses. Once I know more, I will give you a call. And Mia, while it is doubtful that whoever broke in will come back, we can arrange to have an officer monitor the property if you would like."

Mia shook her head. "No, that won't be necessary." Her hands enunciated her decision. She glanced up at Charlie who peered at her over his glasses. It was clear he was not in agreement.

"Well, if you change your mind, let us know. We'll get out of your way now."

"Before you go, Detective," Mia said, "what new information do you have about the hit-and-run?"

"I wish I had good news for you," he said. "We are working the case but have few leads. Our guys are checking chop shops and monitoring the chatter, but so far, no suspects."

"I have a family friend coming into town." Mia paused and avoided eye contact with Charlie. "He's former military and has some connections in the city. He works in the high-tech security business. I'm hoping you might read him in on the case and see if he can be of any help. I want to know who did this to my grandmother. I'm sure you want the same, don't you?"

"Of course, but—"

"Great," Mia interjected. "I'll have him touch base with you when he gets here. I'll give him your number. You can expect a call. Pete Haines. And thanks, Detective."

Nothing else was said as they walked to the front door. Mia turned off lights as they went. Ramirez said something about her calling if she needed anything. The words and events of the day were blurry, and she felt the last drop of her energy evaporating.

Taylor and Ramirez stepped out into the late afternoon sun and Charlie waited.

"You doing alright?" Charlie said.

"I just need a few minutes to myself. I'll be fine." She noticed the lines around his eyes tighten as he looked at her. It'd been a long twenty-four hours for both of them, and they both needed rest.

"I'll be fine," she repeated with a firm tone. "The first thing I'll do is call Henry to come and repair the back door. Then I'll reach out to the security company."

"Let me take care of those things. I have Henry's number on speed dial and the security info downstairs."

Charlie wanted to help, to do anything he could. She nodded an okay. He gave her a soft kiss on the lips and she promised to keep him updated on Louisa, although she hadn't yet told him about her waking last night or that she was now in a coma. But there hadn't been a chance, and now she simply didn't have the strength.

They hugged, a long comforting hug that made her want more, and then pulled away. Just before the door closed behind him, he turned and offered a tired smile. One word, and he would come back. But that would be a mistake.

Standing alone in the front entry, she hung her coat and decided to rest, for just a moment, in the chair used to remove soiled boots. She looked across the floor at the prism of color cast by the sun through the third-floor cathedral windows. The light danced in silence against the walls and the floors. The grandfather clock in the hall ticked steadily, in a way that comforted Mia. The leather chair enveloped her. She kicked off her boots and pulled the footstool over. Fatigue weighed her down. She took one last look at her phone. No call from the hospital. Mia reassured herself that Connie would call if there was a change in Louisa's condition. She stowed her phone and, for now, decided to simply not move.

CHAPTER 22

NIKKI RECEIVED A TEXT FROM MARCO.

Went to the store. They were out of carrots.

Nikki didn't think he was funny. She knew he didn't want to send a message that would be incriminating, but this was not funny. Where was the merchandise? She had just over two days to get her hands on it.

She replied.

Get over here. Now. We need to talk.

Nikki spent the next twenty minutes pacing the length of her suite, feeling like a lion, hungry and prepared to devour whatever stepped in front of it. Only Miguel had bravely remained in the room. The rest of her staff had temporarily disappeared. It was a good sign that Miguel could withstand her brusqueness.

Twenty minutes passed. "Miguel, where the hell is Marco?"

"He's on his way up now, Miss Santos."

She went to the bar and poured herself a bourbon. It numbed her anxiety, but she knew she would need to take it easy on the liquor or else she wouldn't have clarity to navigate the evening's client meetings. She swirled the warm liquid over ice as Marco walked in.

"Marco, am I going to have to do all the work myself?" Her voice seared across the room. Miguel took his hat and jacket. "Well?"

"What can I tell you?" he said walking to the bar. "The merchandise was not at the old lady's house. I had my best guys on it and they had less than fifteen minutes to toss the whole place."

She walked behind the sofa and stared out the floor-to-ceiling windows. The overcast skyline reflected her mood.

Marco poured himself a scotch, a double, and watched her as she roamed from one end of the suite to the other. "Miss Santos?" he said, interrupting her back-and-forth procession.

She stopped at the sofa and sat her glass on the table. "Sit down," she ordered. "Tell me about Mia's routine and what you have for leverage."

"Her routine is simple, really, and has been easy to track. We've spotted her with two people, outside of hospital staff, a Sebastian Armani, and a Charles Baker."

"What do you know about them?"

Marco pulled out a folded piece of paper from his coat pocket. "The first one, Sebastian Armani. He was a bigshot financial investor until he just up and quit one day. Now he drives around a fancy Escalade, seems very familiar with the target and the home. We first spotted him at the hospital. The second one, Charles Baker. He works for the *Trib* as a photographer, lives in the old lady's basement. He's an only child, and his parents live in the city, and from what we found, they are loaded. We've seen him at the hospital and at the house on Astor. They seem close. Want more?"

"Tell me about her phone calls. Emails."

"She's been in contact with a Pete Haines. Former military, rough background, grew up in Sycamore Heights, same as Mia. Currently works freelance as a security consultant. He's headed to Chicago today."

"Anything else?"

"She's had several emails back and forth with some people at the DaVinci House and a couple of clients. Her work contacts are a Lionel McMasters and a Rebekah Summers. Do you want the clients?"

"No, go on."

"The two detectives from the CPD, Detectives Taylor and Ramirez, have been everywhere—at the hospital and the brownstone. Oh, and there is new security in place at the hospital. Organized by one Damien St. Clair, deputy director, State Department."

"I've met the hospital security. A real show of concern by the feds but not an obstacle if we need to bypass it."

She glanced across the room where Miguel was busy typing into his tablet. She held her glass and swirled the remaining cubes. She stared at it like it was a crystal ball.

Nikki moved next to Marco. He straightened and leaned in. "Go with the photographer. Put a twenty-four-hour tail on him. Set it up, but don't make a move until you hear from me, got it?"

He nodded.

"You're sure you can handle this?" She met his oil black eyes head-on.

"Yes, ma'am." She held his gaze until she was convinced.

"Alright." She stood and signaled Miguel. "Keep your cell phone on and keep me updated. Miguel will show you out." She left her glass on the counter and went to dress.

The stylist waited in Nikki's dressing room with a forest-green business suit, pressed and ready.

Nikki glanced at the outfit. "I'll be wearing my onyx-colored pantsuit," she said.

"Yes, ma'am. I'll get it ready. May I ask? Why the change?"

"No, you may not."

CHAPTER 23

Three solid knocks on the door caused Mia to jump. It took a second to get her bearings and realize she had fallen asleep in the foyer at Louisa's. Jasper lay comfortably on her lap. Mia rubbed the cat's head and glanced at the grandfather clock. She'd been asleep for almost an hour.

"Get down, Jasper," she said as she nudged him to the floor and looked through the peep hole.

It was Louisa's handyman, Henry Petrakis. He was built like a bull and had the work ethic of a Clydesdale. For all the years she had known him, the only thing that changed for Henry was his hairline, now receding to the point of desertion.

"Hello, Henry. It's good to see you."

"Hello, Mia." He reached to shake her hand, shifting his toolbox to his left hand. "Charlie called and said you need the back door fixed."

"Thank you for coming so quickly."

"I'm sorry to hear about the break-in and Louisa's accident. How is she doing?"

"She's holding on. Looks like it may be a longer recovery than we had hoped.

"Ms. Louisa, she's a tough one," he said. "She'll be out of that hospital before you know it."

"I'm sure you're right."

"Well, know that me and the missus are praying for her recovery. Oh, and Ophelia sent over some of her homemade Moussaka." He handed her a container. "You can just put it in the fridge for whenever you need it."

"That was thoughtful. And thank you for the flowers you sent. I know Louisa will love them." Mia's voice broke.

"You send her our love, won't you?"

She nodded as she took his jacket.

"Now, why don't I go take a look at that door?" he said as he trotted toward the back entrance.

Mia went to the kitchen and filled the heavy teapot, now a deep gray from use, and placed it on the burner. Mia stared at the flame, her mind still on Henry's comment, "She'll be out of that hospital before you know it." What if Louisa's recovery takes weeks, or even months? What if she doesn't recover? No, she stopped the train of thought and dismissed the later possibility. But the reality remained. Louisa's recovery would most likely be slow, and that meant Mia would need to step in and tend to Louisa's affairs. Graham Mining. The gala. When the water reached a boil, she reached for a large green mug and the cannister of chamomile teabags.

As the tea steeped, she grabbed a notepad and wrote down all the things she remembered Louisa saying.

- No accident
- Santos family

- Cooperate
- I'm sorry
- Collide or cold?
- Soap?

The last two didn't make sense, but Louisa seemed lucid for that brief period. What did she mean? And what did the Santos family have to do with all of this? As she studied the list, Mia rubbed her brow to alleviate the drumming in her head. She breathed in deeply, and the tea's sweet apple aroma worked against her frayed nerves.

Mia walked toward the back of the house, with Jasper as her shadow, and pulled the basement entry door shut to eliminate the draft and muffle the sound of Henry working.

The three-season porch was at least ten degrees cooler than the main house, but the view was worth the chill. Garden beds lined the outer fence and burst with the last bit of color of the season. The roses and day lilies were flanked by white hibiscus shrubs that flowered from late summer to fall. The other plots were filled with vegetables. The majority were herbs, but Louisa always made room for cherry tomatoes and mini sweet peppers. Not one weed in sight. Mia imagined Louisa working the garden wearing her floppy hat the color of tarnished haybales and the worn gardening boots that sat under the bench next to the outside door.

The cold invaded Mia's space, and in defense she covered herself with the heavy plaid throw and held the mug close to absorb the warmth. Two cardinals fluttered near the small ornamental tree and then stopped to bathe in the fountain that sat in the center of the garden. Surrounded by stone pavers, the four-tiered sculpture was a piece of art. Mia's grandfather had commissioned the work when he and Louisa had purchased the brownstone nearly forty years earlier. They met the artist, Constantino Navoli, on a late summer trip to Florence and hired him to create the piece that was now in the back garden. It took him four months to complete. A solid base of chiseled stone supported five plump cherubs that held a copper-edged birdbath. Along the side, just above the cherubs, sat a small cast-iron door the size of a small shoe box. It connected to a small drain and collected loose leaves and dirt. To anyone else, it appeared to be part of the design, but as a girl, Mia used the secret alcove to hide her treasure box. She wondered if she had left anything in it? Curiosity gnawed at her until she slid on the garden boots and went to take a look.

She pulled hard on the outer grate, and to her surprise it opened with ease. Inside was a second door. She turned the knob. Nothing. She jiggled it back and forth but still nothing. She peered into the darkness and saw a hole for a key. Was it locked? She didn't recall ever needing a key. Perhaps she would ask Louisa about it, or maybe if Henry had time, he could get it open for her. Her breath made a small cloud, and her fingers tingled from the cold. Enough of this treasure hunt for now. Better get inside and check her messages.

She slipped out of the boots and retucked the blanket around her. She took a long sip of tea and grabbed her phone. She hit play. Charlie left a brief message saying the security company should be by soon. Mia listened to a second message from Sebastian and one from Lionel's assistant, Rebekah, confirming their appointment for tomorrow afternoon. Nothing from the hospital.

She walked to the kitchen to rinse her mug and called Sebastian. She updated him on Louisa and the break-in and agreed to let him pick her up at five o'clock and drive her to the hospital.

As she hung the mug back in the cabinet, the doorbell rang.

"Afternoon, miss. I'm Matt with Star Security. I'm here to work on your system." The young tech flashed his ID and a large toothy smile. Mia let him in and pointed him in the direction of the security panel and then made her way upstairs. She felt ready to tackle some of the mess from the break-in and decided to start in Louisa's office.

Her stomach tightened as she entered the room. She stood at the threshold and surveyed the mayhem. It seemed clear that they were looking for something specific. Had they found it? She steadied her breathing and made her way to Louisa's desk, carefully refilling the individually labeled folders. After finishing there, she turned toward the floor-to-ceiling bookshelf. The books brought back good memories, and most of her all-time favorites were in this room. She picked up the first-edition copies of *The Adventures of Tom Sawyer, Charlotte's Web,* and *To Kill a Mockingbird* and restacked them. In addition to the classics, Louisa had books on virtually every subject—design, history, earth science, geology, and archeology. Mia first developed her love for the arts and antiquities in this library. One book, *The Treasures of the Louvre,* inspired Mia and her grandmother to take a summer trip to France to see many of the pieces firsthand. Each summer, the duo would pick a new destination, one with a significant world-renowned exhibit, and spend two weeks enjoying the culture and visiting museums. As she stacked the last of the books on the shelf, she heard Henry calling from downstairs. She put the chairs back in their places and shut off the light.

"There you are," he said as they met on the landing. "I'm all done for today. I've temporarily sealed and secured the entry, so you will have to use the front door until tomorrow. I've ordered the replacement door and will pick it up first thing in the morning. What time do you want me to come by?"

"Anytime will be fine. Do you still have the extra key Louisa gave you?"

"Yes, but what about the security alarm?" He bent down to caress Jasper.

"I will call you with the code once the system is back up and running. Looks like Jasper likes having you around." He smiled as he stood. She reached for his jacket and knocked hers from the coat tree in the process.

"Let me get that."

"Thanks, Henry," she said taking her coat.

"No problem. Be sure to let us know if there is any change with Louisa."

"I will."

She shut the door and paused. She looked at her jacket and remembered the key she'd found yesterday. Could this be the key to the portal in the fountain? She removed it and looked it over closely. About the right size and it did seem old. "Come on,

Jasper," she said as the cat rubbed against her leg, "let's go give it a try." She headed to the back of the house and stopped to put on the weathered rubber boots.

"Miss Graham?" The security tech called from the front of the house.

"Yes. I'm back here." The half-opened screen door clicked shut behind her. She slipped the key back into her pocket, her boots squeaking as she headed into the den.

The gangly tech with wire-framed glasses walked toward her with his toolbelt slung over his shoulder. "I'm all done for today." His words spilled out slowly like drips from a faucet. "They really did a number on your system. Seems like a real professional job," he said as he lowered his gear to the floor. "Unfortunately, I was only able to install a temporary fix that will alert you with a chime when a door is opened. Let me show you." He pulled a small remote from his shirt pocket and pushed the button, which activated the system and produced a three-part chirp that made Mia wince.

"Well, you can't miss that," she said.

"Here's the remote. I recommend keeping it with you at all times. Whenever a door opens, you will receive a notification. If you need to deactivate it, you push this button," he said showing her how to operate it. "I'll be back tomorrow with the supplies to repair and upgrade the system. You do want it upgraded, don't you?

"Yes, whatever you need to do." She spoke faster than usual hoping that it might speed the exchange up. "Will tomorrow morning work for you? I will be sure that someone is here to let you in."

"That'll work. Just need you to sign some paperwork," he replied in his no-reason-to-be-in-a hurry cadence.

Mia dug deep for patience as he rummaged through his bag for a clip board with the service order attached.

"Just put your John Hancock here and I'll get 'er taken care of." While she signed, he activated the alarm system.

"That looks like everything," Mia said as she handed him the clipboard. "I'll walk you out."

She outpaced him to the front door and jumped when the temporary alarm sounded. With the door locked, she made her way to the back porch and shook her head as she endured the chirp of the alarm.

In the garden, the sunlight sat low behind the trees and cast long shadows across the impressive fountain. Mia ran her fingers down the long edge of the heavy key. She reopened the outer grating and then finagled the key into the hole. It wouldn't turn. She pulled it out, blew into the hole, and tried again. With some extra pressure, the key met its match and the lock clicked. She pulled the round latch and the door opened. Mia's heart revved with anticipation. She pulled out the metal treasure box and blew off a cobweb and light layer of dust that covered it. Wiping her hands on her jeans, she sat on the rock base and tried to remember what she had last put in the box and how long it had been. She opened the lid and found a notebook, wrapped in plastic, with a small cream envelope on top. Mia recognized the stationery from Louisa's desk. Mia turned the envelope over in her hand. On the front, it said, *Mia.*

With the light fading and her fingers cold, she decided to head inside. Her eyes squinted in anticipation of the alarm signaling her entrance. After locking the door behind her, she sat in the rocker, turned on the floor lamp, and unwrapped the journal.

Mi querida Mia,

If you have found this journal, then, most likely, something has happened to me. I am sure you have many questions. I can only explain by saying life is never simple and is ever complicated by our choices. I am sorry to say I have made choices I regret, and I hope that the effect of these will have a minimum impact on you.

For now, you need to know that my most recent acquisition is safely hidden in the place of broken glass and beauty that changes with the day, just like you, mi Carino.

Stay safe and know that you are cherished.
Todo mi amor,

Abeula

Mia folded the note and opened the journal. The first page simply said, *Book Two*. The pages were filled with entries that included a date, time, dollar amount, and a brief description, most referring to gems or artifacts. The first notation was dated March 6, 1984. She didn't recognize the handwriting. Then, on June 24, 1990, the script changed. These entries were written by her father. His style had an old-school flair and, because he was left-handed, the strokes leaned to the left. The entries remained consistent. Dates, amounts, initials, a variety of symbols. She continued to thumb through until the handwriting changed again. September 15, 2005. Three days after the fire. The entries matched Louisa's cursive style. She ran her finger over the inked text. What was this?

The doorbell rang. Mia walked to the front door and looked through the peephole. The porch light illuminated Sebastian. She had lost track of time.

"Hello, Sebastian. Come on in," she said as the alarm announced his arrival.

"I'm not early, am I?"

"No, I'll be ready in a minute. Make yourself at home."

"Thanks."

She grabbed her bag and the journal and headed upstairs. The fresh pair of leggings and oversized sweater felt good against her goose-pimpled skin. Hair pulled back and fresh lipstick on, she slipped on her ankle boots and jacket. She picked up the journal and considered it, then for safekeeping, stowed it in the office safe.

CHAPTER 24

As she reached the landing at the bottom of the stairs, her phone rang. "It's the hospital," she told Sebastian.

"I'm calling for Mia Graham?"

"This is Mia."

"This is Dr. Cheung from Northwestern."

"Is everything okay?"

"Yes. Just calling to give you an update on your grandmother's condition." Mia stood at the kitchen island and put the phone on speaker. "So far, the medically induced coma seems to be working as we'd hoped. I've looked over her labs and vitals. We are seeing improvement, and her blood pressure is within an acceptable range."

After the call came to an end, Mia and Sebastian shared a relieved look. "Well, that seemed like good news, right?" He nodded. "Since I won't be needing a ride to the hospital tonight, why don't you stay for a while? Can I get you something to drink?"

"Coffee would be great, if it's not any trouble."

"Two coffees coming up," Mia said as she filled the Keurig and popped the coffee pod into its slot.

Sebastian headed to the family room and turned on the stereo. He pulled an album from the record collection Louisa had acquired over the years and gently set the needle onto the spinning vinyl before settling into the large leather chair. With Jasper winding through his feet, he looked like he belonged there.

Before the second cup of brew finished, the doorbell rang. Sebastian stood, but Mia signaled that she would get it.

"Hey, Charlie," Mia said. "Come in."

"I wasn't sure if you'd still be here. Hey, Sebastian." He stepped inside and waved in the direction of the family room.

"When are you heading to the hospital?" He wiped his damp hair away from his face and took off his glasses to dry them.

"As it turns out, I just spoke to the doctor. Abuela remains stable and in a medically induced coma. They said there is no reason for me to be there now. Really, they've insisted. Anyhow, I plan to stay here tonight and head over there in the morning. I'm making some coffee. Would you like a cup?"

"I'll have to pass. I submitted my pics for tonight's edition, but I have to get back to the protest site. Something about some big speeches and possible confrontations."

"Sounds like it might get heated. Better keep your head down just in case things go sideways."

"Think I've seen worse than upscale tenants protesting a building project. But it may take the rest of the night. Duty calls. Wish I could stay," Charlie added wistfully.

"By the way," Mia said, "Henry patched up the door and both he and the security guy will be back tomorrow to finish up the repairs. But for now, everything is taken care of. Why don't we plan on touching base in the morning."

"Okay, but don't hesitate to call if you need anything." He took her face in both hands and moved it to ensure she looked directly at him. "I can always tell Richfield to find someone else to cover for me if you need company."

His thoughtfulness warmed her, and for a moment she considered accepting his offer. "No, I'm fine." She touched his familiar hands and moved them away. She widened her eyes and looked directly at him to emphasize her words. "I'll call if there is any news. I promise." Then she took his arms and pivoted his body toward the now open door. "Now, go take some front-page pictures."

"Talk to you later," he said over his shoulder and then hesitated as if he considered turning back toward her before continuing into the misty night.

With Charlie gone and the door bolted, Mia felt the emptiness of her life. She rationalized that this was the price required to maintain clear judgment and protect herself. But it came at a cost. And now, the cost was being on this journey alone.

"Here's your coffee." She handed the ceramic green mug to Sebastian. He held it loosely in his hand and allowed the steam to rise off the top for a moment before taking a sip.

"Sebastian," Mia started up again. At the sound of his name, Sebastian turned and gave her his full attention. She continued. "Thank you for this. For looking out for me and Louisa. For being available."

She watched his eyes soften as he smiled. "No thanks necessary," he said. "I'm glad I can help out."

The music warmed the room, and Mia found it interesting how comfortable she felt sitting with Sebastian, simply sipping coffee and listening to an old jazz tune.

"Do you recognize the song?" Sebastian said, interrupting her thoughts.

She tilted her head to the left and concentrated. "It seems familiar. Where do I know it from?"

"About ten years ago, we attended the Chicago Celebration of Independence. The group South Town Jazz performed that night. They played this song. It's called 'The Sunny Side of You.' Do you remember?"

"Yes. Wasn't it at the Pier? The Fourth of July?"

"That's right. And Louisa had everyone talking about her dance with the governor."

"I do remember that. He spun her around the ballroom. I remember how her navy blue sequined dress sparkled under the lights that decorated the pier. Oh my gosh. I haven't thought of that in years. She absolutely stole the night."

"I believe a picture of them was featured in the Sunday paper. She wasn't too happy about that as I recall," he laughed, his husky tone filling the room.

"She really is something, isn't she?" Mia said. The question lingered, not requiring an answer. Mia smiled at the memory and then at Sebastian. "I know I said it before, Sebastian, but I really do appreciate you. You've been an important part of my abuela's life for years, and I think I'm just beginning to realize how much that has meant to her."

"Louisa and I go way back. There's nothing I wouldn't do for her or you for that matter." His words sat in the air, and Mia wondered about their history. Perhaps he could shed some light on the journal tucked upstairs. Before she formulated her question, he continued. "Speaking of you, are you getting hungry?" He went to the kitchen and rinsed his cup. "I'd be glad to pick something up for you."

"Actually, I am a little hungry. I thought I'd just run down to Hunan Garden. Do you want to join me?"

Before Sebastian replied, Mia's phone rang. Rebekah, from work, she told him.

"Go ahead and take it. I want to look at the back entry and the security panel if you don't mind. I'll be back in a minute."

CHAPTER 25

Sebastian dropped Mia off in front of the Italian eatery and drove off to find a parking spot and wait. She assured him that her impromptu meeting with Rebekah would not take long and then they'd head to Hunan's for dinner. Mia scanned the cozy restaurant. The black-and-white-checkered floor tiles and café-style seating added to its feel of authenticity.

The hostess approached wearing sensible black shoes, black pants, and a black shirt. Her jet-black hair completed the ensemble.

"I'm here to meet with an associate. Rebekah Richardson. I'm with the DaVinci Auction House."

"Oh, yes, they've reserved the back room. Right this way."

Mia followed the narrow-bodied woman to the space that would soon be filled with the gala support staff. Rebekah started the tradition a couple of years earlier as a pre-event thank-you dinner for the people who handled all of the administrative work. It had been well received, and this year, Pacelli's Pizzeria had been selected for the night out.

The hostess opened the double doors to the small room that held a conference-size dining table, neatly adorned with red-and-white-checkered tablecloth and napkins, fresh greenery down the center of the table, and white plates and sparkling wine glasses. Mia froze at the threshold.

"Is everything okay?" the hostess asked.

"Um, yes, it's fine." Mia swallowed hard.

"The dinner isn't scheduled to begin for another forty-five minutes, but you're welcome to wait."

"Thanks."

"Would you like something to drink? Wine or coffee?"

"No, thank you."

Left alone, Mia experienced déjà vu as she walked around the table. The space resembled, almost exactly, the Little Italy Diner in her hometown. It had been several years since she had been there.

⇒ ⦀ ⇐

Two years after the fire Mia and Louisa returned to Sycamore Heights for the celebration of Pete's adoption into the Acosta family. They cruised along Interstate 90 in Louisa's late-model convertible Mercedes. Mia closed her eyes and let the afternoon sun warm her face while trying to not think about where they were headed.

The Little Italy Diner was alive with activity. Balloons flanked the painted doors on either side of the brick building. Pete's adoptive family owned the restaurant that sat across from the county courthouse. Used by the chamber of commerce and the local book club, among others, the popular diner had been voted "Best Italian Restaurant in the Northern Suburbs" by the *Chicago*

Business Weekly, seven years running. Louisa parked half a block down and the smell of baked bread met them on the sidewalk.

Lively music greeted them at the door, and they followed the chatter of the guests to the private dining area. The back dining room, usually reserved for chamber of commerce luncheons, had enough space to house the entire invited group.

The Acosta kids—Lexi, Eden, and Sam Jr.—ran in and out of the crowd of people playing a game of keepaway until Mr. Acosta instructed everyone to take their seats. Mia settled in next to Pete and across from Mrs. McIntyre, the fourth-grade teacher, and Mrs. Otto, the sixth-grade teacher who'd held Pete back a grade. Pete often mentioned how sore he was over that, yet Mia had seen him develop a respect for Mrs. Otto that he didn't have for the teachers who'd bought into his wit and guise.

Louisa sat between Shelby Katz, the social worker who worked for the Northside Adoption Agency, and Sheriff Reginald Blackstone, the man credited with saving Pete.

On a frigid February night, Sheriff Blackstone responded to a call at the Roadside Tavern. Charlie Haines had drunk himself into a stupor, and the owner, ready to close for the night, called the Sheriff's office and asked if someone could give ole' Charlie a ride home. Blackstone drove Charlie home and found young Pete with no heat, no food, and no supervision. For the next three days, Pete stayed with the Acostas while Charlie sobered up in the local jail. But when the sheriff released Charlie, he walked right back to the bar and reclaimed his stool. The Acostas agreed to keep Pete until other arrangements could be made. The weeks turned into months, and now, after two years, Pete was officially a member of the Acosta family.

Shelby Katz carried herself with a measured kindness that, if tested, would be met, Mia supposed, with an ability to firmly stand her ground. Tapping her glass with a fork, she stood to make a toast. "These are the types of moments that make working within the foster system and work of adoption, worth it." She thanked the Acostas and acknowledged Pete before asking everyone to raise their glasses in a toast. Mia watched Pete grin so hard, his crinkled eyes nearly shut. The happy conversation buzzed on as they ate the extra-cheesy lasagna and breadsticks until Mrs. McIntyre spoke loudly, in a voice that could instantly quiet a classroom of ten-year-olds.

"Does anyone smell smoke?" she said. The room quieted. "I believe I smell smoke."

Silence. Then, smell overtook the moment. Smoke. Fire.

Mr. Acosta jumped from his seat, overturning his chair. Sheriff Blackstone followed him toward the kitchen. Mrs. Acosta asked everyone to exit the restaurant. Smoke alarms screeched overhead. Panic set in and sweat moistened Mia's blouse. Louisa and Pete forced her outside, one on each arm, and kept going until they were a good thirty yards away. Mia waited for the inevitable sound of fire engines, crackling flames, and explosion. Time seemed to stop. Sheriff Blackstone and Mr. Acosta finally emerged, Mr. Acosta waving a red and white napkin in the air. "False alarm, everyone. False alarm." He smiled broadly, his face red. "Just some very burnt bread. Sorry for the scare."

The party was over, at least for Mia. She waited in the car while Louisa thanked the Acostas. Pete opened her car door and they hugged. "I'll see you next weekend," he said.

⸺ ⫼ ⸺

The smell of smoke permeated Mia's senses. She scanned the room and knew that it came only from her memory, yet she couldn't help considering rescheduling when Rebekah opened the door.

"Hi, Mia." The young woman's voice was refreshing against the memory. "Sorry if you waited long. I appreciate you meeting me. How's Louisa?"

Mia updated her and admired Rebekah's ability to extend compassion while still getting work done. It seemed only a matter of minutes, and papers for the gala were signed, the auction and guest lists reviewed, and Mia's spirits lifted at having spent time with Rebekah. The other admins began to trickle in and Mia made her exit.

An awning covered a bench that sat just outside the restaurant. Mia didn't see the Escalade, so she texted Sebastian. The traffic on Rush Street had picked up and the dinner crowd scampered into storefronts. People gave her a quick glance as they entered the restaurant, and Mia met them with a smile. Still no Escalade.

Mia checked her messages and stopped on an email from Sheikh Jabari Ayed, a client and Egyptian collector from just outside of Cairo. He had a job for Mia. Would she come to Egypt to authenticate and appraise a cache of weapons, possibly from the Hundred Years War between England and France?

Contract work combined research and travel to unique locations. Two of her favorite things. Plus, jobs like this paid well and the work was typically drama free, which she was craving today. Not much drama with a fifteenth-century sword, long after its battle days had passed.

She typed a quick response.

Sheikh Ayed,

Thank you for reaching out. It is good to hear from you.

My first availability is mid-November. If you need the appraisal sooner, I completely understand, and would be glad to recommend someone else for the job. However, if you are willing to wait, let me know and Rebekah, from my office, will contact you to find a 3-day window for the appraisal and estimate.

Regards,

Mia Graham,
The DaVinci House.

She scanned a few more emails, forwarding a couple to Rebekah, and then put away her phone. At the stoplight at the top of the block, she spotted the SUV. As she tightened her jacket, a man stepped to the door of the restaurant. He wore all black, except for a crisp white bandage that covered his right hand. His baseball cap hung low on his head, and he avoided meeting Mia's gaze. Sebastian pulled to the curb. Mia watched the man enter the restaurant and considered following him, though unsure of why. The horn honked and she abandoned the thought.

As they made their way north, she sat silent, her thoughts moving to the journal. Her gut told her more was at play than simple tracking of data, and she felt a compulsion to begin digging for answers. She wanted answers for everything. The accident. The break-in. Louisa's warning. As she considered the events of the last two days, Mia felt a darkness looming. It reminded her of the feeling you get on a perfect spring day, but from the smell in the air you'd bet your last dollar that a storm is approaching.

A chill ran down her spine and her body shivered. Then, she thought of Pete. She looked forward to seeing him. For all his good qualities, he, of anyone she knew, understood the darker side of people, and she hoped he could help her find some answers.

⇒ ⫼ ⇐

Sebastian turned off the main road and cut through an alley before continuing north. The residential homes sat just a few feet from the sidewalks. Each of the gray two-story houses looked like a clone of the one before it. Black gates and small plots of grass, now deep green from the cold rain, finished the matching ensembles of the units.

"Trying a new route?" she asked.

"Um hum."

"Um hum? What? Is something going on?"

"Just traffic."

"Sebastian, I don't believe you. Be honest with me. What's going on?"

"Nothing to worry about. I thought someone might be tailing us and I just wanted to be sure."

"And?" Mia swung around to look at the cars behind them.

"If there was someone following us," he said, "I think they are long gone."

"Listen, you don't need to protect me. I need to know the truth and I also know this needs to go both ways. Agreed?"

He smiled. "Agreed."

"So what did the vehicle look like?"

"Dark blue van. Newer model. Tinted windows. I don't see them now."

She turned her body to look. No blue van. "Sebastian, who do you think is targeting my grandmother? What do you think they want?"

"I'm not sure," he paused, "but I'm sure they don't have it yet, and I believe they will keep coming until they get it." His answer sat in the air. "It shouldn't come as a surprise, Mia, that the world Louisa has worked in for the past forty years is full of cutthroat, greedy, and dangerous people. And while she didn't tell me directly, I felt like lately she had some increased concerns."

"What do you mean?"

"She seemed stressed. On edge lately," he said.

"Why didn't she confide in us, in me, if something was troubling her?"

"After your parents died, her top priority was to protect you, Mia. While I don't have details of what is going on, I am confident she did not want you anywhere near it."

"That I agree with," Mia said replaying Louisa's warning in her mind.

Sebastian pulled up in front of the Chinese restaurant. "We're here. What would you like?"

"I can go get it."

"No, I'll make the order and be right back out. What's your pleasure?"

She watched Sebastian exit the Escalade. He locked the vehicle and checked the area before entering the restaurant. Mia scanned the area. A van, midnight blue, passed the Escalade and then turned right at the end of the block. She waited. A minute passed. Then, the van appeared again and pulled into an empty parking spot about four cars back. No one exited the vehicle. Inside the restaurant, Mr. Kim and Sebastian stood near the register. She looked at the van again. Then she decided to confront the problem head-on. Her feet moved quickly as she headed straight for the idling van. The man in the driver's seat jumped as she approached. Two car lengths to go. She recognized him from the Italian restaurant. The man wore a baseball cap that tipped slightly over his thick bushy eyebrows and dark recessed eyes. The van lights flicked on and he pulled away from the curb. Mia read the license plate as he passed and repeated it to herself out loud just as she heard her name.

"Mia? Mia? What are you doing?" Sebastian took long strides toward her. His eyes filled with panic.

"The blue van. It showed back up. I thought I'd see what he wanted."

They watched the taillights of the vehicle fade into the next block, and they walked back to the Escalade.

"Come on, get in," he said opening the door for her. He sat silent.

"Sebastian?"

"What were you thinking?" he said as he twisted in the seat to meet her gaze. "You cannot underestimate what these people might do to get what it is they are after. Please don't do that again." He waited for a response. "Please?"

"Fine. Yes. I'll be more careful. But, for the record, I'm not going to simply hide in fear waiting for something to happen. Fair enough?" A slight bob of his head signaled his agreement. "We need some answers. Let's start with the license plate number from the van. I'll send it over to the detectives. Maybe they'll get a hit. Would you be willing to look into my grandmother's finances? See if there is anything unusual going on? And would you also reach out to Mike Forrester at Graham Mining? You know him, right? See if there is anything going on there that could be tied to all of this."

"I can do that. What are you going to do?" he asked with an eyebrow raised.

There was a rap on the window. Sebastian took the food from Malik and waited for her answer before putting the car in drive. The savory smell of fresh garlic and chicken caused her mouth to water.

"I'll see if Charlie has heard anything new on the hit-and-run at the paper. And I'll try and figure out what they were looking for at the house. Who knows, perhaps I'll find it."

"Sounds good. Anything else?" he asked glancing at her in the rearview mirror.

"Pete's coming into town. He's got connections into, let's say, the seedier part of town. I'm going to ask him to see if there is any chatter that might help us. For now, it's time to gather information."

"I can see you are determined, Mia. But will you take some advice? You need to trust the authorities. Once we have any information that will help, you need to let the guys with the guns handle this."

Mia scoffed.

"You've seen Louisa in the hospital. You've seen firsthand how vicious they can be. This could be dangerous, especially if they haven't got whatever they are after."

She said nothing.

"Okay," he continued. "Promise me that as you dig, you'll keep me, Pete, and Charlie in the loop. And, if you see anyone suspicious, you won't go after them yourself. Again!"

Mia smiled and shook her head, resisting the urge to roll her eyes at him.

"One thing we know is that you're being followed. These types of people are usually single minded and are often easier to spot than you think. If you see someone, stay away from them."

Mia considered the Marlboro man and what level of danger he might pose.

"Mia?"

"Yes."

"Another thing I'm sure of. Your grandmother would not want you to be in the line of fire. She'd never forgive me if something happened to you. You need to think about what she would say."

Mia did. She thought about the jumbled words her grandmother had uttered, but it did not offer answers. Her cell vibrated and she scanned the text.

"Anything important?"

"Pete's on his way over."

Sebastian pulled into the alley and entered the code to the gated garage entry.

"You don't have to walk me in."

"Humor me."

Sebastian walked through the house and checked the doors and windows. As he headed out the back entrance, she promised to keep him updated and call if she needed anything. She threw her things on the recliner and dished a large helping of steaming lo mein onto a plate. The smell made her stomach rumble. Using the chopsticks, she swirled a large helping of noodles toward her mouth. Delicious. Before she could ingest a second bite, the doorbell rang.

She rushed to the door and then stopped. She took a covert peak behind the curtain. It was Pete. "Take a breath, Mia," she said out loud. No need to be paranoid. Clearly, the conversation with Sebastian had gotten to her.

"Hey, slugger!" Mia swung open the heavy door.

"Ellie!" Pete said, unphased by the squeal of the alarm. His tight hug was familiar, like a comfortable pair of old sneakers. His arms were strong and a result of working out, a habit he had not let slide since leaving the marines.

"Come on in."

"Let me take a look at you," he said. He made her turn in a circle. "Oh, Ellie, you look awful. It's a good thing I'm here."

She shook her head. No one but Pete could be so rude and kind to her at the same time. She squared her shoulders and turned away. "I'm fine, considering, and I guess I'm glad you're here. You're in time for dinner. Want to join me? I have an extra egg roll."

Mia grabbed a plate and split the chicken lo mein between them. She told him to head to the family room with the food while she ran upstairs.

"What's that?" he asked when she returned.

"I found this yesterday. It's a journal of sorts."

Mia explained how she'd discovered the key and the box inside the garden sculpture.

Pete read the letter that Louisa had written. "Wow."

"It's full of entries. It goes back a few decades."

"What do you think it is?"

"I'm not entirely sure. I need to do some research. Thought we might dig into it after we eat."

The chicken lo mein didn't disappoint. As they ate, Mia filled Pete in on everything that had transpired over the last day and a half. She told him about the Marlboro man, Sebastian's concerns, and what Louisa had said when she woke up.

They finished eating and Mia checked in with the hospital. No change.

Mia grabbed the journal and her laptop.

As they settled in, Pete offered a suggestion. "It's cold in here. Do you want me to start a fire?" He barely got the words out and came to an abrupt halt. "I'm sorry, Ellie. I wasn't thinking. I'll grab an extra blanket from the closet."

"No, it's fine. It's time to face my demons."

CHAPTER 26

FOURTEEN YEARS EARLIER

Mia checked the kitchen clock. Only 6:30 a.m. Plenty of time for them to make the 7:55 train to Chicago. She popped two slices of bread into the toaster and slid a pat of butter onto her knife.

Her dad walked in still wearing his sweatpants and gray T-shirt. He avoided her...like she had a disease. "Morning, Dad," she said.

"Morning, Mia." His voice lacked enthusiasm. Mia studied him as he poured a cup of coffee. She held her breath, certain something was wrong.

"What is it?" She raised her eyebrows.

No eye contact. No smile. "Your mom has a stomach bug," he said. "We have to postpone the trip to the lake."

Mia shook her head and gritted her teeth to contain her anger. She glared at him, and the bread bolted from the toaster. The butter slid off her knife, missing the plate, creating a creamy yellow lump on the black granite. She glanced at the mess on the counter and back to her dad.

She clenched her jaw and turned toward the pantry her mother had imported from Italy two summers ago, an impressive piece that took up most of the wall. She opened a drawer and rooted through its contents. "I'll fix a cup of herbal tea and take her some antacids. Then you can get her a doctor's appointment in Chicago."

He laid his hand on hers. Without making eye contact, he shut the pantry drawer. She grabbed his arm as he turned back to get his coffee.

"No," he said. "We are not going. I am sorry."

"Dad, you gave me your word. Please." The request sounded half demanding, half begging. She knew she'd already lost the battle. Teetering between panic and fury, she made one last attempt at salvaging the trip. "How about we take the car and let Mom grab a cab tomorrow and meet us there? I know she wouldn't mind. I'll ask her." She turned toward the stairs.

"No, Mia." The volume of his voice rose, but the tone remained flat and unwavering. "We are not going." He blocked her path.

She stood her ground and met his gaze straight on. This was the third time the trip had been postponed since her birthday nearly four weeks earlier. The first two were work emergencies, according to her parents. After the second cancellation, Mia had stepped up her game and created a formal agreement that, after a brief but succinct presentation, had been signed by all parties ensuring a Graham family overnight trip to Chicago on September 12.

"Eric." Mia heard her mom calling from upstairs. "Can you bring me some water and an aspirin?" He filled a pale blue crystal glass with water, grabbed the aspirin bottle, and his coffee, and easily slid past Mia.

Her face grew hot. As she watched him mount the curved staircase, she tasted blood, realizing she'd bit into her cheek.

"This is your fault." She planted her feet and yelled after him. "You and Mom…and Grandma. You three are always fighting. That's what makes Mom's stomach hurt and gives her headaches. Why can't you all just get along?"

She grabbed her overnight bag and thundered her ninety-pound body to the back of the house. She slammed the screen door. Picking up steam, she continued her stampede outside, throwing her duffle as far as she could into the yard. She let out a high-pitched scream, not caring if the neighbors heard, and made her way to a small, gated door that opened to the crawlspace under the porch. She opened the rusted latch and pulled, the bottom dragging in the dirt. Squatting, she moved inside, and duck-walked under the porch toward her secret place.

The space was used for storage of forgotten items—a hose, splintered 2x4s, a couple of buckets, and empty planters. She liked it.

In the hollowed-out middle section, she sat comfortably against the concrete beams that had old pillows she'd duct-taped to them. A thick yellow quilt and her old sleeping bag sat at the base and provided a much-needed cushion. The leaves from the oak tree had accumulated under the porch, and she busied herself by scooping the remnants of summer into a tidy pile. She sat crossed-legged and searched for another task to keep disappointment away. But she could think of nothing to do and allowed the disappointment to join her.

With her knees tight to her chest, she retrieved her stuffed elephant from inside the sleeping bag and sobbed until the tears blurred her vision. She wiped her nose on her new sky-blue cardigan, given she had no other option. Who cared anyway? So what if it had been a birthday gift from her parents?

Streaks of sun sliced through cracks in the floorboard, bringing life to the dull, gray dirt. One beam was especially bright, and, like a spotlight, drew her attention to the pile of rocks that she and Pete had collected over the summer.

She peeked through the lattice toward the tree line and scanned the lot. The Acostas' cottage-style house, where Pete lived, sat silent. She wished hard for him to be outside, or just wandering by, but the landscape was empty. She leaned against the pillar and unearthed the Hello Kitty lunch box the two of them had buried using Pete's old pocketknife and a bent spade from the garden shed. It didn't take long.

Shaking the dirt from the metal container, she dumped her stash on the yellow blanket and took inventory. A couple of small candles and matches from Pete's last birthday. Seashells from her last trip to Columbia. A bag of crushed Cheetos. A Harry Potter book. A notebook and pen. And the three birthday cards she had received almost four weeks ago.

She opened the first card. It was from her dad. *You are my sunshine*, the card read with a glittery smiling sun on the cover. *Sure*, she thought. She tore the card to pieces. Bit by bit, they floated to the hole where the lunch box had been. She grabbed the matches and struck one against the red strip. Nothing. On her second try, the match burst into flame, and she touched it to the largest piece of paper. The glittery sun caught fire.

The second card was from her mom. It easily ripped in half, and she added it to the miniature campfire. The third card, pink with flowers, was from her grandmother. She held it a moment and then crushed it and tossed it on the now-inviting glow.

Using her hands like a basket, she scooped the leaves and let them float through the air, merging them with the burning paper. The blaze calmed and excited her at the same time. She widened her search. She reached for a rotted board and pulled it toward her campsite. Using her foot for leverage, she broke it in half and tossed it in. The flame leaned into the dry wood, consuming it like a meal. A breeze sifted through the lattice and her body shivered against the warmth of the fire.

She picked up the notebook and ripped pages from its spine, a handful at a time, and tossed them forward, encouraging the flame to dance. The smoke thickened and worked its way through the porch boards threatening to expose her hiding place. Her arms and legs warmed as she reached for the Harry Potter book.

"Mia?" her father yelled from the upstairs window interrupting her trancelike state. "Do I smell smoke?"

She froze. What should she do?

"Mia Eleanor Graham. Where are you? Answer me."

She waited a few seconds longer. Panic filled her body. She scrambled to her knees, knocking the heavy book into the gluttonous flame. Her knees scraped the hard ground, and she felt the hair stand on the back of her neck.

"Mia, I smell smoke. Where are you? Answer me."

She threw two handfuls of dirt at the fire, shoved the empty lunch box to the side, and half crawled toward the gate, her back and knees scraping the wood. Once clear of the porch, she ran hard to the far side of their property, as if being chased by a lion, stopping only to grab her duffle. Safely at her fort, she squinted and looked to the house. Her dad was perched at his bedroom window, scanning the yard. She breathed deeply through her nose and blew out through her mouth before answering. "I'm right here. I don't smell anything." With her fingers firmly crossed behind her back, she dropped her bag and waved. Mia watched as relief spread over his face.

A deafening blast met her ears. An explosion reverberated in her skull. The force carried her backward and she landed hard. It hurt to breath. She felt debris on her face and tried to look up, but her eyes blurred. Gasping for air, she could feel heat coming from her home. She rolled to her stomach and pulled her arms to her face. Her skin burned where the pea gravel dug into her wounds and her ripped leggings exposed a deep gash just below her knee.

The bright yellow blaze succumbed to blackness, and then the flames returned, more orange now. She opened her mouth to scream, but no sound came out. She grasped at the cold grass and listened to the crackling as the porch yielded to the heat. Her home caved in, and she wanted to melt into the ground with it. The smell of smoke rolling out of the windows burned her nostrils. Mom screamed for help.

Mia forced herself to look through slatted fingers. The demon-sized flames seemed to laugh at her as it consumed her home. From blocks away, she could hear sirens. Mia pulled herself up to her knees and tried to stand, her eyes transfixed on her parents' bedroom window. Flames poured from the opening and waves of dark smoke escaped from the rectangle, turning everything black. Blue and red lights flashed as firefighters yelled orders and dragged hoses across the lawn. Neighbors appeared but kept their distance as the flame and smell of burning wood overtook the day.

"Ellie, are you okay? Ellie, what happened?

She turned toward the voice, her ears ringing still. Pete.

She looked at him but could not speak. Tears stung her face and deep, unfamiliar sobs flowed from her. His arms wrapped around her shoulders. Another explosion and flames erupted, not as strong, but still making a statement. Pete shielded her from the image and the heat. They held each other tightly as her world crumbled and her childhood came to an end.

CHAPTER 27

PRESENT DAY

Mia and Pete shoved aside their dinner plates and opened the journal. The notations began on the second page. She flicked through the pages and estimated a couple hundred entries, give-or-take.

5.2.81 - NY / A / BD / $ / 5M / EXP % / ✓ / M.S.

6.23.81 / ART / TR / AUS / PR / 7.6M / MONT ACQ / ✓ / D.R.

7.6.81 / M.S. EM / ✓

With no legend, Mia and Pete searched the dates on page one and worked to establish a pattern. It was hit or miss. After about an hour, they decided to work backward and turned to the last page.

"Let's see. The date is *September fourteenth*. That's this Saturday," Mia said rechecking the calendar. "The date of the gala?"

"Well, maybe this is a list of all major functions she, your dad, or your grandfather attend or have attended?" He stared at Jasper, who'd temporarily joined them, as if the cat might have an answer to the question. "But, that wouldn't make sense, would it?"

"I agree. If that's all it is, why all the secrecy? Why would Louisa hide this in the garden? Let's keep going."

8.19.19 / JO.SA / PA / IV / $ / 2M / EXP % +1 / N.S / ✓ .

Mia's fingers flew across the keyboard as she searched DaVinci House's secure database. With her access, she was able to track every fine art and gem event and trade worldwide for the last fifteen years. She typed in the date August 19. Just last month.

"Listen to this. There was a private auction off the shores of Johannesburg hosted by the Adrian La Roux. He's a bigtime property tycoon and easily one of the richest people in South Africa."

She followed the link that displayed a photo of La Roux and a feature article in *Architectural Digest* that gave readers a full tour of his private yacht. Pete and Mia scanned the photos of the 365-foot-long yacht, which included a billiards room, a pool, and a helipad. She clicked the link to the article.

Only three of the top auction houses had items listed. Among the items, an impressive sphinx from the first century. She recalled Louisa mentioning it.

"So, let's see if this makes sense. 8.19.19 is the date of the event. The JO.SA seems to indicate Johannesburg, South Africa, the site of the event. PA stands for private auction."

"Agreed."

"IV. Not sure what that stands for—any ideas?"

Pete shrugged.

Mia looked over the list of sold items, the sellers and buyers. Nothing seemed to match. Unsure, she moved on. "The dollar sign must indicate money and 2M seems obvious—two million dollars?"

"Nice chunk of money."

"And then EXP percent plus one. Not sure, maybe something to do with costs or expenses."

"I would say it might have to do with payouts. Similar to gambling. Maybe meaning the expected payout plus or minus. Just a thought."

"I'll jot it down." She added to the legend and tried to not let her mind wander to Pete's past gambling trouble and the night he had showed up at Louisa's with a black eye and split lip in need of a place to sleep.

"What about NS?" she asked, checking with Pete who shook his head.

"I'm not sure about that one either," he admitted.

"And finally, a check mark. Assuming the transaction was completed?"

"Makes sense to me."

Every three to six weeks, a new entry. Most were easy to match up with events on record. The locations and amounts varied, but the initials at the end seemed less random. The last six entries all had the initials NS, and before that, they were MS, GS, or CRS. Was it a location, a person, or a reference to an auction house?

Pete yawned. Then he yawned again and she couldn't stop herself from mimicking his signs of fatigue.

"Knock it off," she said.

"Can't help it."

Around two a.m., they conceded their need for sleep. Mia shoved the computer and papers aside, and Pete adjusted the thermostat. She watched him pull his cap over his eyes as she snuggled under the warmth of the blanket. With her feet on his lap, she let sleep overtake her.

CHAPTER 28

Friday

Mia woke to the smell of frying bacon and followed the aroma to the kitchen. She found Pete whisking eggs and wearing Louisa's checkered apron. "That's a fetching look," she said as she pulled up a stool at the counter.

"Thank you," he said as he tipped an imaginary hat. "Coffee?" He poured her a cup and set it in front of her. "Sorry no cream or almond milk, just the good stuff."

"It'll be fine. Thanks."

"Breakfast will be ready in about ten minutes."

"I think I'll go get a quick shower. Won't take me long."

The hot stream felt good on her stiff muscles. The couch had been comfortable but still not her bed. She wrapped her hair in a towel and put on her black slacks and white blouse. The doorbell rang as she made her way down the wide staircase.

"I'll get it," Pete said as she arrived at the landing.

He unbolted the door, triggering the high-pitched chirp, and there stood Charlie holding two large cups of coffee. His expression was more than surprise, almost shock as he looked at Pete and then Mia and then Pete again.

"Hi, Pete. Mia. I didn't realize you had company," he said as his face turned a deep shade of red. "I, um, just thought you might need some coffee, so I grabbed you a cup this morning. I'll just drop it off and come back later," he said handing a cup to her. Pete headed back to the kitchen. "Sorry I don't have any for him," Charlie added.

"It's fine," Pete said over his shoulder.

Mia opened the door wider. She forced him to meet her eyes. "Hey, why don't you come in while I finish getting ready. I have a lot to catch you up on."

"I have some calls to make." He looked out toward the sidewalk and then at Pete. "Yeah, now's not a good time. I've gotta run."

"Well, I'm going down to the hospital later this morning. Want to walk with me? I mean, if you're free?"

Charlie glanced at Pete. She reached out and touched Charlie's arm. He looked at her hand and then met her eyes. They stood silent, reading each other's intent, until he softened a bit.

"The three of us?" he asked.

"Pete is going to check in with some of his contacts. There are some strange things going on and he's offered to ask around."

"Well, I agree that there are some strange things going on. And sure, I'll go. Text me when you're ready."

"Thanks for the coffee. It was very thoughtful," she said, and she meant it. She didn't understand men. Charlie was acting strange. Because Pete was there? Charlie had to know that she and Pete were just good friends. Yes, she loved him, but differently. They were best friends. Always had been, always would be. Besides, there was nothing serious going on between her and

Charlie. When it came to Charlie, she had kept things casual, never giving him the impression of a commitment. They offered each other companionship, dinners out, an occasional kiss, and sometimes more. But they weren't exclusive. Not "in a relationship." Couldn't everyone understand that? Mia marked the discomfort up to the two of them simply being men. Territorial.

She shut the door and walked to the kitchen island shaking out her hair.

"Well, that was awkward," Pete said as he dished up his military-style breakfast of scrambled eggs, bacon, and toast. "Hope I didn't run ole Charlie away."

"No, it was fine. He was fine," she said as she dug into her eggs. "Why would your being here matter anyway?"

He sat down at the island next to her with a look of honest surprise on his face. "You're kidding, right? Charlie has it bad for you, Ellie."

"No, we're friends. Our relationship is casual. And even if he wanted more, I'm not interested in a relationship. Not going there." She washed a bit of toast down with her coffee.

Pete turned away and wiped the bacon grease off his hands. He seemed exasperated.

"Hey, Pete." She put her fork down and nudged him. He turned and looked at her. "What is it?" she asked.

He finished his eggs, saying nothing.

Pete pushed his plate back and faced her.

"Why aren't we more than friends, Ellie? I mean, we are best friends, right? And we love each other, right? I've always loved you, you know that."

She worked to contain the surprise on her face. What he said was true, but he had never spoken that bluntly to her before, about her. While she couldn't imagine her life without him, she was content with being single and independent.

"What's stopping us from being more?" he said.

Mia looked deeply at him. She looked at the medallion he wore around his neck and then at the sincerity in his eyes. He looked like he wanted to kiss her. She had seen that look once before.

⇒ ⅲ ⇐

April 2007

Pete arrived on the train, holding the silver bar for balance, and wearing his signature faded blue jeans, white T-shirt, and bomber jacket. Wafts of his dark hair spilled out around the edges of his Cubs ballcap. She watched as his brown eyes searched for her. She waved.

"Hey, slugger, how was the ride down?" she said.

"Same as always." He turned to look at her. "How are you?" His question penetrated the moment, and she smiled as he waited for her answer.

"Couldn't be better. Are you ready to see your team lose?"

"Ha, not a chance." He pulled on the rim of his ballcap. This is going to be the Cubs' year. You'll see."

"Yeah, right." They hugged tightly.

"Still up for a slice from Rizolli's?"

"You bet. You don't want to see your team lose on an empty stomach."

"Very funny."

They ordered two large slices of stuffed crust, and Mia told him about the summer plans her grandma had made for them. Travel to three different continents over a six-week period, and then in the fall she would be attending both the Dinner for the South American and African Contingency of US Ambassadors and the Annual Charity Gala in September. Mia kept the conversation light and moving, not wanting to pause long enough to consider that Pete was leaving for boot camp soon and this would be their last ballgame for the immediate future. Maintaining the charade, they headed toward Lincoln Park, taking time to walk through the zoo and grab a hot chocolate from a street vendor.

They found a bench at the Diversey train station and waited for their ride to the ballpark. Mia leaned back, her elbows resting on the worn seat, and acted as if she was studying the buildings beyond the station platform.

"What's on your mind, Ellie?" He knew her as well as she knew herself.

"You know what."

He waited.

"It's only a week until you head to boot camp," she said. "I know you've made your decision. And I know you always planned on joining the marines, but it doesn't make it any easier. I wish you weren't going." She let out a deep breath. There—she said it.

"We've talked about this. You'll be fine. We can still write every week. Besides, you'll be gone all summer and then back in school. Christmas will be here before we know it and I'll be home for a visit."

"I know. But I won't be happy."

"Really? Thanks for making this hard on me too." He stood.

He seemed sincere. "Okay, I'm sorry. Let's change the subject. I won't spend any more time talking about you deserting me. In fact we won't even think about it. Agreed?"

He shook his head and gave her a cock-eyed look of frustration.

"Besides, today is a celebration. You have a birthday this week and a graduation. Sit back down. I have something for you." She reached into her seventies-style sling handbag and pulled out a box wrapped in blue and white paper. "Here, happy birthday."

He jostled the present from hand to hand and lifted it to his ear. He shifted his gaze to her and raised one eyebrow. "It's not booby trapped, is it?"

"No, you dork. Open it already."

With one fluid movement, he removed the lid and unrolled a Chicago White Sox T-shirt.

"Of course," he said. "You just can't resist, can you?"

"You're gonna want it when they win the World Series. There's more. Keep looking."

He pushed aside the tissue paper and pulled out a velvet-covered box. "What's this?"

She signaled for him to open it. He held a bronze-hammered medallion in his palm.

"The lion was engraved by an artisan in Senegal named YeTu. He said the lion represents strength, courage, and protection. It's supposed to bring you good luck."

"It's amazing. I love it, Ellie. Thank you." He ran his finger over the face of the feline that looked as if it were ready for battle.

"Here, let me put it on you." He took off the baseball cap and she clasped the leather strap behind his neck. "Now turn around so I can see it." She surveyed the gift.

The brass medallion lay comfortably on his chest. She looked up at him. His eyes were fixed on her. Her breath caught and he leaned forward and kissed her. He paused and then kissed her again. They pulled apart and she tried to read his eyes. This should not be happening, not now. Probably not ever.

"Well," she said in an unsure tone, "I think you must like your gift."

"I do. And I like the person who gave it to me. Thanks, Ellie."

"You're welcome. Look, our train is coming. Let's go watch some baseball."

Holding hands, they boarded the El. *The kiss*, she thought, *means nothing. Just let it go.*

⇒ ⦀ ⇐

"Ellie?" Pete lifted her face until she moved her eyes to meet his. She scanned the contour of his face. His face, she knew. His heart, she knew. She loved him, and he held her secrets. Yet, in the moment, she knew that it would never be more. But how to respond? She pushed the stool back and picked up both their coffee cups to warm them. She needed a minute before responding.

"Isn't what we have enough? Besides, you're dating someone, aren't you? Courtney or Candice or something?"

He shook his head and turned back to one remaining piece of bacon. She knew she should say something, something to repair this, but what? As she sat back on the barstool, she wrestled with what to say, anything to fix what was unraveling in front of her.

Pete stood. "I need to clean up the kitchen and get going," he said. Are you done with your plate?" He reached toward the plate as if the last ninety seconds were only in her imagination.

She grabbed the last of her toast. "I guess so," she said as he took her plate to the sink. The dishes clattered as he rinsed and loaded them into the dishwasher. In one fluid leap, Jasper bounded to her lap, rubbing against her face. "Get down, girl. I need to see if Henry will watch Jasper for me, at least until Louisa comes home." She stopped as the words took hold in her mind. Louisa would be coming home, wouldn't she? She dropped the last bite of toast in Jasper's cat bowl and wiped her hands on the towel.

She headed to the front door and sat to put on her leather boots as her phone rang. "Hello, this is Mia Graham."

"Miss Graham. It's Connie Wilson, your grandmother's nurse at Northwestern."

"Yes. Is everything alright? I was just heading over."

"Everything is fine. However, Dr. Cheung has asked for a consult with you and the medical team at ten thirty this morning to review next steps for your grandmother. Can you be here at that time?"

"Of course. Are you sure nothing is wrong?"

"Yes. She is stable. No change. You'll receive a full update when you meet with the medical team."

"Thank you. I'll see you soon."

Pete put away the last of the breakfast skillets and wiped his hands on the towel as she ended the call. "The hospital?"

She nodded.

"Everything okay?" He walked around the island and joined her on the landing.

"I think so. They want me to come at ten thirty to meet with the medical team. I guess that's a good thing. Maybe they'll have some answers as to when Louisa might wake up."

He opened his arms and she leaned into his familiar embrace as if the awkward conversation had never happened. His time in the Marine Corp had further developed his already solid frame, and his muscles tightened as he held her close. "She's going to pull through this, Ellie."

"She has too," she replied. "She just has too."

Pete released her from his hug. "Do you want me to come to the hospital with you? I can if you want."

"No, I'm going to stay here for a while and catch up on some work calls. I'll be fine. What's on your agenda this morning?"

"I'm going to check with a few people I know and see if there is any word on the street about the break-in or the accident. And I'll stop by the police precinct."

"I gave you Detective Taylor's number, didn't I?"

"Yep. You'll let me know what the doctors say?"

"Yes. Be careful," she said giving him a concerned look.

"That goes for you too. By the way, where's Sebastian? I was hoping to visit with him."

"We're going to touch base later this morning. I haven't told him about the journal yet. But I'll fill him in today. I think the more we work together, the better, agreed?"

He nodded, grabbed his worn bomber jacket, and kissed her on the top of the head.

"You call me, Ellie, if you need anything. And don't forget to lock the door after I leave."

"Copy that, Sergeant Haines." She saluted him.

He returned the salute with a smirk as he shut the door.

CHAPTER 29

MIA TURNED THE DEADBOLT and settled on the sofa. She sent a text to Sebastian and then to Charlie to let them know about the change in plans and read through her work messages. Jasper made himself home beside her.

"So, let's see, Jasper," she said to the half-attentive feline. "Lionel would like me to come to the museum early tomorrow. Looks like there are some final appraisals that need my sign-off. We'll try, won't we?" she said as she stroked the cat. "But for now three o'clock will have to do." She typed in her response.

"What's next?" There were two messages from private collectors who had questions about items on Saturday's auction list. She would hand these off to another appraiser. She forwarded the emails.

"This is interesting," she said. "A Mr. Brisbane emailed. He's the executive director of Sotheby's Auction House in London. He's going to be at the gala and hopes to have a few minutes to visit with me, privately. I wonder what that is about?"

With emails caught up, she listened to her voicemails. Most could wait. She hit play and the resolute voice of AD St. Clair blasted through the phone. Would she please meet with him at the federal building? That was not likely to happen. At least not today. But, despite his arrogant behavior, she admitted he might be useful in getting some answers. He did have access to resources. She sent him a text and assured him she'd be in touch.

She stowed her laptop in her bag, along with the journal, and tidied the front room. With time on her hands, she moved to the library to pick up the mess. It was a beautiful room and Louisa's favorite place to entertain guests, serve tea, and talk business mergers and politics. Framed photographs of family, trips, and special occasions lay on the floor. She picked them up and gently re-placed them on the shelves. She paused on the last one. It was from a trip to Costa Rica. Louisa, and her mom and dad, were in the picture, along with three other people. As Mia looked closer, one of them resembled Nikki Santos. Much younger, but yes, that could be her. Nikki's parents reminded Mia of the foreign dignitaries Louisa worked with. The woman, Nikki's mother she presumed, stood a foot shorter than the husband, yet her presence could not be avoided. Her demeanor demanded attention and her dress looked ceremonial. Multicolored with gold flecks that caused her to stand out. Nikki's father carried himself like a military man. Shoulders back, chin up. His face serious. Mia sat the picture on the fireplace mantel as Louisa's jumbled words from the day before replayed in her mind. What did the Santos family have to do with all of this? And what did she mean by *"Cooperate"*? Mia considered her upcoming meeting with Nikki Santos. If she is involved, as her grandmother suggested, then why not face it head-on?

Near the back wall, a handmade kaleidoscope lay on the floor. Mia and Louisa purchased it during a layover in Italy the summer of Mia's fifteenth birthday. With time on their hands, they took a day trip to Caldogno, a small town outside of Vicenza, during its annual arts and crafts fair. They ambled past the open-air booths of handcrafted fare and stopped to watch a woman, her hands weathered and her back hunched, piece together a kaleidoscope. Wood shavings and colored glass pieces covered the small bench that served as her workshop and store. Mia watched, amazed at how the old bent fingers were able to craft the magnificent instrument. When Mia peered through the wooden ring, the vessel burst with color. Mia shopped the display of kaleidoscopes and picked this one as her favorite. It favored silver and ruby tones and provided a burst of beauty with each turn of the shaft.

Mia picked up the treasure and returned it to its wooden stand and then continued returning books to the shelves. As she worked, her grandmother's words kept replaying in her mind. *"Collide. Soap."* Was she referring to a kaleidoscope? She replayed the scene back in her mind. Collide. Soap. Kaleidoscope? Mia allowed her mind to freefall through the significance of the piece.

After the last of the strewn items were picked up, she turned to shut the pocket doors. Then, she stopped and returned to the kaleidoscope. She raised it to her eye, aiming for the light coming in from the windows. It felt heavier than she remembered, but the colors that filled her view matched her memory. She turned the outer shaft and heard rattling. Maybe broken glass? The piece appeared intact, but that sound... She flipped on the piano lamp and sat on the ebony bench. Twisting the top counterclockwise, she pulled the viewer away. No doubt about it.

Something was loose inside. She grimaced at the thought of the scum who had violated their space.

She pulled off the wooden top, hoping she'd be able to put it back together, then tipped the oblong shaft to release the loose pieces. Dozens of small uncut diamonds filled her palm. The glistening gemstones overflowed, and she let them pour onto the black lid of the piano. She rose and looked around, wondering if anyone was watching, then her eyes returned to the jumble of glitter in front of her. There had to be five dozen diamonds, maybe more, sparkling in front of her. Mia ran her fingers through the magnificent jewels and held one to the light. Its beauty was flawless. These had to be worth millions. What were they doing in her kaleidoscope?

Like tentacles, the sun's rays reached toward the gems, casting prisms across the room. Mia softly touched them one-by-one. Then, as if struck by reality, she realized someone could stop by at any time. She reloaded the tube and replaced the lid. She set the benign-looking kaleidoscope on the shelf, surveying the scene to make sure nothing looked out of place. She replayed Louisa's words. *"No accident...you must stay safe...cooperate."* Perhaps Louisa knew exactly what she was saying. And now, Mia knew what they were after.

The ringing doorbell caused her to freeze where she stood. She stared at the cannister holding millions of dollars' worth of diamonds. To anyone else, it looked just like a kaleidoscope, and it blended in with the books and photos and knick-knacks. *Calm down*, she said to herself, and took a deep breath. She turned off the lights and shut the pocket doors.

CHAPTER 30

THE BUTLER REFILLED NIKKI'S COFFEE CUP and set the table with the breakfast entrees Miguel had ordered. Nikki and Miguel spent the next hour reviewing the seven clients she had met the night before. It had been an evening of wining and dining, one client at a time, and an opportunity to discuss each individual's unique import/export needs. It was a dance she had to do, and she excelled at it.

Only one of the seven clients, Bruno Hastings, said he would have to run the deal by his parents. Bruno's parents owned thousands of acres of rice farms and provided product to nearly every continent. Nikki had seen this before—a second-generation business owner having to seek their parents' approval for every major decision. She empathized with the forty-year-old Bruno and the exhausting plight of living with familial chains.

She admired Miguel as he finalized the documents for the business she had acquired, noting that he had found time to get his mustache trimmed.

"Miguel."

"Yes, ma'am," he responded without looking up from his work.

"Didn't you get your education in the states? Georgetown?"

"Yes, I went on scholarship for a business degree."

"Why didn't you stay? In the US, I mean?"

Miguel stopped typing and met her eyes. "My grandparents. They relied on me after my mother passed away."

"And your father?"

"He is in prison."

She waited, wanting more, giving him her full attention.

"He had a small coffee plantation, until the price of coffee declined, and he could not pay his debt to the government. Some people prospered during those difficult economic times, but we lost our land, and he was sentenced to prison. I was very young and could do little to help. My grandparents took me in, raised me, and made sure I did well in school."

"Your grandparents, what are their names?"

"Senor e Senorita Montague. Perhaps you know them? They both worked in your household—my grandfather in the stables and my grandmother in the kitchen."

"Yes, I remember them. They retired several years back, didn't they? How are they?"

"Not well, I'm afraid." He offered nothing more.

She got up to stretch before refilling her coffee cup. "Let's review the itinerary for the reception." He nodded and pulled out a file. "Is everything set for food, drinks, entertainment?"

"Yes, ma'am. The caterers will be setting up at six."

"You've hired additional security? And our hosts and hostesses are, well, professional and attractive, is that right?"

"Taken care of."

Miguel continued reviewing the details while Nikki stared out to Lake Michigan. A large cargo ship made its way across the horizon, partially obscured by the morning mist. Miguel rambled on, in an oddly calming beat. Occasionally she nodded in his direction. But her mind wandered, like the ship, to how she would find the merchandise.

"What items are the Bannister brothers interested in?" he asked. Nikki was somewhere else. "Miss Santos?"

"Yes Miguel?"

"The Bannister brothers. What items are they interested in?"

"A set of chenets." She turned and watched him scour the list in front of him. "You won't find them on the list yet," she continued. "The final appraisal is being done today and then they will be added."

"Do you find it odd that the Bannister brothers have interest in this piece? I mean, they don't really seem the type."

She turned, her eyes boring into him. "Oh, and what 'type' are they?"

He set down the tablet and replied coolly, "They seem the type to play in a bigger league. Bigger, anyway, than a set of lions. Is there anything else they have interest in, something you might be willing to share with me? Perhaps I can be of some help in securing their business."

He had never been so bold, and she wondered if it was ambition or dangerous curiosity. "They have been our customer for many years. I don't question what they are interested in, and neither should you. It is simply our job to supply it."

"Yes, Miss Santos." His response sounded compliant, but his demeanor seemed too sure for someone conceding the point. "Please let me know if I can be of assistance."

"What appointments am I scheduled for this morning?"

"Muriel Docking, MLB owner from Austin, and Clinton McDermott, managing partner at MDX Investments. Then of course, Brian Caseo from *Time* magazine will be here. Are there any other clients you need me to reach out to?"

"No, I will be able to visit with everyone else this evening. Is my prep team on their way?"

"Yes, ma'am."

"What time do you expect them?"

"Ten thirty. One more thing, Miss Santos. You have two messages from your mother. She says it's important."

"Important?" Important meant that Mother simply wanted an update. Urgent would mean there was news on Papa. For now, it could wait. "I'm going to go dress. I will call her this afternoon."

CHAPTER 31

THE FRONT-DOOR ALARM pierced her ears as it announced Charlie's arrival. "Come in. It's getting cold out there." Mia stepped aside as he darted into the warmth of Louisa's brownstone. "I'm ready to go, just need to grab my bag and coat."

Charlie helped her into her jacket. As she turned to slide her arm through, a lock of hair caught in the button of his peacoat.

"Hold on, I can get that," he said. His fingers worked the tangle as the scent of his nutmeg aftershave danced between them. Mia's skin tingled as Charlie's breath hit her face.

"There, got it." Their eyes met and neither of them moved. He leaned in. His lips brushing hers. Mia reminded herself to breathe.

"Thanks for rescuing my hair," she said nervously and wondered if it was a reaction to the kiss or the fact that there were several million dollars' worth of diamonds hidden forty feet away. As she turned to set the alarm, Henry and the service tech arrived. Mia left Henry in charge.

"You sure you want to walk?" Charlie asked.

"Absolutely," she said and slipped her hands deep into her pockets. The movement helped to lighten her anxiety but could not keep her mind from thinking of the diamonds and, now, out in the open, the man she'd seen following her. Perhaps she should have locked the diamonds in the safe.

Charlie's phone rang. She listened, but he said little to the voice at the other end. He furrowed his brow and kept his eyes on the sidewalk. He mumbled something and then hung up.

"Who was that?"

"Richfield. Said we should expect a visit from MacKenzie Miller today. She's working up the story and they plan to go to print tomorrow."

"I don't want to talk to her." She spun and looked directly at him. "No, I won't talk with her. Why does she want to visit with me anyway?" she said as they resumed their walk.

He shrugged. "You know you don't have to answer any questions."

The thought of people reading and gossiping about the accident and her family irritated her. Investors and old acquaintances would be reaching out, wanting updates. Mia felt a sense of desperation. A deep yearning for Louisa to get better and for them to be left alone.

Inside the hospital, Mia pressed the up arrow on the elevator panel and noticed her hand trembling. Charlie reached for her as they entered.

"Hey, are you okay?"

"I'm just cold," she said. But clearly the past few days were getting to her. She vowed to get her nerves under control.

He touched her chin and moved her head until their eyes met. He waited.

"Fine," she said. "I'm a little rattled, but I'll be fine. There's a lot going on, so maybe I'm entitled to have a few nerves.

Mostly, I need Louisa to get better. She will get better, won't she?" He gently pulled her in as the elevator moved toward the fourth floor.

"Everything is going to be fine. You'll see."

Before she could respond, the lights flickered, and the elevator came to an abrupt stop. She stumbled against the back wall, grabbing the bar. "Oh my God. What is happening?" Charlie went to the panel and pressed one button and then another. Nothing. The glow of an emergency light cast a gray tone to the box they were trapped in.

"Try calling someone."

Mia grabbed her phone. No service. She tried again. "I can't get a signal."

Charlie pushed the emergency button and began to yell for help. Mia crumbled to the cold floor; her knees pulled to her chest. Charlie joined her.

Inside her, panic took root. She did not care for small spaces, not since the day of the fire. She'd been lucky to have gotten out of the cramped crawl space. She looked at Charlie, his face full of concern. "Mia, we are going to get out of here. They will have the door open in just a few minutes."

They sat in silence. Time crept forward. Her eyes darted from Charlie to the doors, to the panel and then to Charlie again. She thought of Louisa, just a little more than a floor above her. Was the power on in the ICU? She needed to get to her. The sound of her heartbeat reverberated like a hammer hitting the inside of a hollow tube, and then she heard her own voice as she stood and pounded on the metal doors.

"Help! Get us out of here! Can anyone hear me? We need help!"

She looked to her left. Charlie was there, pounding and yelling with her.

CHAPTER 32

The elevator jolted back to life. Mia and Charlie grabbed the rail as it moved and opened on the fourth floor. The maintenance supervisor, along with three hospital staff members, looked surprised as Mia and Charlie lurched from the open doors.

"Whoa, are you two alright?" the super asked.

Mia scanned the situation, not sure if she was relieved or angry.

"What happened? Why did the elevator stop?" Charlie asked.

"Well, we're not sure. But, as soon as we received notification of the system shutdown, we came. We didn't know you were in there."

"Did someone shut down this elevator intentionally?"

"That's highly unlikely," he said as he took off his cap and scratched his head as he considered the situation.

"But it's not impossible?" Mia came within inches of the man who was now walking backward toward the wall. "Did you do this on purpose?" She held her position when a second maintenance worker stepped past them and headed to the staircase. "Where are you going?" she yelled in his direction.

Charlie pulled Mia aside and the man ducked to safety. "Mia, we are out and everything is fine."

"Maybe you'd like something to drink or to sit down a minute?" the man offered. "To make sure you're okay?"

"No, I just need to go see my grandmother. Let's go, Charlie."

They rounded the corner toward the busy ICU waiting room. Everyone was staring. Mia slowed for a moment and then continued toward the intercom. As she hit the button to announce herself, a woman with a notepad approached them.

"Mia? Mia Graham?"

Mia looked at Charlie and then at the woman.

"I'm Mackenzie Miller from the *Chicago Tribune*. I'd like to ask you a few questions. I only need a few minutes."

"Sorry, I'm busy," Mia said and then announced herself to the nurse on the intercom.

"I can wait. Say in thirty minutes or so? Maybe we can get a cup of coffee?"

"Sorry, Mac," Charlie interjected. "She's not available for comment."

"Come on, Charlie. I only need a few minutes. I don't mind waiting."

MacKenzie followed them into the ICU. A nurse stopped the group and worked to identify everyone who was entering. Mia made a beeline toward Louisa's room, relieved to have left the others behind her. She glanced over her shoulder to check on Charlie. He waved her on. She would have to thank him later. She made it to Louisa's room. No Nurse Connie in sight, but the State Department's security duo was still there. She looked up at Samson. "Anything new I need to know about?" she asked. He shook his head and she moved past him into the room.

As soon as the door shut, the adrenaline of the past thirty minutes expelled from her like air leaving a balloon, and the cold stillness of the room surrounded her. Louisa lay there. No response to the closing of the door. No response to Mia's presence. No change. The only sign of life came from the growing collection of flowers covering the windowsill. Louisa joined the silence, laying there as if suspended in time. Mia remained at the door, sensing the vast difference between the world behind her and the one before her, wishing for what life was just two days earlier but knowing that the world she longed for might never return.

She made her way to the side of the bed and held Louisa's small hand. She surveyed the monitors and then her grandmother. The ventilator created a steady rhythm, fulfilling its purpose. She shook her head in disbelief, not knowing herself how to breathe without the woman in front of her.

"Good morning, Miss Graham."

Mia turned. Nurse Connie and four white coats filled the room.

"Miss Graham," Doctor Cheung began. "These are the doctors who are helping with your grandmother's care. Dr. Mills from neurology, Dr. Nagar from internal medicine, and Dr. Yahn, our intensivist, who specializes in critical care."

Mia acknowledged them as they were introduced.

"As you know," Dr. Cheung continued, "your grandmother is in a medical coma to allow her brain and body to heal. The brain swelling does seem to show a slight decrease, which is a good sign. However, we have run into a few additional complications."

"Such as?" Mia scanned their faces.

"The accident caused damage to Mrs. Graham's spleen and kidneys," Dr. Yahn said. "Removal of the spleen is recommended, but not in her current condition. We will delay the surgery as long as possible. However, if it ruptures, we will have no choice but to operate. It would be a risky surgery, and as such, we will wait as long as possible. In addition, her kidneys have sustained damage. We are monitoring their function and hope they will recover from the trauma. If not, we will need to consider dialysis or a kidney transplant. However, that is not our most pressing concern, but we wanted you to know we are keeping a close eye on this."

"So, what is the most pressing concern?"

"Because of the spleen injury, we will need to begin blood transfusions, and your grandmother has a rare blood type. We are working on getting a supply shipped here as we speak."

"She and I have the same blood type. I can donate blood."

"We can have your blood tested to see if it is a match. Nurse, would you see to it?" Dr. Cheung said. "I have also reviewed your grandmother's paperwork. Are you aware that you have medical power of attorney? Did you and your grandmother ever visit about her final wishes?"

"Yes, but you don't think that..." Mia glanced at the tiled floor, at Louisa, and then searched the eyes of the medical team. "You don't think we need to consider that now, do you? I mean, are you giving up?" Her stare demanded an answer from the team of professionals.

"Certainly not. We are giving her the best possible care, and we will continue to do everything we can. I am only confirming that you are aware that all final decisions will be yours. For now, the best medicine is time," Dr. Cheung said.

The room began to shrink, and Mia found the chair.

Connie broke the silence. "Do you have any other questions for the doctors, Mia?"

Mia shook her head and mumbled a "thank you" as they exited.

Connie remained. "Mia, if you can stay for a while, I will ask the tech to come and get your blood sample now." Mia nodded.

Connie checked Louisa's monitors before leaving. Mia moved her chair so that she could easily hold Louisa's hand and look directly at her. How she wished Louisa would open her eyes, for good this time.

"Abuella, can you hear me? The doctors were just here, and it looks like your recovery is going to take a while. You are going to have to fight. I can't have you leaving me, okay?"

Determined to be positive, she spoke to her as if they were sitting on the back porch enjoying tea and watching the setting sun. "You know, Abuela, it's been quite a day." Mia imagined the two of them sitting on the back porch having a normal conversation. "Besides getting stuck in the elevator, which was quite something, I found some things at the house. For starters, I found your journal hidden in the garden. Very clever, by the way. I could use your help in understanding what it all means." Mia's voice strengthened as she spoke. "I also looked inside the kaleidoscope. Now *that* I did not expect. I'd like to know why you put them there or why you wanted me to find them. You wanted me to find them, didn't you? I think that is what you were saying when you woke up yesterday."

There was a knock on the door.

"Come in."

Charlie entered the room, along with the phlebotomist.

"What's going on?" Charlie asked, eyeing the tray of empty vials.

"Louisa needs a blood transfusion," she said as he pulled up a chair.

"Where do I sign up to donate?"

Mia smiled at the swiftness of his generosity.

"After I'm done," the young nurse said, "we'll go out to the desk and talk to the charge nurse."

CHAPTER 33

"Thank you for meeting this morning, Clinton," Nikki said to the impeccably dressed bachelor as she offered her freshly manicured hand. "I am confident we can locate a Superleggerra for you. And when we do, it will be a wonderful addition to your exquisite collection. I look forward to seeing you at the reception this evening. Miguel, will you show Mr. McDermott out please?"

With the final meeting of the morning complete, Nikki headed to her bedroom to get ready for her interview with *Time* magazine. She felt like a girl who was about to get a pony for Christmas. She had looked forward to this day and had spared no expense in putting together her outfit. A pinstriped navy Armani pantsuit with a mint-green blouse. The pièce de resistance was the diamond-encrusted vine-drop necklace and dangle earrings. A combo of bold and subtle, just the image she hoped to cast on the watching world. The hair and makeup team had set up shop in her bathroom and went to work prepping her for the photo shoot. While they worked, she reviewed the anticipated questions that her PR team had prepared.

Three stylists worked simultaneously. Perched in a director's chair, Nikki felt like a star. She was ready for the spotlight.

The cover of *Time*. It was the type of publicity that would solidify her as the head of Santos Distributing, and garner the company fresh business opportunities, not to mention give her one more opportunity to prove to her mother that she had the savvy needed to lead the organization.

Outside the bedroom she could hear Miguel ushering in the magazine's crew. The excitement nearly distracted her from the most important issue of the day, but not quite. She dialed Marco. After a short visit, she learned that there were no changes in Louisa's condition and the next step was clear. Mia would have to find and transfer the diamonds. Nikki would be sure to communicate that message when they met later. And then, Nikki would work to get Mia on board with the entire operation, seeing as though Louisa would be out of commission for the foreseeable future. *One step at a time*, she told herself.

Miguel informed Nikki that the man interviewing her, Brian Caseo, had arrived. She'd read several of his articles and knew his expertise lay in international business. However, his true gift was his ability for pulling out personal and heartfelt moments from those he interviewed. She would need to be careful and make sure she controlled the narrative of the conversation.

Nikki walked into the living quarters. Every eye turned to her like a magnet, and a collective *aah* filled the air. Brian approached her, hand extended.

"Miss Santos. It's a pleasure to meet you. And may I add you look exquisite. The camera will love you."

"Thank you. I hope your readers will love me as well."

"No doubt. Before we begin, they'd like to take a few photos. Then we'll visit, okay?"

Nikki was ushered off and let herself enjoy the photo shoot. After fifteen minutes, a staffer led her to a high-backed parlor chair that faced Brian. Her adrenaline still high from the session, she felt ready for his questions.

"Miss Santos...or may I call you Nikki?"

She nodded. He began with softball questions, gathering the basics about her past and building rapport with her. She answered them easily, working to add interest and intrigue with her replies. Then, he turned his journalistic prose toward the personal side of her life.

"Your parents have been the face of Santos Distributing since its inception. Why are they choosing now to transfer leadership to you? There are rumors that your father is ill. Is there any truth to that?"

Good try, she said to herself. Her eyes narrowed and she held his gaze. "The leadership transition of our company is a strategic move and one that has been in play for some time. This change will allow my parents to commit more time to philanthropic ventures and the needs of the people in developing countries."

"And your father's health?" Brian asked.

"Brian, my father and my mother are strong and healthy and enjoying the warmth of Costa Rica. A much better trade-off than this cold Chicago weather, don't you agree?"

Brian laughed. "I suppose so."

Nikki repositioned her legs and leaned slightly forward. "What else should we talk about, Brian?" Her eyes bore playfully into his. She waited until he readjusted and moved on to topics of the upcoming gala and impact of world markets on the import/export business as well as the expanding capabilities of her family's company. She gracefully led the conversation to highlight her successes.

As if on cue, once Nikki had covered all she wanted, Miguel came and tapped her lightly on the shoulder. "Excuse me, Ms. Santos. It is time to get ready for your next appointment." She said her goodbyes to Brian as his crew packed up the lighting and cameras.

In the private office off her bedroom, she removed her jacket and shoes as the butler brought in a fresh Perrier for her. She paced the room as she reviewed the interview. "Miguel," she said, "I'd like for the PR team to find a few more news outlets and set up interviews. I want a global reach. Perhaps we can coordinate the interviews with our year-end financial reporting. Once they have a list of options, send them to me."

"Yes, ma'am."

He seemed nearly unflappable, taking shorthand-style notes and never missing a beat. She wondered if he could truly be trusted. Nikki hoped he would be loyal and would richly reward him for it, but it would take time to know for sure.

A slight knock on the door told them that lunch had arrived. "Miguel, have the car brought around," she said, inspecting the salmon salad and tropical fruit that brightened the crisp white china. "I'll have a bite of lunch and then will be down. I don't want to be late for my appointment with Mia."

CHAPTER 34

Charlie headed down the hall with Nurse Connie to complete paperwork and have a sample of blood drawn. Mia dialed Pete's number as the phlebotomist connected the IV to her arm. Relieved that she could do something that might help Louisa, Mia settled in with a small pillow propped under her elbow as the blood defied gravity and made its way up the tube and into the clear bag.

Pete filled her in on the buzz from the Rat Hole, a dive bar on the south side of town that was run by an old marine buddy. He'd learned that an out-of-town crew had asked around for local hires for a high-security job. He had a lead but hadn't been able to follow up on it yet. The bar jockeys jabbered about the hit-and-run, but no one seemed suspicious or indicated firsthand knowledge. He promised to keep digging.

As she updated him on Louisa, there was a knock. She waved Sebastian in. His good looks caught the breath of the nurse who was attending to Mia's blood donation. Mia guessed Sebastian was in his late sixties, but probably in better shape than most men in their thirties. His salt-and-pepper hair swept over his brow as he removed his black fedora. She watched his deep gray eyes as he glanced at Louisa, a flicker of warmth rising to their surface.

"Hi, Mia," Sebastian said, looking around the room. "Where's Charlie? I thought he'd be here." Sebastian pulled a chair up next to Mia's.

"He went down the hall with the nurse to see about donating blood. Then going to visit his parents. He wanted to update them on Louisa."

"I know the Bakers," Sebastian said. "Really nice people. He's a retired surgeon, isn't he? And Charlie's mother was an attorney."

"Yes, they and my grandparents go way back. I asked Charlie if he could fill his dad in on Louisa's case and see if a second opinion might be in order."

"Do you have a concern about the staff here?"

"No, they seem competent, but I want to be sure that this medical coma is the best treatment for her. It doesn't hurt to ask, and I need to do everything I can to make sure she has a full recovery."

"Speaking of doing what we can, am I able to donate blood?"

"Sure. We'll leave your contact info with the floor nurse."

⸻ ⫼ ⸺

Sebastian drove the Escalade out of the hospital parking garage. Dirty clouds filled the sky, and the wipers smeared at the cold spit of rain. Traffic crawled at a slow beat matching the song being played on the oldies station. Swept up in the rasp of Stevie Nicks, Mia found herself mouthing the lyrics to "Landslide." *How fitting*, she thought. The last couple of days had indeed been a landslide.

Sebastian turned down the volume. "Mia?" His voice brought her back to the moment. "What are you thinking about?"

Mia looked at Sebastian. "Before they placed Louisa in the coma, she woke up, for just a minute and spoke to me. She only said a few words, and I'm still sorting out some of what she said."

"For instance?"

"Well, for one, she mentioned the Santos family and gave me what felt like a warning. She told me to 'stay safe.' Those were her exact words. She also said 'Cooperate.' What do you know about the Santos family?"

"Well, they have a reputation."

"For what?"

He glanced at her in the rearview. "Corruption, bribery, illegal trade, you name it."

"You're kidding, right?"

"No, I'm afraid I'm not. Louisa may have been tangled in something that she doesn't want you involved in. Did she say anything else?"

"No, she was only awake for seconds." Mia considered telling him about the diamonds and that, as they spoke, Nikki Santos was heading to the brownstone, but decided to not worry him. She sensed that he was a bit like Pete and would only overreact if he knew. If the meeting felt off, she would fill him in on everything.

The Escalade came to a stop outside the brownstone. "How long will you be here?" he asked.

"I have an appointment at the museum at three. I'm going to freshen up and make a few calls."

"Then I'll be back at two thirty."

"Thanks, Sebastian."

He escorted her to the door, she disarmed the alarm, and after he did a quick check of the house, he climbed in the Escalade and pulled away. She set the teapot on the burner and hustled upstairs to change her outfit.

With the tea steaming, she took her cup and saucer to the desk near the back porch, pausing at the library to peak at the kaleidoscope. It remained where she'd left it. Safe for now. She set up her laptop and reviewed the list of items scheduled for auction. She closed her eyes and rested her head in her hands. After a deep inhale of air, she straightened her body. She should be on guard after Sebastian's comments about the Santos family. She sipped the ginger-infused tea and hoped the encounter with Nikki would not provide any truth in her grandmother's warning.

CHAPTER 35

Nikki cursed under her breath. Her security escort held a large umbrella over her head, yet beads of sleet covered her coat. Next year, she'd work to have the gala location changed to Miami or perhaps Key West. New leadership, new rules.

She shivered as she rang the bell a second time. *What is keeping her?*

The stately door finally swung open. "Ms. Santos," Mia said. "Sorry to keep you waiting. Come in."

As they walked past the kitchen, Nikki scanned the room for signs of the break-in. Nothing looked out of place. The doors to the parlor, where she and Louisa usually met, were closed. She considered asking Mia about the break-in but thought better of it. Other things were the priority, and her curiosity would have to wait.

"Let's sit back here," Mia said as she led them to the family room. The brownstone was as Nikki remembered it, rustic and modern and a reflection of Louisa. Mia only partially fit here. She had a modern vibe. She could see it in her outfit choice. A classic ivory blouse and maroon fitted slacks paired with expensive tan flats. Nikki settled into a leather wingback chair next to the fireplace and let her mind go to work, discarding thoughts of much-needed warmth and a question of why there was no fire burning to warm the space.

"Before we begin, can you tell what is the latest on Louisa? Have there been any improvements?"

Mia rested her hands on her lap, on top of documents presumably for the auction. "She's resting comfortably, and we hope to have her home soon." Nikki had to maintain a concerned and then relieved look when what she really wanted to do was clap and say, "Bravo!" The heir of the Graham family wore a calm and convincing poker face. Marco had updated her this morning saying that Louisa's chances of recovery were slim at best. Mia might very well be a good asset for the Santos family.

"Shall we visit about the gala?" Mia asked. Without waiting for a response, she continued. "First, on behalf of my grandmother, we appreciate your family's involvement in this event. The funds raised have positively impacted many small businesses throughout the world."

"We're glad to assist. And we were also happy to accommodate the foundation's request to raise the level of proceeds donated to 7 percent of every sale. That should have a significant impact, don't you think?" Nikki noted the professional feel of the banter and enjoyed the balance they seemed to strike. "We also appreciate the assistance of the DaVinci House in disbursing collected funds to the appropriate parties. It's unfortunate your grandmother will not be able to join us. Her presence not only encourages generous bids, but she has the ability to pull off a seamless event."

Mia's stare told Nikki that she did not appreciate the challenge to her grandmother or the DaVinci House. "Rest assured," she said decisively, "the team at DaVinci has great processes in place. Nothing will seem amiss. Because this event is so important to my grandmother, we will make sure this year's gala is one for the record books."

Mia handed her a document, several pages thick, that outlined the auction items. Nikki scanned them. Each entry included a detailed description of each individual piece along with its condition, an estimated value, the authenticator, and a beginning bid. The last item was the set of chenets. No details were attached.

"I see the chenets are on the list. Have they officially been put on the docket?"

"Not yet." Nikki caught Mia's suspecting stare. "Why are they so important?" Mia asked.

"Well, in addition to client interest, their entry is important to Louisa."

"And why is that?" Her question was direct.

Nikki leaned back in the chair as if considering a poker hand in Vegas. There would be no gentle transition into this. "The chenets are carriers for precious gems. Gems Louisa smuggled into the country for a client."

Mia's eyes grew wide, and then she laughed as if to say, *yeah, right.*

"I'm serious, Mia. Twenty-three million dollars' worth of diamonds, to be exact. Louisa's job is to transfer the diamonds into the set of lions prior to the auction. After the auction, she gets a cut, I get a cut, and the buyer is happy."

"I don't believe you." Mia had regained her poker face. If she had any knowledge of Louisa's part in their transaction, her tone and body posture did not let on.

"It's true. And I have a buyer who insists that the transaction be completed, as planned, with or without Louisa."

"And if it's not?"

"Well, they mean business. Consider what happened to Louisa." Nikki paused to let the statement sink in. "Your grandmother, well actually the entire Graham family, has played this game for many, many years. Unfortunately, just a few weeks ago, Louisa decided to grow a conscious. Clearly, that is not going well for her."

"What do you mean? You had her hit? And left to die?"

"I admit, it was an egregious error. The ploy was only meant as a warning. To bring her back in line. She was not intended to be injured." Nikki straightened her shoulders and leaned closer to Mia. "The people in this game do not care who gets hurt. And believe me when I tell you that worse will happen if we don't see this transaction through."

"Worse? What could possibly be worse?"

Nikki grimaced. Such a naive girl. "We are expecting you to pick up where your grandmother left off. Do you understand?"

"And if I don't?"

"Your grandmother is at risk. You are at risk. The people you care about are at risk." Nikki threw each word at Mia, like darts aimed at a bull's-eye.

Mia tossed the papers aside and stood. "Nikki, you need to leave," she said as she walked toward the front door.

"Listen to me," Nikki's voice rose. "I need you to get the chenets on the official docket, and put the diamonds inside of them before the auction." She reached for Mia's shoulder and turned her. She probed Mia's eyes. "You do know where the diamonds are, don't you?"

"I don't know about any diamonds." Mia involuntarily moved backward, and the color in Mia's face paled. A light bead of perspiration formed below her hairline. She had lost the poker game. She knew the location of the diamonds.

"Where are they, Mia?"

Mia tightened her mouth and said nothing.

"Transfer the diamonds to the chenets before the auction. And you are expected at the reception tonight. Our client wants to meet you."

"Not my client."

"They are now. I will send a car for you at eight forty-five."

"No. If I decide to come, I have my own transportation."

Mia stood facing her directly now. Shoulders squared, eyes flaring. Nikki smiled at the fire in her new partner. "I will see you tonight at the LeBlanc."

As Nikki grabbed her coat, Mia nearly shouted, "Don't count on it."

Nikki turned. With a tone of victory she replied, "Mia, you don't have a choice. You clearly have a lot to learn about your grandmother and your family, but regardless, know this—you are in this, by default, and there is no exit strategy. Move the diamonds to the chenets and be at the reception by nine o'clock."

CHAPTER 36

MIA BOLTED THE DOOR. Her insides swirled like a tornado filled with anger, fear, and shock. She went to the living room and paced, working to dissipate the flow of her emotions. Jasper approached and then disappeared under the safety of the sofa.

She tried to sort the confusion in her mind. Her grandmother involved in black market trading? And Nikki Santos threatened her if she didn't cooperate. Was her grandmother responsible, in some way, for all that had happened? And what about her parents? How long had this been going on? The questions ricocheted like ping-pong balls with no real answers appearing. In a horrible way, it all made sense. She went to Louisa's office and retrieved the journal, looking at the entries as she walked.

The Westminster melody from the grandfather clock slowed her march. She'd been walking the length of the brownstone for thirty minutes. Her emotional tank near empty, she sat on the sofa. Jasper reappeared, as if asking, *now what?*

"Now what, indeed," she said to her companion.

Mia considered telling Pete, Sebastian, and Charlie about the diamonds and the threats. They would want to know, but she decided to keep the information to herself, for the time being. With the diamonds tucked safely away, guards stationed at Louisa's door, and Sebastian keeping close tabs on her, she felt the bases were covered and she had time to mull things over. What about the authorities? If she tipped off the detectives about Nikki's involvement in the hit-and-run, they might discover the motive behind the attack and that could lead back to Louisa, and, if she transferred the diamonds, her. For now, everything she knew, and the revelation of her family's criminal activity, should remain a secret.

It would be an hour before Sebastian returned, and Mia needed a distraction. Tackling the mess upstairs would be a good way to pass the time. She headed for the stairs but stopped at the closed parlor doors and considered the hidden diamonds. Jasper rubbed against her leg.

"Am I really supposed to give these diamonds to them?" she said as he scooted up the stairs. "I won't be a pawn in this... transfer of stolen goods? In a crime? Oh Abuela, what have you gotten me into?"

In her old bedroom, Mia looked out the window at the gray clouds and wondered why her grandmother had recently "grown a conscious" as Nikki said. If she had been smuggling stolen merchandise for apparently years, why stop now? Mia replaced the chair cushion and then the desk drawers.

She restacked the albums that had been pulled from the closet and then opened the storage bin that had held her gemology set. She carefully replaced the replicas of rubies, sapphires, and emeralds into the velvet bags. The fake diamonds covering the base of the container were smooth, and she thought of the real ones downstairs. Balancing several in her hand, she found the imitations heavy and quite convincing for fakes. Perhaps they would be useful. As if on automatic pilot, she returned the bin to the shelf, the black bag of counterfeit diamonds still in her hand.

She jiggled the fakes in her hand, and her mind juggled the possibility of using them to fool Nikki and her clients. It seemed foolish. But it could work. She needed to think this through.

She checked the time. She headed downstairs and rubbed her forehead hoping to remove the crease above her eyes. The one she was afraid would be her first permanent worry line. She stopped when the chime of the doorbell announced that her ride had arrived.

CHAPTER 37

AFTER AN HOUR AT THE SPA, Nikki lounged in her private quarters. Dressed only in the plush hotel robe and slippers, she sipped her sparkling water while catching up on the business news. She scanned the market reports, the international news, and then local media.

The Chicago paper had a teaser piece on Louisa on page two. Nikki had heard of the star reporter, MacKenzie Miller. She had a reputation for cover stories that led to indictments. This was not good news for Nikki's operation. She considered reaching out to the reporter. Perhaps she could entice her to spin the story toward the gala and the deserving recipients of the auction proceeds. She made a mental note to run the idea by Miguel.

There was a knock on her door.

"Come in."

"You have a call from your mother," Miguel said. "She said it's urgent."

Nikki took the phone.

"What is it, Mama? I'm rather busy."

"It's about your papa. Are you too busy for him?"

Nikki tossed the tablet to the side and sat up. "Is he okay?"

"No, Nikkole, he is not okay."

"What is happening?"

"His labs just came back. The doctor said it is not good news. His major organs are shutting down. They are adjusting his medication, but I honestly don't know what else they can do for him."

"That can't be. I need to talk to him. And to the doctor."

"Your father is resting now, and the doctor is returning in an hour. I will call you when he returns. If you are not too busy to take my call."

The line went dead.

CHAPTER 38

The Bradbury Museum and Event Center housed some of the most important early American artifacts on the continent. Mia had studied the displays on every floor and could discuss them as fluently as any tour guide. The historic building sat on the banks of the Chicago River, and the views at night were breathtaking. Despite the events of the last two days, she looked forward to returning to the venue and to something work related.

Outside the great hall, Mia heard Lionel's voice before she saw him. His words floated through the rotunda like pixie dust at a Disney parade. "It's decided," Lionel said. "We'll go with the calla lilies for the centerpieces, but be sure they are fresh. We do not want them to wilt before the end of the night." The team of people nodded and made notes as they waited for his direction. "Rebekah, do you have the updated itinerary? I want to go over it with Mia when she arrives."

Lionel could brighten any room and always brightened Mia's spirit. "Did I hear my name?" Lionel turned his tall frame toward her, arms open. She smiled at his fashion choices, which were never left to chance. His gray dress pants were accented by a gray-and-purple-striped bowtie. A buttoned vest and purple suede hat brought a finishing touch to the ensemble. He handed a stack of papers to his assistant and adjusted his rectangle-shaped glasses as he headed toward her.

"Oh, Mia, darling. It's so good to see you." He wrapped her in his long arms and then pulled back to kiss both her cheeks. "I'm so sorry about Louisa's awful accident. How is our girl doing?"

"She's hanging in there. I don't think she'll be wearing her dancing shoes at this year's gala, though. I know she would not want to miss it."

"It won't be the same without her. We are praying for her quick recovery."

"It looks like you have everything in order. Everyone knows you are the brains behind the event." The round tables were in place and covered with silver linens that sparkled. The makeshift stage for the orchestra was already set, and strands of tiny lights were tastefully hung around the edges of the room.

"Yes, but Louisa played an important role and now I am going to need you more than ever."

"Hold on," she held up her finger in protest. "My job is acquisitions and appraisals, remember?"

"Yes, but these are special circumstances, and everyone is expecting a member of the Graham family to guide the evening." He grabbed her elbow and urged her forward. "And, as it turns out, Mia, that means you. Don't worry. I will make it easy. You just have to play along." Before she could debate the point, he moved on. "I know you are very busy, so let's head to the vault so you can do a final inspection of the entries. I need to get the final docket sent to print. Most of the items you've seen. We did set aside the late entry, the stunning set of chenets, for you to give your stamp of approval on."

Lionel led her down the narrow hallway and launched into a nonstop gusher about this year's guest list. As he talked, they passed a rare collection of early nineteenth-century paintings. Under their feet, the crimson carpet cushioned their steps and the familiar smell of the old building provided the comfort of a familiar friend.

The hall came to a T, and they turned to face a museum guard in front of the locked vault.

"Hello, Bernie," Lionel chirped.

"Afternoon, Mr. McMasters."

Bernie scanned their IDs before allowing them to pass through the door that was made of bullet proof glass and 15-gauge metal. Once inside, he opened a second door, a round swinging mass of metal that you would see on most bank vaults from the 1900s. The lots for the auction lay on tables, each numbered with its own catalogue. To the far right lay the set of chenets. Lot number 36.

Lionel handed her a manila envelope. "The appraisal, provenance, and everything else you need is in here. Angela did the initial appraisal, and as always, did a thorough job. Take all the time you need, but come find me when you are done." He scooted through the gates. Rebekah waited for him in the wings, and the two of them reviewed seating assignments as they left her in the cavernous room.

The items along the tables were carefully displayed. Original artwork, sculptures, jewelry, even some baseball memorabilia, which Pete would love. She did a quick review of the first thirty-five items, and their appraisals. Everything checked out. Last in line were the chenets. They were beautiful, but not nearly as valuable as many of the other items. At least not without the diamonds. She wondered why Lionel hadn't questioned Nikki's or Louisa's insistence that they be added to the auction. Perhaps he was too busy to argue about it. Or maybe this wasn't the first time Louisa had submitted a late-addition request. Mia would try to find a time to ask him.

The gilded lions were exquisite, but she felt this way about most handcrafted artwork. She admired the detailing. The craftsmanship. Spectacular. It took both of her gloved hands to lift the first chenet. The lion sat on its hindquarters, looking as if it were ready to lunge. Its ferocious eyes met her gaze. The threat to not cross it was implied.

Mia's hands skillfully traced the surface of the piece. The wooden base was made from Brazilian teak wood and finished with a thick piece of black felt. If someone wanted her to insert diamonds, there was no place to do so here. The piece was solid and secure. The second item was the fraternal twin of the first, similar but not identical. The face of the lion exhibited a docile, almost tired expression. It was if he wanted only to nap in the African sunshine. He seemed approachable despite being a predator. Her hands examined the piece as before. She moved her finger along the base. As she traced the back left corner, she felt a small ridge, almost like a hair line crack in the wood. The routed edge had two small cuts, almost too insignificant to notice. Placing two fingers on them, she gave a push, and a panel opened under the beast. Only two inches wide, it gave way to the hollow belly lined with velvet but otherwise empty and waiting. She gasped and glanced back at Bernie who was seated comfortably outside the vault, his back to her.

She set the sculpture on the cloth-covered table, her eyes boring holes into the beast as if it was somehow responsible. This was real. Artifacts were being used to smuggle items. How could she have been so naïve to never consider that people did this? Not just people, her family.

The echoes of Lionel's voice sifted down the hallway like a mist. She heard him ask Rebekah to check on Mia's progress. She only had seconds. What should she do? She could deny entry of the lions into the auction. That could be the end of it. But would they still come after the diamonds? Or Louisa? Her fingers trembled as she pulled out the black velvet bag in her pocket and considered it. She slowly jostled the sack in her hand and wondered how long it would take for them to figure out these were fake. Probably not long, she surmised.

The shape of the bag shifted. It could slide easily into the cavity. The lion lay waiting. She conducted an internal debate. There were four options. She could leave the chenet empty, insert the imitations, return with and transfer the real diamonds, or contact the police. The first and last options were a huge risk to Louisa and herself.

Two options remained. If she went with the imitations, they'd eventually figure it out, which put her and Louisa at risk again. *I need to transfer the diamonds*, she said to herself. It might bring an end to all of this. There is no other way out.

She scolded herself for not bringing the real ones with her. She'd have to find a time and an excuse to come back to the vault without raising suspicion. The black bag of fakes easily slid into the stomach of the beast. The wood base clicked into place. She used her gloves to wipe down the chenets.

"Mia?" Rebekah called from behind her. "Lionel sent me. Is there anything you need?"

"No, I'm just finishing up. I'll be right there."

She signed the paperwork allowing the lot to be entered into the auction and returned it to the envelope before making her way back to the grand hall.

"Are you okay, darling? You look pale?" Lionel asked. "Why don't you sit down for a moment?" Without waiting for a response, Lionel waved for Rebekah to bring a glass of water and he walked Mia to a settee.

"I'm fine, really. It's just been a long couple of days. I should probably get back to the hospital."

"Of course. I will take care of everything here. Rebekah will send over a draft of the welcome statement and an acceptance speech for Louisa's award for you to review."

"Lionel," she said in protest.

"You will be fabulous. Don't worry. Will I see you at the reception tonight?" he asked.

"I plan to stop by, but only briefly."

"I totally understand. And don't worry, my dear, parties are my specialty. I look forward to seeing you there."

Mia smiled. Just the thought of attending a high-society party and Lionel glowed. Star-studded events, five-course dinners, and rooftop parties were his wheelhouse. While he knew the business almost as well as anyone in the industry, he left the nitty gritty work of research and appraising to her while he stepped into the limelight of the client-facing events. They were a good match.

CHAPTER 39

THE SETTING SUN INTENSIFIED the gray hue of the hospital as Mia and Sebastian entered through the revolving doors. It was quiet. Only a few people milled about as they waited to board the elevator. The metal door slid open, but she hesitated. She eyed the contraption as if to question its ability to perform its job. Perhaps the stairs were a safer bet.

They exited the fourth-floor stairwell. When they rounded the corner, they found Charlie pacing the freshly mopped floor and carrying a sack with the bright green logo from Capelli's Sandwich Shop. Mia's eyes narrowed in Charlie's bright red, swollen lip and the white butterfly bandage above his left brow.

"What happened to you?" Mia asked.

"Oh, this?" He gingerly rubbed his jaw. "Got into a bit of a scuffle at the protest. Turns out someone had an issue with their picture being taken. They went for the camera, the police came, some arrests were made, you know, all in a day's work."

She evaluated his fresh bruise and grimaced at the thought of him wrestling for his camera and getting clocked in the mouth over it. She was also mildly impressed and had no doubt he could hold his own when needed. Even though Charlie had a quiet demeanor, he was not the type of man to back away from a challenge, which made him good at what he did.

"Does it hurt?" she asked, finding this new scraped-up Charlie appealing.

"Just a little sore. My ego hurts worse. Let's talk about you," he said. "How are you? Any update on Louisa?"

"We were just going to check on her. I can check with the nurse to see if we can all go back."

"No need for that," Sebastian interjected. "Charlie, you go in with Mia. I need to go fuel up the Escalade and I'll be back in about an hour," he said. "Call me if there is any news?"

"Of course." Mia knew what Sebastian was up to. She was doubtful that he needed gas; he most likely wanted Mia and Charlie to have time together. But she didn't mind and she needed more information about the brawl he'd gotten himself into.

"I brought some sandwiches. Are you hungry?" Charlie said.

"I am. Let's go see Louisa. Maybe she's awake and will want to join us," she said with a wistful smile.

He tilted his head and gave her a sad look.

"I know," she said, "a girl can hope."

He reached for her hand and led her forward. "Well, let's go see."

A new set of guards were posted at Louisa's door. Mia visited with the nurse on duty while they conducted the now routine interrogation of Charlie and gave them the go-ahead to enter.

The hospital room seemed unchanged. Same monitors, ventilator, tubes, and boxes of latex gloves. The only difference was a shift in color. Louisa's bruises had become a fusion of purples, blues, and yellows working together to mask the ashen color of her skin. The thin gown and blanket that covered her were now a pale shade of mint green. And the fragrant flowers on the sill had been joined by a bouquet of bright yellow daisies. But the dreadful gray remained. Gray, now Mia's least favorite color. She wanted to trade in the gray for the blush pink of Louisa's skin and the pine-colored green of her eyes.

"Guess it's just the two of us for dinner," Mia said trying to lighten her own mood.

She went to the side of the bed and held Louisa's hand. Charlie joined Mia, his arm around her thin shoulders. "Hey, Abuela. It's me. Mia. And Charlie is here too. I spoke to the nurse. She said your vitals are stable, and you're responding well to the blood transfusions. I need you to get better."

Charlie squeezed her gently. "She's getting the rest she needs. She'll be better in no time, you'll see."

"Did you hear that, Abuela? Charlie says you'll be better in no time. I'm counting on that. I have a lot to tell you. It's been quite a day. For Charlie too. In fact, he got beat up today. But don't worry, just a few bruises and scrapes," she said smiling up at his scuffed-up face. Their eyes met and electricity moved through them. Their muscles froze and their breathing paused, before they reflexively moved apart. "Well, we better have that sandwich," she added to break the tension.

Charlie made light conversation, filling her in on the growing hostility of the crowds at the protest. His story amplified Mia's awareness of the greed, violence, and evil that existed around her. Her mind shifted to the threats from Nikki and the diamonds she needed to get to the museum.

"Mia? Hey, Mia?" Charlie worked to bring her back to the present.

She turned toward him. "Sorry," she managed.

"Did you hear what I was saying?"

"No. Sorry."

"It doesn't matter." His eyes settled on Louisa and then back on Mia. "Louisa will get better. If anyone can, it's her. She has a way of getting what she wants. I've seen it firsthand."

"What do you mean?"

"Like the time I went with her to the Kennedy Center Honors. About four years ago."

"What? Where was I?"

"Studying for finals or something like that. She said you couldn't get away and asked if I would like to escort her. Of course, I said yes. The next morning, we flew first class to DC. When we arrived at the Kennedy Center that evening, they didn't have us on the guest list. They had gotten news that she wasn't attending and gave her seats away. Your grandmother asked to see the executive director. The manager escorted her into a suite of offices, and less than five minutes later, the maître d' was escorting us to seats on the second row, directly behind the president and his wife, who she introduced me to."

"You're kidding."

"Nope. That woman, your grandmother, has an ability to get what she wants. I've never met anyone quite like her. If she wants to pull through this, and I'm sure she does, then she will."

Mia ruminated in the image of Louisa and Charlie jetting off to Washington and her not even knowing they had gone. Secrets of the past seemed to be coming to light this week.

Turning back toward Charlie, she refocused her thoughts on Charlie and her half-eaten sandwich.

"How are your parents? Did you have a nice lunch?"

"Yeah, it was good to see them. They are doing fine. I did ask my dad about the medical team in charge of Louisa's care."

"And?"

"He had a lot of wonderful things to say about them. Dr. Cheung has a great reputation and is very respected. Based on what he said, your grandmother is in very good hands."

"That's good to know," she said and looked back at her grandmother. "Thank you for asking."

"So, are things coming together for the gala? Did you meet with your boss today?"

"Yes. Lionel has every detail accounted for, including pulling me in as Louisa's replacement. You know, he's expecting me to accept the award for philanthropist of the year on behalf of Louisa and give the opening remarks. I'll probably pass out from nerves alone."

"If you don't want to do it, tell him no," Charlie said.

"If you knew Lionel, you'd know that's almost impossible. He is a good partner, though. Like tonight, at the reception, he will carry the load of making the connections. Both he and Louisa love these sorts of events. I wish I weren't going.

"You'll have a great time, you'll see."

"Ha," she replied. "You think so?" She crossed her arms and sat back. "Since you think it will be so much fun, you can go with me. Besides, you can meet Lionel and Nikki."

He looked at her as if to say, *are you serious?* Mia continued. "Really, I'd love to have you there with me. I could use a wingman."

"Well, Richfield did give me the night off. But I'm pretty beat up. You'll have to play the role of Beauty. I'll be the Beast."

"You look fine. Sebastian is planning to drive me. I'll let him know to pick you up at your place. Say eight thirty?"

The idea of Charlie joining her at the reception brought some relief, yet that feeling seemed misaligned with the fact that her grandmother was in the fight of her life. Mia silently repeated the words Charlie had said. *Louisa will get better. Louisa will get better.* The mantra helped her to enjoy the normality of sharing a meal and chatting with Charlie. Perhaps everything would be alright.

A nurse tech entered the room. "Excuse me. Mr. Baker? The lab called," she said to Charlie. "You can head down anytime. Second floor. Just to the left of the elevator."

"I'll be right down."

"Thanks for doing this," Mia said as he gathered their lunch trash.

"I'm glad to help. I'm guessing Sebastian will be back soon, so I'll probably just see you tonight."

The warmth of his hug lingered after he left, and she realized how much she had grown to enjoy Charlie's company, his touch, his companionship, and how fast the time had passed.

Silence, and the familiar hum of the machines, surrounded her.

"Hey, Abuela. I'm heading to the LeBlanc for the big Santos reception soon. Charlie's coming with me." Mia shifted her weight.

"I met with Nikki Santos earlier. Seems the diamonds you have tucked away in the kaleidoscope need to be put into the set of chenets before the auction Saturday night. I don't know how you got involved in all of this or how long it's been going on, but I've made a decision. I am going to do it. There's no doubt her threats are real. Her family is responsible for the hit-and-run, for you being here, fighting for your life. And even though there are two strong, capable men guarding your door, I'm going to do whatever I need to keep you safe. And then, once she has the diamonds, it ends. I'll make sure Nikki understands that."

Mia swallowed and considered what else she needed to say to Louisa. "I have a lot of questions, Abuela. So, you need to get better while I handle the Santos family. Then, we'll talk. Okay?"

The ventilator-induced breathing answered in a steady in-and-out pattern.

"I'll take that as a yes."

She kissed Louisa on the forehead and left to find Sebastian.

CHAPTER 40

Miguel entered her dressing room. "Your mother is on the phone."

Nikki snapped her fingers, and the hair and makeup stylist, along with Miguel, exited the room.

"Your father is awake and would like to speak to you."

Nikki adjusted herself in the chair and waited to hear his voice.

"Hola, mi bella." He spoke slowly and struggled for the breath needed to expel the words.

"Papa." Relief flooded her and tears fell softly.

"Hold on, mi Bella."

"What is it, Papa?"

"I can't find my phone. What did I do with it?"

"Papa, we're on the phone. Isn't it in your hand?"

"Oh, yes," he said, sounding relieved. "There it is." He moaned softly as if preparing to sleep.

Nikki swallowed down the lump that had formed in her throat. "Papa? Do you remember the day we hiked to the Sendero Bosque Nuboso Trail? It was so beautiful. The clouds surrounded us, and you said this is what heaven must look like. We sat for hours. Remember how the wind sounded, Papa? Like the current of the river. We hiked to the viewpoint, and when we got there, we could see for miles. The bright color of the grass reminded us of ripe zapote, and the wildflowers bloomed white and pink and yellow. It was incredible. We didn't want to leave. Do you remember, Papa?"

He said nothing.

"I love you, Papa. Can you hear me? I love you."

"Nikkole? Your father is sleeping."

"Mama, I need to talk to the doctor. Get him on the phone."

"I have spoken with the doctors. There is nothing they can do, Nikkole. His organs are failing."

"Then I need to come home. Tonight."

"Nonsense. You will do no such thing. It is of no consequence, whether you are here or not. He is unaware. You have business at hand and that is where he would want you to be."

"But Mama, I need to be there."

"Are you that weak, Nikkole? Do you not understand that weakness will not run this empire? This is your time. Are you ready for it or not?"

Nikki gritted her teeth and breathed through her nose fighting the urge to scream.

"Nikkole. What will it be? Will you make your father proud or come home and sit by the bed like a scared child? I can easily take over the work you are doing if you wish to be his nursemaid. So, tell me now. What do you want to do?"

"You are right. My place is here."

"Very well. You have made the wise decision."

Nikki set the phone on the counter and leaned against the tan wall. Deep breaths rolled from her, but she gritted her teeth and buried her sobs deep inside her core knowing that if they were given an outlet, they'd be heard all the way to the Hancock Building. And that she could not allow.

Her throat hurt from controlling her emotions, and her shoulders ached from the tension she held. She focused her mind on the evening, on her staff, on anything but her father, lying on his bed, perhaps for his last day.

Nikki cleared her throat, took a deep breath, and steadied herself. Using the mirror, she looked directly at herself.

"This is where I am supposed to be. This is what he wants. This is my time. I am a Santos, after all." She picked up her drink and held it up. "Cheers to you, Papa," she said toasting her reflection. "Now it is time to focus on the future, Nikkole."

She sat in the dressing chair and swiveled toward the door.

"Miguel," she called.

"Everything okay?" he asked.

"Yes. Call in my style team."

CHAPTER 41

Mia stood in front of her full-length mirror and inspected her outfit. The pecan-colored pantsuit with the white blouse fit perfectly. She slipped on her brown pumps and unlocked the safe to pull out the Gucci flora and diamond necklace. She held it to her neck and then returned it to the safe. After the last two days, she was not in the mood for expensive jewels. Instead, she pulled her hair into a low bun, letting a whisp of hair hang from her bangs, returned to her closet, and selected a leopard-print scarf that hung to her waist.

The apartment phone rang as she headed to the closet to get her coat. Adam, the night doorman, was on the other end. Her car had arrived. She slipped her wallet, phone, keys, and lipstick into a brown snakeskin satchel and headed to the elevator. The gold mirrored elevator doors opened to the lobby, and there stood Charlie, looking as handsome as she could remember despite his colorful bruises. Dark brown trousers, a cashmere camel jacket pulled together by a rich brown patterned tie. His hair waved gently past his bandaged eye, and he flashed her an unrestrained smile.

"You look fabulous," he said.

"You look pretty good yourself." She tucked her hand into the crook of his arm.

Sebastian stood waiting with the door open, smiling like a proud parent. As Mia neared the Escalade, she noticed a man across the street. He looked familiar. The oversized man from the hospital waiting room. Sebastian followed her eyes as the silhouette evaporated into the darkness of the alley. Sebastian stopped her before she entered the car. "Is everything alright? Did you see something?"

"No. Well maybe. I'm sure it was nothing." Sebastian didn't look convinced.

Before Charlie could enter the car, Mia's phone buzzed. She had missed a call from Pete. She listened to the message, letting Charlie know she would be just a minute.

"Mia," Pete said in the message. "I have a solid lead on the break-in. The out-of-town crew is South American. They've been hiring locals with specific skills, the kind that would be useful in a burglary. The group is professional and well-funded. Mia, if these are the people targeting Louisa, they are dangerous. You need to be careful. Please call me. We need to talk."

Mia smiled as she listened, not wanting to tip Charlie or Sebastian off to who she was talking to or about. She passed off the call as work related and worked to maintain a calm facade, but their furrowed brows and back-and-forth glances told her they weren't buying it. But they didn't press. She'd loop them in later on what Pete had discovered. For now, surviving the dreaded reception remained her top priority.

CHAPTER 42

Nikki pushed thoughts of her father to the far recesses of her mind. Twinkling lights lit up the pier like fireflies while a lone cargo ship floated silently across Lake Michigan, illuminated by the full moon. Inside, the fingers of the handsome lounge pianist, who Nikki had hired for the night despite protests from the lounge's manager, danced over the keys, and a soft jazz tune flowed from the baby grand piano. Along the wall, a top-of-the-line bar had been assembled. A steady flow of drinks would help to remove the pretenses of her rich and famous clientele who always arrived with their guard up, and their image and defenses in place. Understandable. But to get them to make deals and move her business forward, she needed to deflate some air from their tough facades. Mia included.

At nine o'clock, the room filled with high-fashioned people and the reverberation of polite chatter. Nikki greeted guests, introduced them to others, and made sure they were taken care of by the wait staff. Miguel stayed close, providing an outlet if she needed to gracefully excuse herself. He looked especially dashing in his black Hugo Boss suit that fit his sculpted body to perfection. He continued to prove himself an exciting and valuable asset to her team. After finishing her first martini, she decided to keep him.

"What time is it, Miguel?" she asked as they made their way to welcome Michael Frazier, the manager of the largest hedge fund in North America.

"Nine fifteen, ma'am."

"Please find Marco. And make sure he's dressed appropriately." He nodded and headed toward the second set of doors at the far end of the suite. "Michael Frazier." Nikki drew out the man's name as she welcomed him, pouring all her attention toward the George Clooney lookalike. "It's so good to see you."

"Nikki." He gave her a familial kiss on the cheek. "You look delicious," he added.

She watched him react to her form-fitting coral wrap dress. The neckline made a long V, the opening nearly reaching the leather belt that accentuated her waist. The coral was balanced by black Louis Vuitton shoes and an 18K black onyx necklace with diamonds. Her hair waved gently just past her shoulders. She stood and enjoyed his silent applause.

With his hand positioned snuggly around her waist, she led him to a server and introduced him to Jamarcus Knight, owner of Knight Aeronautics, a custom supplier of private jets. They should have a lot to discuss.

Marco slid in beside her and Nikki excused herself. "Where's Mia?" she asked as soon as they were alone.

"She's on her way. They left her apartment fifteen minutes ago. Hold on…" He put one finger to his earpiece and tilted his head as he listened. "She just arrived."

Sure enough, Nikki saw her new accomplice enter the suite. Marco attempted to peel away, but Nikki grabbed his sleeve.

"Make the move, now. No harm. Just send a message." He nodded. She waited until Marco maneuvered across the room and out of site before heading in Mia's direction.

"Mia, I'm so glad you could make it." She leaned in to hug her but met a cold shoulder. She found Mia's nonverbal message an intriguing challenge. "And who do we have here?" Nikki continued. She evaluated Charlie, her eyes stopping longer than necessary at his bruised chin and bandage.

Mia made the introduction. "Charlie Baker. Nikki Santos."

"I've heard a lot about you, Miss Santos."

"Please, call me Nikki. And it's very nice to meet you, Charlie. I'm so glad you both could join us this evening. I was wondering, Charlie, if I might have a moment with Mia alone. Would you be so kind as to get Mia and me a drink? Martini for me. Mia?"

"Nothing for me. I'm not planning on staying long."

"She'll take a sparkling water with a twist of lemon. Thank you, Charlie."

Nikki watched as Charlie waited until Mia gave him a nod. They were tight. Not easily pushed around. She made a mental note.

Walking Mia toward the back expansive windows, Nikki inquired about Louisa.

"Let's cut to the chase. You don't want to know about Louisa. Frankly, she's not your concern. What do you want, Nikki?"

"Are the diamonds in the chenets?"

"Worried? Afraid everything you worked for will blow up in your face? It'd serve you right after what you did to my grandmother."

"Don't mess with me, Mia." Nikki locked eyes with her opponent like a fighter before a match. "Move the diamonds before tomorrow night's auction."

"Or what? What can you do? You've already put Louisa in the hospital. There are guards there 24/7. I am not playing your games. If I do this thing for you, then no matter what deal you might have had with Louisa, it doesn't transfer to me. And she and I are out. For good."

"They really have kept you in the dark, haven't they?" Nikki couldn't hide her surprise. Once Nikki became heir apparent, her father introduced her to their operatives, involved her in transfers, and taught her the ropes of the business.

"Do you not even know who your family is? What the Hernandez-Graham family is known for?" Mia looked puzzled. Nikki walked her a few steps away from a couple who had stopped to enjoy the lights from the pier. "Your family, starting with your grandfather, is one of the most respected linchpins in the world of black-market trading." Nikki spoke slow like an attorney providing life-or-death instruction to their client, assuring that they fully understood the words spoken. "The Grahams provide exclusive items, mostly rare and valuable gemstones, for resale." She paused so she could relish the moment and see the confusion form in Mia's eyes. "My family. We are brokers. We find clients, your family delivers the merchandise. Everyone wins. When your grandfather passed away, your dad took over. But after a few years, he became reluctant. Uncooperative, shall we say. And then the fire. Very unfortunate. He and your mother were killed, isn't that right? After their premature deaths, Louisa took over operations. And now, dear Mia, since she is unavailable, you are the acting CEO. You are in the family business." She let the information sink in and watched Mia stagger, her hand reaching toward the window for support. Nikki's informative punch had connected. "Do you need to sit down?"

Nikki watched as the softness of Mia's face hardened into resolve. Mia regained her poise and turned to face Nikki. "You listen to me." Mia's finger inched close to Nikki's face. "Even if any of this is true, I am not going to be a part of it," she said through clenched teeth.

Nikki laughed and pushed Mia's finger away. "You will. We have a job in motion, and you must fulfill your part. After that, we can talk. But make no mistake. You. Are. In. Understand?"

"What are you going to do? Have someone run me over with a car? You've got no one if I'm gone."

Nikki's laugh escaped their bubble. "Mia, darling, my family, the people we deal with, do not take no for an answer. And speaking of the people we deal with, our clients are here. They want to meet you." Nikki grabbed Mia's arm as she attempted to bolt. "Smile and be nice," she said into Mia's ear. They walked toward the entrance where Miguel was taking the coats of the Bannister brothers.

"Andrew. Jonathon. I'm so glad you could join us. I'd like you to meet someone. Mia Graham. Meet Andrew and Jonathon Bannister. They are one of our top gala supporters and have a strong interest in the set of chenets that are to be auctioned off tomorrow evening."

"Mia. Nice to meet you," Andrew said as he reached for her hand. Nikki noticed Mia's insolent refusal to offer the return greeting and inched Mia's arm forward from behind. Andrew's large hand enveloped Mia's. "You resemble your mother. Yes. Same eyes. Same beautiful skin tone." By the look on Mia's face, it seemed as if heaven and hell had just collided.

"Your parents were frequent guests of the Bannister family," Nikki said, "at their estate in Columbia." Mia pulled her hand away and wiped her fingers on her pant leg. "They actually became good friends."

"They never mentioned it," Mia said.

"Well, you were very young when they passed," Jonathon said. "We are very sorry for your loss. And we hear your grandmother was involved in a terrible accident. How is Louisa?"

Nikki watched as Mia's jaw tightened and her cheeks turned the color of a blood moon. She stood silent. Seething.

"Louisa is recovering," Nikki said, "and, unfortunately, won't be able to join us at the gala. No worries. Mia has agreed to fill in for Louisa. The gala should be a great success. Isn't that right, Mia?"

Before she could speak, Charlie moved between the ladies. "There you are," he said handing Mia and Nikki their drinks. "I thought you had disappeared." He looked at Mia and then the two mafia-style men and then back at Mia. "I'm Charlie Baker." He offered his hand to Andrew. "And you are?"

Andrew looked wryly at Charlie. "Friends of the family," Andrew said, keeping his hand to his side.

"Miguel," Nikki called. And as if from nowhere, he appeared. "Miguel, will you take our guests to get something to drink?

Gentlemen, once you are settled, I will find you and we can visit." They nodded and moved toward the bar with Miguel.

Before Charlie could ask any questions, Lionel burst into the small circle smiling as if this was his reception. "It is so good to see so many of our clients, face-to-face," he gushed. The plaid double-breasted jacket looked heavy on his wiry frame. He held his cocktail to the side as he scooped Mia into a gentle hug. "Isn't this suite spectacular?" he said. "The views alone are worth a million dollars. Nikki, it's so good to see you, darling. Marvelous reception." He kissed her lightly on both cheeks.

"Lionel, have you seen the view from the balcony yet?" Nikki asked him. He offered a look of anticipation as he glanced toward the back of the suite. "Oh, you must," she continued. "Why don't you take Mia and Charlie so they can enjoy it as well. Go. Get the full experience." He agreed and led them to the far end of the suite.

CHAPTER 43

The chilly night air did nothing to lower Mia's internal temperature. She worked to sort out the garbage Nikki had hurled at her, hoping the twisted words were lies.

Lionel blathered on about the venue, the gala, and the guests. Mia's mind felt like it had entered a disorienting blizzard, and Lionel's ramblings brought unwanted shards of ice into the winter nightmare. Having had enough, she pointed to Louis Merrington, a stocky, buffalo-sized investor who was obsessed with early sixteenth-century Chinese art. Shouldn't Lionel go say hello? He bounded off.

Even with Charlie's coat around her, she couldn't stop shivering.

"If you are cold, we can go in," Charlie said.

"I don't want to go back inside."

"Did something happen in there?"

"No. Nothing." She knew she should talk to Charlie, but she was trying to make sense of everything. Anyway, where would she even start?

"Mia, it's not nothing. You are really shaking. Please, tell me what is going on."

She bit her lip. *How do I tell him that these people are trying to extort me? To force me to participate in a crime? That I come from a family of criminals?* She stared out into the moonlit night ignoring his pleading eyes.

He reached for her. She pulled away sharply. Too abruptly she realized, but too late. He turned away and leaned against the railing, giving a nod to a couple passing by. They stood in silence. The seconds moved like the dripping of molasses. She wrestled with Nikki's words and sensed Charlie's longing for her to open up, but she was not willing to share her tangled thoughts, at least not yet.

"Mia, it's really cold out here."

"You're right. Let's go inside," she said. "I'm ready to go."

His jaw tightened and his face turned hard. He held the door, out of some expected obligation, and accepted his jacket back as she entered. She did not want him to be angry, but given time, he would be fine. He would understand, wouldn't he?

Without being asked, Charlie headed to retrieve Mia's coat. She took a seat on an empty barstool, surrounded by the festive party, but feeling as if a cloak of darkness surrounded her. And she felt lost. Her parents gone. Her grandmother fighting for her life. And tonight she learned of this family legacy. An inheritance she didn't want.

"Can I get you a drink?" asked the bartender who looked like he'd just left the tanning salon. A ladies' man, she guessed, by the way he flashed his ivory smile and exposed his dimples.

"No. I'm getting ready to leave."

He tried once more. "You sure? Anything you want."

Perhaps she should have considered a shot of something, just to calm her nerves. Maybe another time.

Mia called Pete.

"Where are you?" she asked.

"Still on the south side. I've got a solid lead on a chop shop, one that might be dismantling the car that hit Louisa. I'm on my way now to meet with Detective Ramirez. Once they confirm the information, they're going to raid the location. With any luck, they'll have a match to the piece they found at the accident site and will be able to connect it to the Santos family."

"Well, that's some good news." She tried to muster some enthusiasm.

"They're also looking into the name I got, a Marco Peretti, a real piece of trash, that may be associated with the break-in. Making some progress here. What's going on there?"

"Well," she lowered her voice, "I can't say much." She paused as the bartender gave her a glance. "There's no doubt who's behind all of this—Nikki Santos. And from what I've learned, it's clear that Louisa...," she stopped and considered adding her parents and grandfather into the sentence, "has been mixed up in something pretty awful."

"We'll figure it all out. Listen, I just got to the meet-up with Ramirez. He's waiting. I've gotta go. Call you later?"

"Okay." Mia put away her phone.

The noise of the party swirled around her. The pianist was playing an up-tempo Elton John number. People laughed at one another's jokes whether they were funny or not. Everyone carried on chatting about stock trades, social events, and exotic destinations. Mia looked closely and could see behind the façade. One by one, she sized up each person and imagined what they were each hiding. If they were lined up and stripped bare, their souls exposed, what atrocious acts would be revealed?

She imagined herself in that line. By tomorrow night, would she be guilty of a new transgression? Participation in smuggling stolen diamonds? The sins of her family were multiplying like weeds. This was not how Mia wanted to live. Hiding secrets. Carrying guilt. Looking over her shoulder. Needing protection. Yet for the moment and regardless of the possible outcome, she remained committed to her decision and would do what was needed to protect her grandmother. She looked for Charlie, hoping he'd return soon with her coat so they could leave.

"Excuse me, Miss Graham?" Someone tapped on her shoulder. It was Nikki's well-dressed assistant. "There are two gentlemen here to see you," Miguel said. "They said it's an urgent matter." He handed her St. Clair's business card. She looked at it and then back to Miguel. "I've escorted them to a private conference area. May I show you the way?"

She wondered if St. Clair had stumbled across unfavorable information that might implicate Louisa. Her nerves tightened as she told the bartender that her friend, Charlie Baker, would be looking for her. Would he pass on a message and ask him to wait?

Miguel led her through the perfumed crowd to an obscure door in the far-right corner of the room and slid the pocket door open. Inside, St. Clair, and another man, whom she had not seen before were waiting expectantly.

"Mr. St. Clair? I didn't expect to see you here. What's going on?"

"Sorry to interrupt your evening, Miss Graham," St. Clair said. "This is Special Agent Moore, FBI."

"What's this about?" she asked again.

"There has been a breach at the hospital."

"A breach? What does that mean? Has something happened to my grandmother?" Her eyes pounced from man to man and then to no one, trying hard not to jump right out of her skin in attack of answers.

"An incident. Louisa is fine, but we were required to bring in the FBI. I'll let Agent Moore fill you in."

"Miss Graham, here's what we know. A person, posing as a member of the hospital's housekeeping staff, entered your grandmother's room at ten fifteen this evening. We do not know what their intent was, only that they were not a registered hospital employee. The suspect was interrupted by the RN on duty. The nurse questioned the individual who quickly exited the floor before they could be apprehended. The nurse is providing a detailed statement, and our team is reviewing security tapes as we speak."

"You are sure that Louisa is alright?"

"Yes. She was unharmed."

"And you're sure this intruder wasn't an employee? That they had ulterior motives?"

"It appears that way, yes ma'am."

"What about your guards, St. Clair? What were they doing all this time? Taking a smoke break?" She could feel the temperature under her skin increase to a near inferno as she stared down the man who had been so demanding of her.

"The suspect had a valid hospital ID. We are strengthening security protocols, and only pre-authorized individuals, including hospital employees, will be permitted to enter your grandmother's room," St. Clair said. "In addition, the FBI will be providing extra security for your protection as well. They are assigning two agents to escort you until we find out what exactly is going on."

"No. Not necessary. I can take care of myself." She inched closer to him. "I do not want an *escort*. I have a driver and people around me that have my back." She steadied her feet under her. With hands on her hips, she continued. "Right now, I am leaving. I'm going to the hospital to see Louisa."

"Well, with all due respect, ma'am," Agent Moore said, "this situation requires precaution, and we will have our agents follow you to the hospital and remain in close proximity to you at all times. This is not up for debate."

She pulled the pocket door open and stormed to the bar. Her coat lay on the barstool, but no sign of Charlie. The bartender handed her a folded cocktail napkin.

"Your friend left this for you."

Although the ink was smeared and the handwriting jagged, she recognized it.

Mia,

Had to run a work errand.
Sebastian is on his way up. Call me later if you want to talk.

C

She hadn't meant to push him away, not really. She knew that she could make him angry, but he always got past it, re-engaging in chats out in the garden or over lunch at Ozzie's . Surely, he would understand once she explained. She would make amends with Charlie, but for now she needed to get to the hospital and check on Louisa.

She picked up her coat and headed toward the entrance. As she wiggled through the relaxed crowd who seemed to be swaying in tune with the music, she felt a presence by her side. In a Jasper-like move, Nikki matched her pace.

"Leaving already? I do hope everything is okay."

"Everything is fine. Good night, Nikki."

Nikki continued. "Has something happened to Louisa?"

Mia stopped abruptly, nearly causing a man behind her to toss his drink. He gave a high-eyebrowed look at the two women and moved on.

"Why would you ask?" Mia looked directly into Nikki's dark eyes.

"I heard she had an unexpected visitor this evening. I do hope everything is okay."

"You? You are behind this? You know the FBI is here. They will want to talk to you."

"Oh Mia, dear. Let's not complicate the matter. And for heaven's sake, let's just handle this between us, like civilized businesspeople. I told you," her voice softened into an icy cadence, "you need to make this transaction happen. It is in everyone's best interest. I will touch base with you tomorrow to confirm that the transfer has been successfully completed. Have a good night."

Mia's teeth were clenched so tightly that her jaw ached. She could feel her nostrils flaring. She had never hated anyone so much as she did in this moment. Not even herself. Who did this woman think she was?

"Once this is done, I am out. We are out." Mia's canter matched Nikki's. "You need to move on, Nikki Santos. Find another family to do your dirty work. Stay away from me and my grandmother. Do you understand?"

They stood, toe to toe, Mia unable to move. Afraid if she released her muscles, her next move would be to punch the devil in front of her. She almost hoped that Nikki would provoke her. It would feel good to put an exclamation point on her message.

From their left, a rotund woman, early eighties and weighted down with expensive jewelry, appeared. "Nikki, there you are. I was hoping to visit with you. Do you have a moment?" Mia and Nikki maintained eye contact, neither of them flinching. The woman evaluated the situation and paused before continuing. "Oh, have I interrupted something?"

"No, I'm just leaving," Mia responded and headed for the door. The Bannister brothers were leaning against a high-top table and nodded as she passed. They seemed amused, and she wondered if they had just taken in the show.

Sebastian stood at the door and wore a worried expression. She grabbed the crook of his arm and they moved down the corridor to the elevators, two FBI agents in tow.

Sebastian pointed at them and offered Mia a quizzical look.

"An unwelcome shadow. Courtesy of the FBI. Please take me to the hospital."

He held the elevator door for her and hit the lobby button, telling the dark duo they would need to catch the next car down.

CHAPTER 44

MIA FILLED SEBASTIAN IN on the hospital security breach, divulging that Nikki Santos had confessed to her involvement. He didn't push for more information. She liked that about him. Sebastian's ability to listen with great patience, watch carefully as she spoke, and offer insight also impressed her. She trusted him.

With the main entrance of the hospital closed for the evening, Sebastian and Mia entered the building through the ER. After the night security received permission for them and the two FBI agents to enter, they snaked their way through the building's maze, following the signs to the elevators and the fourth floor.

In the ICU, Mia received a flicker of recognition from the nursing staff stationed behind the counter, their faces focused on their computers. At Louisa's room, the night guards remained vigilant, giving Sebastian the once-over, before permitting him to enter.

With her coat still wrapped around her, Mia went directly to the bed and reached for Louisa's hand. Her grandmother slept, unaffected by the touch. Mia's face was moist with tears when Sebastian entered. He pulled a chair over and Mia sat.

The clock on the wall clicked steadily. Five minutes. Fifteen minutes. After thirty minutes passed, Sebastian suggested he take her home. *Home. Where was that anyway?* she thought.

She did not answer, but Sebastian pressed. "I'll come back and sit with her tonight. Let me take you home."

She looked at him to consider his offer.

"I'll come straight back," he continued, "and call you if there is any news. Anything at all. I won't let anything happen to her. And tomorrow, I'll make sure someone we know is with her at all times. How's that sound?"

She didn't argue.

Mia reviewed the list of approved guests with the guards and told the charge nurse that Sebastian would be returning and sitting with Louisa for the remainder of the night.

She dialed Charlie's number as they walked. He didn't answer, and in truth, she didn't know what she would say if he did. But she did need to talk to him and make amends. She left a brief message and would try again first thing tomorrow.

The Escalade was cool from the clear night air, and she buttoned her coat up to her neck. Sebastian asked if she would like the radio on. She shook her head no. He turned his eyes back to the road but left the partition open for her. She dialed Pete, who answered on the second ring.

"Hey, Ellie. Everything alright?" Jukebox music blasted behind him from what sounded like a pool hall.

"Just leaving the hospital. It's been quite a night."

"You're not alright, are you? Why don't I come by?"

"If you aren't busy, that would be great. Sebastian is taking me to my apartment. I'm going to grab a shower, but I'll leave word with the doorman that you're coming up. Thanks, Pete." She felt relieved and could see that Sebastian was too.

The clock chimed midnight as she entered her apartment. The moon and a speckling of lights from the nearby buildings broke through the ebony canvas of her space. She kicked off her shoes and headed to the bedroom, tossing her coat, handbag, and clothes on the wingback chair. As the shower warmed, she glanced at her messages, hoping to see a reply from Charlie. Instead, a long message from Lionel filled her screen. Rebekah had sent the scripts for the pre-gala run-through. She considered Lionel's energy and passion for their business. She did not share his enthusiasm and hadn't for a while. Maybe, she thought, she should consider taking a break after all this, an extended vacation of sorts. Besides, once Louisa was home, she might need help until she was back on her feet. Time off sounded almost as appealing as the now steaming shower.

Ten minutes later, Mia slid on soft terry cloth sweatpants and a hoodie. With the towel wrapped perfectly on her head, she walked to the kitchen. Her stomach grumbled and she tossed a bag of popcorn in the microwave before heading back to the bathroom to return the towel. She heard a knock at the door and the sound of the electronic lock whining.

"Hey, Ellie. It's me," Pete said.

"I'll be right out," she replied from the bathroom.

She found Pete in the kitchen looking through her wine options. "Want a glass? To go with the popcorn?"

She walked to him with one intent, to be hugged by her best friend. The stress that had knotted in her shoulders began to loosen as he held her tightly. She had a lot to tell him and felt sure he could help her make sense of all that had happened. But most importantly, he could tell her if she was doing the right thing.

CHAPTER 45

THE LAST OF NIKKI'S GUEST LEFT the suite as the staff loaded dirty plates and wine glasses onto carts. The man who looked more like a GQ model than a bartender wiped down the counter for the final time and headed toward the service elevators. A bluesy tune wafted through the overhead speakers giving life to the otherwise quiet room.

Nikki summoned Marco. He assured her that everyone and everything was in place. He reviewed the details of the plan. She considered each move like a high-stakes chess match. And then, she gave the go-ahead and Marco scuttled off.

Nikki kicked off her stilettos and curled into a lounging couch that had an expansive view of the city and replayed the plan in her mind. It was solid. She sipped her chai tea and waited. This part of the business reminded her of a slow game of chess that required patience. She settled into the couch and sighed. Things were in motion and now she would wait.

CHAPTER 46

SATURDAY MORNING - THE DAY OF THE GALA

The apartment door closed, and Mia stirred from her sleep. She found herself sprawled across her gray sofa, a soft teal throw covering her. The morning sun peaked just above the horizon and gave enough light for Mia to get her bearings. She looked for Pete but found instead a note on a paper towel.

Went to grab coffee and muffins.
You need to do some grocery shopping!

Back soon, Pete

She straightened the pillows and dialed the hospital. "Connie Miller, please," she said to the floor nurse.

"She's with a patient. Would you like to leave a message?"

Mia left her name and phone number, and tidied the coffee table that was covered in papers, empty bowls, wine glasses, and her grandmother's journal.

Last night, she recounted everything that had happened since the accident. For the first time since Tuesday, she breathed easier.

They discussed the man she'd seen on the street, at the hospital, and in front of her building. She told him about the short conversation she'd had with Louisa in the hospital and recounted the threats from Nikki, the discovery of the diamonds, and the hidden cavern inside the lion currently filled with fake gems. It took until 3 a.m., but they researched the journal entries and were able to confirm that the initials indicated a member of the Santos family. They identified twenty-six transfers, including one on September 2005, just a week after her parents died. The reality that her entire family had been involved in black market trading carried a bitter stench that caused her stomach to churn.

They visited about it all. Everything except Charlie and how he'd left during the reception. That was a knot she would have to untie on her own.

Mia went to her bedroom to change. When she returned, she found Pete in the kitchen with a box of fresh muffins, a container of fruit, and two large mugs of coffee. She breathed in the sweet aromas that wafted from her hot cup. "You'll make someone a wonderful house husband someday," she told him.

"No doubt," he replied. "It'd be like winning the lottery." Their laughter lightened the air.

As the coffee warmed her insides, Pete's demeanor turned serious. He cleared his throat. "Ellie," he handed her a newspaper, "I thought you would want to see this yourself. Not hear about it from someone else."

The bold headline read: AMBASSADOR TARGETED IN ATTACKS.

Dressed in a navy-blue suit with the American flag propped in the background, the official government photo made Louisa appear senatorial. Mia ran a finger across the newsprint. Louisa looked beautiful.

Louisa Hernandez-Graham, Former US Ambassador to Costa Rica, was struck by a vehicle Tuesday morning near the corners of East Scott and Division Streets. According to Chicago Police Detective Franklin Taylor, the incident occurred at approximately 8 am. The suspect fled the scene. There were no witnesses, and the investigation is on-going, according to Taylor. The former ambassador is being treated at Northwestern Hospital and is reported to be in serious but stable condition.

Mia scanned the next couple of paragraphs that summarized the burglary and read a line out loud.

"Federal authorities have joined the investigation and are working to identify what was taken from the victim's home."

Mia paced in front of the windows as she skimmed the section on Louisa's work history.

The following paragraph focused on the upcoming gala, and when Mia read her name in print, her walk turned into a stomp, pummeling the unsuspecting carpet.

In Mrs. Graham's absence, her granddaughter, Mia Graham will host the event, according to sources. Ms. Graham is Chicago resident and currently employed by the DaVinci Auction House.

Mia looked at Pete, her frustration growing, and then continued.

Ms. Graham's parents were killed in a residential fire in the subdivision of Sycamore Heights, IL in August of 2007. The Fire Marshall indicated the official cause of the fire was an explosive device and arson was suspected. No suspects were apprehended.

Having read enough, Mia crumpled the paper and considered setting it on fire. And then self-corrected her thinking.

She turned to the window and glared at the golden hue that had taken over the sky. She hated the brightness it offered, and she felt a growing loathing toward it. In fact, she loathed everything. Her family's secret history. The fact that Louisa lay in a hospital bed fighting for her life. She loathed the Santos family and their bully tactics. She loathed MacKenzie Miller, even though the paper had every right to publish private information about her or her family. She stared into the cheery sky, but felt a storm brewing inside her. Anger. Frustration. And now, maybe the need for revenge or justice? Everything fell silent around her as she wrestled with her emotions. She stayed in the mindset until she felt Pete's arm reach around her shoulder and pull her in. "It's going to be alright, Ellie," he whispered. "It's going to be alright." It was as if this was his life's calling. To calm and comfort her. How many times had she heard him say this? They stood, the ticks of the clock breaking the silence, her breath slowing, the fumes dissipating, and watched the city come alive beneath them. "Come on." He took her hand and led her back to the kitchen. "Sit down." He patted the barstool at the island. "I'll warm up the muffins. No need to take on the world on an empty stomach." His comment made her smile.

Pete went to work, trying to make things seem normal, and magically made the pre-packaged food look inviting. The fruit was displayed on an oval platter—pineapple, blackberries, melon, and grapes. There were two forks on the plate, one at each side. He had transferred the coffees into large ceramic mugs, each steaming. A fresh blueberry muffin with crystals of sugar beckoned her. He knew all her weaknesses. He handed her a cloth napkin, their hands touching, stopping there. She studied his familiar face and kind eyes. "You know," she said as she placed the napkin on her lap and picked up her mug, "if this security gig you're doing falls apart, you could always open a restaurant."

"Only if you will be a regular." He moved around the counter and sat at the island with her. They locked eyes. They shared a rare type of friendship. One that she knew would go on forever. He gave her a knowing smile.

"Well, I might need a reserved seat, one right at the counter."

"I could arrange that." They clinked their mugs together. "So, what's the schedule for today?"

She appreciated the question and hoped the day would provide answers and closure. Time to get her head in the game.

"I need to go to Louisa's house and get the diamonds. Then I'll head to the event center. Lionel's scheduled a run-through at ten thirty. That's when I plan to transfer them to the chenet. After that, I'll stop by the hospital, check on Louisa, and then head to the gala. What about you?"

Before Pete could answer, there was a knock at the door. "It's probably Sebastian. He's here to drive me, well everywhere. Self-appointed chauffeur, it seems. He's very insistent," she said.

Pete invited Sebastian in as Mia took a bite of muffin. "Hi, Sebastian. How are things at the hospital?"

"No change. Ophelia Petrakis is sitting with Louisa this morning."

"Thanks for staying with her last night."

Mia gathered her computer and files when her phone chirped. She looked. "It's Nikki Santos."

"Put it on speaker," Pete said. Sebastian nodded.

They clustered in a circle and placed the phone on the island. "What do you want, Nikki?"

CHAPTER 47

Nikki sat comfortably in her yoga gear, her hair pulled up in a ponytail and a towel hugging her neck. She motioned for the personal trainer to leave. The golden hue of the morning cast optimism on Nikki.

"Good morning, Mia. Hope you had a pleasant evening."

"What do you want?" Mia repeated.

Nikki waited until the trainer had left the suite. "Just making sure you plan to transfer the diamonds today," Nikki emphasized, "like we discussed." She patted the towel against her moist brow.

"Worried, are you?" Mia replied. "Afraid your client will turn their wrath on you rather than a defenseless old woman? Perhaps I should let you suffer whatever fate comes to those who disappoint the Bannister brothers."

"You think you're cute," she said, sensing Mia's resolve. "I don't find this funny, and I can't risk you dropping the ball. So, perhaps I can offer you some extra incentive to stop playing games." Nikki stood and walked the length of the windows of the suite and sipped her smoothie.

"I'm not interested in anything you have. The only thing I want from you is out."

"Now, now, Mia," Nikki interrupted. "Why do you have to make this so difficult? Listen carefully." Nikki stopped and stared across the city, her tone turning icy. "You will cooperate. Assuming you want to see your friend Charlie Baker again."

"What are you talking about?"

"You know, Charlie your date from last night. We have him." Nikki waited as the message settled at the other end of the phone. "You transfer the diamonds and Charlie will be released unharmed. Understand?"

"I don't believe you."

Nikki sighed. "What is it with you and not believing in me, Mia? We are just getting to know one another and already you don't trust me." Nikki began pacing again as Marco entered the suite. "Believe this. If you want to see the photographer again, transfer the diamonds. Today."

"Are you crazy? What have you done? Where is he? I want to talk to him."

"Well, he's indisposed at the moment, but I will see what we can do to prove it to you, if you insist." Nikki stared at a passing cargo ship and cleared her throat. "Mia, believe me when I say, I am not playing around." She turned as she gave a catlike smile to Marco. "I'll see you soon."

She hung up the phone before Mia could reply. Marco took off his hat and waited. Dark circles weighted his eyes, yet they remained overly large as if he had guzzled a double espresso to withstand a night of no sleep. He wore a smirk of respect for her. As she walked toward him, he finger-combed his hair into place and waited.

"How is our guest?" Nikki asked him.

"A little feistier than we had anticipated, but not a problem."

"I need a proof-of-life photo. This morning." She picked up the morning paper. "Use this," she said handing him the front page. "It's perfect."

Marco looked at the headline and then at Nikki, and his smirk turned into an unrestrained smile of agreement. "I'll take care of it."

CHAPTER 48

"Don't worry, we'll get Charlie back," Pete said.

"If she has him," Mia replied. "You don't believe her, do you?"

"She has him," Sebastian replied. Pete nodded somberly in agreement.

"I don't believe this." Mia looked out the window and began to piece things together. No answer from Charlie. No call. Yes, he would have at least returned her call. She grabbed her phone and checked once more. No messages from him. Her pulse quickened and she felt the coffee resurfacing from her stomach, burning the back of her throat. "We have to get him back," she said. She looked at Pete, and then Sebastian.

"Bring me up to date," said Sebastian.

Pete filled Sebastian in on everything that had transpired while Mia paced the room, occasionally tossing tidbits of information into the synopsis. They formulated a plan. Pete would utilize his contacts to locate Charlie. Sebastian would take Mia by the brownstone to collect the diamonds, and she would put them in the lion during the run-through.

"Okay, we all agree?" Sebastian asked.

"Yes," Mia said. "Our first priority is getting Charlie back."

A dark recess of Mia's mind considered what might be happening to Charlie. Scenes from old movies depicting horrible beatings of hostages raced through her imagination. The crease between her eyes tightened into a V as she paced the apartment.

"I'll find him," Pete said, stepping to her, "and I'll bring him home to you. Don't worry." His words were soft.

"Thank you." She knew he offered more than a rescue. He offered his blessing. Her feelings for Charlie were clear, and Pete would help her once again.

"Alright, Mia. You ready to go get the diamonds?"

She nodded and Sebastian went to get her coat. "Pete, can we talk for a minute? In private?"

He already had his bomber jacket on when he met her near the kitchen. "I'm sorry you have to be the one to help find Charlie." She swallowed and met his eyes.

"You know I'd do anything for you, Ellie. All I want is for you to be happy. Charlie makes you happy." He offered a familiar smile. "We need to get going," he said and kissed her lightly on the forehead.

At street level, Pete turned toward the south. Mia and Sebastian went north toward the Escalade. "Hey, Pete," Mia called over her shoulder. "Be careful." She threw it out as an offering. A simple way to say "you matter to me."

"Copy that." She watched him disappear around the corner.

"Let's get in the car," Sebastian said. He nodded at the two agents, who were ten paces back, then scanned the area. He had been on alert before, but now, it was as if a switch had been flipped and he appeared able to handle any potential threat.

Sebastian parked the Escalade in the back alley behind Louisa's house, shutting the gate before exiting the vehicle and opening Mia's door. She unlocked the newly installed back door and entered the security code. No more annoying chirp. Light streamed through the cathedral windows, and a haze of dust drifted through the air. Sebastian joined her in the parlor.

She unscrewed the metal end of the kaleidoscope then pulled out the outer tube. Mia and Sebastian both stopped. A sound. Perhaps a light thud on the stairs?

"What was that?" Mia said in a whisper.

Sebastian signaled her to get down as he pulled a black steel handgun from the inside of his jacket and moved quietly to the left of the door. Mia grabbed the kaleidoscope and ducked under the piano. In a quick move, Sebastian pivoted to the far door, where he could get a view of the staircase. Mia watched. He slowly leaned toward the stairs, his body tense and eyes unblinking, then, just as quickly, he relaxed.

"False alarm," Sebastian announced as Jasper rounded the door with his back arched, clearly agitated that his domain had been disturbed.

Mia released a long breath.

Sebastian holstered his weapon and Mia shot him a relieved look. "Do you carry that with you all the time?"

"It's just a precaution," he said.

"Let's hope we don't end up needing it."

The kaleidoscope tube was heavy and her heart beat in anticipation. She poured the contents on the ebony backdrop. Sebastian whistled as he looked at the sparkling mound.

"Well, that will catch a person's attention," Sebastian said, his eyes taking in the display.

Mia didn't respond. The site of the diamonds made everything swirl inside of her.

"We need something to put them in, other than the kaleidoscope," Sebastian said.

He instantly returned to an objective place, devoid of emotion. She decided to do the same.

"I have some extra jewelry bags upstairs. I'll be right back."

She retrieved a black pouch from her gemology set, and they inserted the diamonds and secured the plastic clasp. She and Sebastian met eyes, weighing the magnitude of what they were involved in. She was participating in a crime, and although coerced, she still knew it was wrong.

"I'd put them in the chenets myself if I could," Sebastian said. "But there is no chance they would let me in the vault, would they?"

"No chance. I can do this."

"Until you complete the transfer, you need to be careful. If anyone knows that you have the diamonds with you..."

"I'll be fine, Sebastian. It will be fine." She stashed the contraband into a small, zippered compartment inside her shoulder bag.

She carried the kaleidoscope to the shelf and realized it was no longer important to her. The magical memory of her and Louisa perusing the open-air shops in Italy had been ejected and replaced by this moment. She wondered if she would ever see beauty in a kaleidoscope again.

"Ready?" Sebastian asked as they closed the parlor doors.

Mia looked around the room, and then at Jasper. "Can you give me a minute?" Sebastian nodded and headed toward the kitchen.

"Come on, Jasper. Let's see if you need some food," he said.

She closed the door to the powder room and took in her tired reflection. "You can do this," she said. "Just push through the next twenty-four hours and you can get Charlie and Louisa home. Everything will be okay."

When she emerged from the powder room, her hair was pulled back, a light foundation covered the signs of sleep deprivation, and a pale rose lipstick freshened her look. Her eyes up and shoulders squared, she felt ready to face the mayhem the Santos family had created.

Mia waited inside the back door and tried to appear relaxed while Sebastian checked the perimeter. Slipping out of the shadows, he nodded, and she opened the door. From her left, Jasper appeared, and with the speed of a gazelle, he slipped between her legs and out into the garden. The cat bounded the back fence and onto a branch of the pink dogwood tree that filled the corner of the yard. Mia let out a grimace and knew there was no coaxing him down. She and Louisa had played that game before, only winning after Louisa tempted the feline with fresh tuna.

"We need to go," Sebastian said.

"Jasper," Mia said, "you're on your own."

CHAPTER 49

Forty-foot banners hung from the roof of the Bradbury Event Center, two on each side of the columned entrance. Welcome to the Annual Hope for Tomorrow Gala and Auction. Long cables tethered the banners at all four corners, and their royal blue color accented the gray columns perfectly. *All Lionel*, Mia thought. The red carpet extended from the large entry to the curb, and velvet ropes and gold stanchions completed the walkway making it feel like the entrance to a movie premiere. Inside, three sets of double doors welcomed guests into the big hall, each door with wooden benches between them. A woman sat on the bench to the right. Mia recognized her. The reporter, MacKenzie Miller. Before Mia could signal Sebastian, the reporter cut off their entrance to the hall. Sebastian moved between the two women, acting as buffer.

"Mia, a moment?" MacKenzie asked. "I'd like a statement about your grandmother's condition. Is she going to be able to attend the gala?"

"No comment," Mia said trying to slide past her.

"Are you planning on assuming your grandmother's role at Graham Industries, at least in her absence?"

"No comment."

Sebastian opened the door and let Mia slide under his arm, blocking MacKenzie from getting through.

"Well, perhaps you'd like to respond to the allegations that your grandmother is involved in illegal activity related to both the hit-and-run as well as the burglary."

Mia stopped. Her face red and eyes glaring as she turned toward the reporter.

"She has no comment," Sebastian said. "Come on, Mia, we're late for your appointment." He took Mia firmly by the arm and led her into the banquet hall. He nudged her ahead. "You go on in. I'll be right there," he said before turning to face the persistent journalist.

Mia glanced at Sebastian who pointed for her to keep moving. She did. Moments later, he was by her side, MacKenzie nowhere to be seen.

"Thanks," she said. "How'd you pull that off?"

"Got a little help from our FBI friends. But Mia, you have to keep your cool. You can't let her get to you."

"You're right."

"Now, let's go take care of business," he said as they entered the main ballroom.

Underneath the cathedral ceilings, round tables, adorned by shimmery linens and flowing florals, filled the room. Handwritten name cards were placed in front of elegant dinner plates and goblets. A wide ornate carpet runner, the color of pasta sauce, created an aisle between the tables and led to the perfectly set stage. Jumbo screens were mounted, one on each side, and a cluster of people stood in the center discussing something that seemed of utmost importance.

As they neared the front, Rebekah spotted Mia. "Look everyone, Miss Graham is here."

Lionel bounced down the steps. He looked taller and thinner in his monochrome mustard ensemble, which was completed by a woven scarf wrapped twice around his neck, and sage green glasses. "Alright, everyone. Places. Let's begin." He gave her a double kiss. "Are you ready?" He was in all-business mode, with a dash of enthusiasm. Mia glanced at Sebastian. He nodded and took a seat at one of the tables.

When Lionel cued her, Mia stepped up to the microphone and read the opening remarks prepared for her. It took several attempts to acclimate to the teleprompters while still looking natural, a must according to Lionel. They went through the program, step-by-step, as well as a "fake" auction. After Lionel read his closing comments, he clapped his hands and called the group to attention.

"Gather around, everyone, gather round." Lionel steered the group to a large desk and chairs that were camouflaged by a banner and floral arrangements. "Well done, everyone. You have all done a great job preparing for this event, and, in light of the fact that our event's matriarch, Louisa Hernandez-Graham, cannot be with us," his pinched voice cracked as he nodded at Mia, "we want to make this an event that will make her proud, set new records, and set the art and philanthropic community abuzz."

Everyone agreed. Mia gave a thin smile while inwardly fighting the urge to chew her nails. She hoped that the busyness of the evening would distract Lionel, or anyone else, from noticing the slight weight difference in the docile lion, once she inserted the diamonds. And she hoped the buzz Lionel was referring to did not come from someone finding out that she was transferring stolen gems.

"So, let's do this for Louisa. Are you with me?"

Everyone let out a cheer that echoed against the seventy-foot-tall ceilings.

"Are there any questions? Any other items that need addressing?" No one responded. "If not, I'd like to briefly meet with each of you, to review some final details. Mia, can you wait around for just a bit? Maybe fifteen minutes?"

"Sure," Mia said. "Is there a problem?"

"No, just want to compare notes on a couple of our VIPs. Give me a few minutes and then I'll find you. Okay?"

"Of course."

Mia split away and descended the stage, looking for Sebastian. At the table farthest to the right of the stage, waiting in the shadows like a vulture, sat Nikki Santos. Mia paused and strode straight for her.

"What now?" Mia asked her unwelcomed visitor.

"I have something for you, my skeptical friend."

"We are not friends," she said as Sebastian joined them.

"Maybe someday. I've come to remove your doubts and make sure you finish the business deal your grandmother started." Her large phone came alive with a photo of Charlie. He sat on a metal folding chair, a concrete block wall behind him. The floor was gray and dusty, and the only light came from a bulb that she could not see. Charlie's hands and feet were bound with black zip ties. The dark circles under his eyes aged him by several years. His glasses were missing. His lip looked more swollen than before, and now had a large cut to its side. He stared angrily toward whoever was taking the picture, his eyes showing exhaustion and defiance. In his hands, he held the morning paper. The bold print read, AMBASSADOR TARGETED IN ATTACKS.

"Where is he?" Mia grabbed the phone from Nikki and examined the photo of Charlie. "You need to let him go." She felt like she was on an amusement ride that suddenly dropped her twenty feet, but her insides had yet to catch up.

"You deliver the diamonds; we will deliver dear ole Charlie." Nikki pried the phone from Mia. "It's simple, really. A simple transaction."

From the left, two of Nikki's men appeared. Mia had seen them both before. The man with the hat and trench coat. The other at the hospital. They were cleaned up, but she recognized them. Her skin crawled, and she unconsciously took a small step closer to Sebastian.

"Hello, Ms. Santos." Lionel entered the circled conversation. "We weren't expecting you today. Is there something we can help you with?"

"Hello, Lionel. No, just a quick stop to say hello to Mia. I'm on my way out. Looking forward to this evening." Nikki's voice sounded like a schoolgirl's, and she gave Mia a light hug as if they were old friends. Mia bristled.

From the left, the FBI agents approached and without warning, Nikki's two minions split off into the shadows and Nikki followed them toward the exit.

Mia leaned against one of the sparkling dinner tables and watched the event prep team scamper around tables, setting crystal and straightening chairs. The lead decorator clapped her hands to get everyone's attention and said, "I need three of you to freshen the flowers at these back seven tables. We don't want it to look like a funeral."

Fresh purple orchids were added to the table arrangements, and their coconut scent floated through the air. Sebastian stood halfway between Mia and the oversized double doors, where Nikki slipped into her zebra print mink coat. She wore a smirk and gave Mia a wave with her gloved hand. She looked like someone who'd been given the prize-winning numbers for the lottery. The heat inside Mia grew as she watched Nikki leave.

"Ready?" Sebastian offered Mia a hand and she accepted. The sounds of the workers faded as they neared the vault. They rounded the corner and the guard came to life.

"Miss Graham. Can I help you?"

"Hi, Bernie. I need to check some paperwork."

Bernie went through the required protocol to allow Mia to enter the secured area. As she waited for Bernie to finish, she glanced at her phone and scanned a text she'd received from Pete. Have a location. Heading there now with backup. Will call as soon as I know more. Had he found Charlie? She glanced back at Sebastian, who was watching her attentively from about five yards back. She pointed to her phone. He nodded as if he understood.

Alone in the vault, she headed straight for the docile lion, still the last item on the far-right table. Mia reached inside her bag and unzipped the pouch. She set the black bag on the table. She hated the idea that Nikki or the Santos family or the Bannister brothers would win, but in the end, she told herself, she and Louisa would win if indeed this final act ended their part in the smuggling ring.

A tense exchange echoed outside the vault.

"You can't be down here," Rebekah said.

"I'm looking for Mia Graham. I was told she went this way."

The second voice belonged to MacKenzie Miller.

Rebekah's voice became firm, like an elementary school principal directing an insolent child. "Excuse me. This is a restricted area. You need to leave Miss...what is your name?"

"Miller, MacKenzie Miller with the *Chicago Tribune*."

"Well, Miss Miller. This is a restricted area. You can leave with me or I can have security escort you out. Should I ask Bernie to call for reinforcements?" A pause and then Rebekah continued. "What will it be, Miss Miller?"

Mia heard the conversation continue, but it faded off into the distance. She smiled at the toughness of Rebekah, and Mia made a mental note to send flowers and a bottle of wine after the gala.

Mia felt the embers of her anger rekindle as she slipped on the gloves, turned the lion upside down, found the crack in the wood, and slid and pushed the latch. The secret panel didn't open. She tried again. Nothing. Again. Her back dampened from nervous perspiration. Using all her strength, she pushed again. The panel did not open.

A stack of papers lay next to the exhibit. They were bound together with a paperclip. Mia slipped off the gloves and grabbed the clip. She looked over her shoulder toward Bernie as she unbent the metal fastener and returned her attention to the lion. The silver tip just fit into the tiny slot. Mia felt something blocking the gap. She could see a small piece of black fabric from the bag that held the fakes. Her hands ached as she pushed the small piece of fabric, back, back. Still nothing. She dug in again and pushed the blockage until it reversed its path, and the spring gave and the secret panel opened. Mia expelled a large breath—a sigh really—and the sound echoed in the chamber. "Everything okay, Miss Graham?" the guard said.

Mia took a deep, calming breath, and wiped her brow with her forearm. Looking over her shoulder, she offered a forced smile and said, "Everything is fine. Just a few more minutes." She waited until Bernie repositioned himself in the metal chair and then turned back toward her work.

The black bag of fakes slid out of the belly of the lion, and Mia deposited them into her handbag's hidden pocket along with the destroyed paper clip. The duplicate bag of real diamonds weighed heavy in her hand. *This act*, she thought, *is a felony*. She swallowed hard knowing that the consequence of stopping now could implicate her grandmother and put Charlie at risk.

From the hall, voices sifted toward her. Bernie began the entrance protocol for Rebekah to enter the vault. Most likely, they were coming to collect the final dossier before closing the vault until the start of the auction. She only had a minute or so. She needed to move fast.

She adjusted the bag into a cylinder-like shape. The real diamonds were bigger and proving to be a tighter fit. She squeezed it to get it in the opening. Just as the velvet pouch began to morph to the required size, the plastic clasp broke, and diamonds spewed across the table. Mia gasped. Dozens of diamonds glistened like stars as they lay scattered on the black tablecloth. From behind her, she heard keys jangling as Bernie prepared to open the gate. They would be there any second.

Mia scooped up loose diamonds and dropped them, a half dozen or so a time, into the lion. They stuck to her palms, and she still had half of the diamonds to go. Her heart raced as the light chitchat grew closer. She took the document that lay next to the chenets and scraped the remaining loose diamonds into her handbag as the ladies entered.

"Oh, hello, Mia," Rebekah said. "Anything I can help with?"

Mia remained at the table, her back to Rebekah. She closed the bottom of the lion, returned it to its place, and picked up the paperwork that sat in front of it, scanning the area for any runaway stones.

"No. Just double-checking some paperwork. Everything seems to be in order. That should do it." Her voice raised a bit. She smiled and turned toward the entrance hoping Rebekah didn't notice her damp shirt or shallow breath.

"Bernie, I'm all finished," Mia said. The guard completed his protocols, in reverse, and Mia and Sebastian walked back to the banquet hall. The FBI followed close behind.

CHAPTER 50

The end-of-summer sun battled against a chilled autumn breeze blowing down Michigan Avenue. Mia had convinced Sebastian to walk the half mile to the hospital despite his protests and those of the FBI agents walking behind them. The brisk pace helped to alleviate the tension she carried from the mishap at the vault and a temporary distraction from the resentment churning inside of her after the encounter with Nikki.

She looked to Sebastian who kept an easy pace beside her. "Any word from Pete?" she asked, already knowing the answer.

"No. I'll give him a call when we reach the hospital."

Mia dug her hands into her pockets and stretched her face to the wind, letting its sting replace the lingering anger, worry, concern, frustration, and confusion. Or was it loneliness? She wasn't sure. Maybe all of them.

They entered the hospital, and the change in the temperature made her skin burn. The weekend brought about a change of pace that defied the urgency of a weekday. Medical staff, dressed in scrubs, casually walked along the corridors carrying coffee and cell phones.

Sebastian and Mia reached the elevator bay but opted for the stairs. She needed to keep moving. They reached the ICU unit and buzzed in. Nurse Connie met them at Louisa's door and told them they would need to come back in about thirty minutes. Louisa was being bathed and they were changing sheets. Mia's stomach tightened into a ball of barbwire. How were they at this point? She felt the whisp of hope slipping away, and the weight of the past few days catching up to her.

Mia said nothing. She did not move. It didn't matter that she felt ridiculous. All her social cues, even her instincts seemed to have left her. So she stood in silence, looking at the nurse, and hoping that maybe—just maybe—if she waited just long enough, Connie would say, "Just kidding. Louisa is awake and doing fine. Go on in and say hello."

"We'll be back in a half hour," Sebastian said, interrupting the clumsiness of the moment, and led Mia to the empty waiting room. Concern stretched across Sebastian's brow. Before he could say anything, she said, "I'd like to go downstairs."

Sebastian's eyebrows raised.

"To the chapel." She averted her eyes, trying not to wonder what Sebastian thought of her request. "I'd like to go sit in the chapel."

"Okay," he said.

He said nothing more, and Mia welcomed the silence between them.

She entered the space alone. A familiar hymn played over the speakers. The plush carpet muffled her steps as she moved toward the front of the makeshift church. Warm tones of rust and golden rod softened the room. The chapel felt small and private, even though it could hold a few dozen people. In front, two stained-glass pieces, one on the right and a second on the left, flanked the elevated stage. The artist had used richly color glass to create landscapes brandishing deep, leafy trees and a sloping path that curved along a river. The scene reminded her of the cemetery that housed the bodies of her parents. She dropped onto a silky wooden pew and closed her eyes.

How had her world unraveled so quickly? It had only been a couple of days since she first walked by this chapel, and now she faced her own ugly truth. She was desperate. And despite the sense of desperation, a tinge of thankfulness overcame her. Thankful she had not been drawn to this pew to mourn.

She looked up at the cross that hung in the center and recalled the words from the Sunday services she attended with Louisa. "God is in control, and He can be trusted."

Mia shook her head. That was asking a lot, but perhaps she should consider it. There was no guarantee Pete would find Charlie or that he would be returned safe. The doctors and nurses were doing all they could, but there was no guarantee that Louisa would recover. Nikki and the Bannister brothers wanted the diamonds, and half of them lay nestled in her handbag.

With nowhere else to turn, she looked up to the cross and prayed. Not just for one miracle, but for three.

⇒ ⦀ ⇐

Mia moved away from the hospital room window where she'd been watching people scurrying from their parked cars to the hospital door and restarted her routine. She paced, checked her phone, sat by Louisa's bed, and checked her phone again. Her nerves frayed, she chatted aimlessly with Louisa about the gala, hoping for some response, but receiving only silence. With nothing more to say, she paced. Five steps exactly from the door to the window and four steps from the window to Louisa. Mia's right hand never left her phone, while the nails of her left hand became victim to her nervous habit.

The bowl of soup Sebastian had brought from the cafeteria sat cold and untouched. The night nurse, Sophia, came in and introduced herself. She was about five months pregnant and seemed kind and capable.

Just before dusk, Sebastian entered the room, and without a word, Mia and Sebastian asked each other if there was any news. There was none.

"Are you ready to go?" he asked.

She nodded and did a last check on Louisa when her phone chirped.

"Pete, I've been worried. What's going on?"

Sebastian leaned in and listened.

"We've located him. They have him in a warehouse on the southeast side of town. I don't have much more to tell right now, but I have a team in place. We're going to attempt an extraction."

"Do you know if he is okay?"

"That's all I know right now. I'll call later if I have an update. One other thing—I received a call from a Miguel Montoya, says he works for Nikki Santos and wants to meet with me. Do you know him?

"I know who he is. What did he want?"

"I don't know, but he said it was urgent. I haven't decided if I will meet with him. Charlie is the priority right now. Listen, Mia, I have to go."

"Hey, Pete?"

Sebastian walked to the window.

"Yeah."

"Thank you." She waited. Long seconds passed. "Pete?"

"I'll talk to you soon." The phone went dead.

"Excuse me, Miss Graham." The security guard Mia referred to as Samson leaned his head around the door. "You have two visitors. A Henry and Ophelia Petrakis," he said reading from the two drivers licenses in his hand.

"Thank you. Yes, let them in."

"I'll wait for you down the hall," Sebastian said after greeting the salt-and-pepper couple who asked if they were intruding.

Mia updated the couple, telling them there had been no change in Louisa's condition.

"I know you both just arrived, and I'm sorry to do this, but I have to head out," Mia said. "The gala is this evening. I'm expected there. In Louisa's place.

"We understand. You go ahead. We'd planned to stay with Louisa for the evening. Run along."

CHAPTER 51

"What do you need, Marco? I'm in a meeting."

"Sorry to interrupt, Miss Santos. May I have a word with you? In private?"

"About?"

"I have some important information about an associate of Mia Graham. Pete Haines."

Nikki raised her pointer finger as a signal to Miguel and the suited woman sitting on the sofa.

Nikki stood. "I'll be right back," she said to Miguel.

She stepped out to the balcony. The cold wind carried the smell of the lake, and she wrinkled her nose and shivered. "Go on," she said hoping the conversation would be quick.

"This associate of Mia's, Pete Haines, has been poking around. Asking questions. Word is he may have a beat on where we are stowing our guest. I think we might want to consider transferring him to another location, which could be tricky. This guy is feisty."

"Listen, Marco, everything is on track. We should have the transfer compete by end of today. Early morning tomorrow at the latest. I don't think you should risk a move. Can't one of your men throw this guy off the scent?"

"We'll do what we can. There is one other item."

She waited.

"The police raided a chop shop. Ours."

"And?"

"Some arrests were made."

"What about the car? Was it still there?"

"Yes, at least part of it. I doubt they will be able to trace it back to us. The driver is out of the country."

"Marco, how could this happen? This could jeopardize everything."

"I'm aware. But don't forget, my neck is on the line. My prints are in that car and the owner of the shop can ID me. I'm going to need to get out of town pretty soon."

"As soon as the merchandise is delivered, you can release our guest, and you and your associates can fly off into the sunset with a nice wad of cash in your pocket. Understood?"

"Yes, ma'am. Just wanted to keep you in the loop, Miss Santos."

She appreciated his loyalty and realized he had a lot at risk as well. "Just a few more hours, Marco. Just a few more hours. Get back to me if anything changes."

Miguel joined her on the balcony, wool shawl in hand.

"Everything okay?" he asked.

She allowed the wrap to absorb the cold and stared out to the pier not seeing the ships as they passed.

"Miss Santos?" Miguel said. "Would you like to go back in? Or should I tell Madelyn that we will finish the financial review later?"

Nikki turned and looked into Miguel's dark eyes. He waited.

She looked at him, her right-hand man, so to speak, considering putting their newly placed trust to the test.

"We might have a problem that you could help me with."

She had his full attention.

"There is an important transaction occurring tonight and there is a person who I've been told may be trying to disrupt it."

"Tell me how I can help."

Nikki briefed him and explained that a friend of Mia's, Pete Haines, needed to be distracted until after the gala. She watched his breathing, his eyes, his tone. He remained calm and seemed unaffected by the information as if it was the kind of news he heard every day.

"Visit with Marco. Let him know you'll reach out to this Pete Haines and keep him busy for a while. Can you do that?"

"Yes, ma'am. Right away. And I will arrange to have someone step in while I am out and help you with anything you need this evening. Anything else?"

"That's all. I'm glad I can count on you. Keep me updated."

She detected a masked excitement from him as he opened the door to the suite and escorted her inside. Perhaps he also shared her hope that a mutually beneficial relationship had taken root.

CHAPTER 52

"It's a lovely evening, Miss Graham," Adam, the night doorman said even though the cold night air said otherwise. "It's always good to see you." His uniform fit him snuggly and showed off his rugged good looks that he most likely used on the young tenants, but not on Mia. Not that he wasn't willing. She suspected his restraint had something to do with Jerome and his desire to keep his lucrative job.

"Good to see you, Adam."

"Is there anything I can do for you this evening?"

"I'll be going out later, but Sebastian will be driving me. Have you met?"

Sebastian gave a professional nod to the young buck. Adam tipped his hat. Before Adam could open the building door for Mia, two solid men showed up next to them. Adam eyed them but stood his ground as they approached.

"They are with me," Mia sighed as she gestured toward the security detail. "Try to pretend they're not there."

"Yes, ma'am," Adam replied.

"I'll park the car and wait in the lobby," Sebastian said as Mia entered the elevator. "You can let me know when you're ready."

"No. Come upstairs. I insist."

"Okay. I'll be up in a few minutes."

Mia brewed two cups of coffee and warmed up the leftover blueberry muffins from Pete's morning trip to the bodega. Halfway through, she wondered if Charlie had eaten. Could he be injured? She pushed back her plate.

The doorbell rang. Sebastian skirted past the FBI agents, hung up his coat, and followed her to the kitchen. "I brought a change of clothes. Do you mind if I use your restroom to freshen up?"

She pointed him to the guest bath, took a seat on the sofa, and watched the city below. After a few minutes, Sebastian reappeared.

"Nice tux, Sebastian. You look great." She stood and took in the detail of his appearance. Polished black shoes, his silk bowtie perfectly tied, and a clean-shaven face.

He accepted the compliment with a nod.

"I made you some coffee," she said handing him a mug of steaming, dark roast. "Help yourself to a pastry. Sorry I don't have much else to offer. I'm going to get ready. Make yourself at home."

The refreshing smell of mint shaving lotion met her as she headed to her bedroom.

Thirty minutes later, Mia assessed her appearance in the three-way mirror. The black mermaid dress fit her well, although just a little loose through the waist. She heard her grandmother's voice scolding her for not eating enough. The thought nearly made her smile. Her hair bounced onto her bare shoulders as she applied a deep mauve lipstick that reminded her of a hellebore flower. She and Louisa had once grown the flower in the garden until they discovered the sap from the seed pods caused an allergic reaction. The ER doc had told them that some species are even poisonous. The thought that her lips looked like the hellebore gave her confidence. Perhaps tonight Nikki Santos would discover that she was more than a pretty flower.

Mia found an aspirin bottle and emptied the last pills into the trash. In the bedroom, the last of the day's sun puddled on Mia's bed, providing enough light to find the loose diamonds floating in her handbag. The pieces sparkled as they caught the sun's reflection. Mia scooped the stones into the bottle, making sure not to miss any, secured the lid, and placed it in her clutch. The remaining bag of fakes created a large black velvet dot on her white down comforter. She felt the urge to bring them along, although she wasn't completely sure why. She hesitated and then buried the black bag in the bottom of her patent leather satchel and turned off the light.

Sebastian stood as she entered the living room.

"I guess I'm as ready as I'm going to be," she said. "Would you mind grabbing my black cashmere coat from the closet?"

Sebastian did not move.

"Is something wrong?" she asked.

His face softened as he looked at her.

"What?" She gave him a quizzical look then looked at her dress, and her shoes. "Did I forget something?"

He let out a musky laugh. "No, you didn't forget anything. You look perfect. And, well, you look so much like your mother. Do you know that? She was beautiful as well."

"Thank you, Sebastian." Her throat tightened as she accepted the compliment. She cleared her throat. "Would you be so kind as to escort me to the gala and help me end this nightmare of a day?"

He took her hand and helped her with her coat.

"It would be my pleasure."

CHAPTER 53

Saturday Evening - The Gala

The assigned FBI detail tailed the Escalade as Sebastian snaked the car past poncho-covered protesters. The community activists carried large, slightly wilted signs that read, PRESERVE OUR CITY. According to the paper, the project would most likely be approved at the next council meeting, and it appeared not much would stop the demolition and building of new condos. The people in the street seemed undeterred. Their efforts, at best, might slow progress but chances were slim that they could avert the inevitable outcome.

A woman in a yellow slicker, streaks of black mascara painting her face, looked right into Mia's tinted window, chanting loudly with the small mob as the car creeped by. Mia searched the faces of the people. She wanted to see Charlie there. He should be here, doing his job, not held in some basement. She felt the beats of her heart increase as she thought of seeing Charlie. Hopefully soon.

At the Bradbury, the event host welcomed Mia and Sebastian and asked about the two men in matching black suits who stood behind them. The FBI agents hovered over Mia like drones, and in light of what she carried in her clutch, she didn't like that they were monitoring her every move. Besides, when it came to her safety, she felt perfectly secure with Sebastian close by.

The coconut scent of the floral arrangements met them as they entered the great hall. Twinkling lights hung on white strands and encircled the room, their light reflecting against the gold-rimmed dinnerware. The crystal sparkled and the flower arrangements were lightly glittered. The polished marble floors gleamed next to the ornate runner that led to the stage. The finished backdrop reminded her of the ballroom scene from *The King and I*, one of her and Louisa's favorite plays. Neither she nor Sebastian could stop the "wow" that simultaneously expelled from them. Lionel's team had outdone themselves.

Uniformed servers stood at the ready. Fully stocked bars lined the edges of the room, and black-vested bartenders worked quietly on final preparations. To the right, a woman dressed in a deep navy, backless gown, her ash blond hair falling halfway down her back, stood visiting with a group of servers.

After a moment, she turned and smiled. "Mia. Mr. Armani," she said.

"Rebekah?" Mia said. "I'm sorry, I didn't recognize you." Mia worked to reconcile this woman with the Rebekah who helped to run the DaVinci Group. "You look fabulous," she said trying not to sound too surprised.

"Thank you. So do you. I believe everything is ready for the evening. We are going to do a quick test of the teleprompters and microphones before our guests begin arriving. Lionel is expecting you up front."

"Before we go," Mia said, "I want to thank you for handling that reporter earlier today. I owe you one."

"No problem. And just so you know, I've placed the media table, with Ms. Miller, all the way at the back of the room." She pointed to the far back corner. "Should at least give you a running chance at avoiding her this evening."

"Thank you."

"No worries. Now, may I take your bag and coat?"

"I'll keep my bag, thank you."

"And I'll check our coats," Sebastian offered.

"Okay then, I need to meet with the caterers. Lionel is right over there." Her manicured finger pointed toward the stage. "I'll join you in a minute." Rebekah turned and headed toward the kitchen.

"I would never have known that was her," Mia confessed to Sebastian as he helped her remove her coat. "Just goes to show that sometimes people can surprise you."

"You're right about that."

"Listen, would you try to detain the dynamic duo for a few minutes?" She pointed to the FBI agents. "I want to get the rest of the merchandise transferred, and I'd just as soon them not know where I'm going."

"I'll see what I can do."

"Thanks."

She waited until Sebastian momentarily distracted the two men and slipped behind a group of servers who waited in the wings. She took long strides toward the hallway that led to the vault. A heavy velvet rope hung across the corridor. A sign read

NO ENTRY. Mia skirted past it, ducked under the rope, and headed down the empty hall.

"Hello, gentlemen," she said to the vault guards as she turned the corner. The two men stood to attention, nearly knocking over their metal folding chairs. She recognized Bernie who had been there yesterday. The second guard she had not seen before. "I'm Mia Graham, with the DaVinci House," she said.

"Hello, Miss Graham," Bernie said. "How can we help you?"

"I need to check on an item for tonight's auction. Just a last-minute clarification. I only need a few minutes."

"I'm sorry, Miss Graham. The vault is on a timed lock, and we have no way of opening it until ten minutes before the start of the auction. Eight twenty p.m. to be exact."

"Are you sure? It's really important." She glanced behind them and saw that the large metal door to the entrance shut tight.

"There's nothing we can do. If you come back at eight twenty, we'll be glad to assist you."

Mia swallowed. The temperature seemed to be rising. Perhaps there would be time just before the auction to insert the remaining diamonds without anyone noticing. It remained her only window of opportunity.

"I'll stop back after dinner. Thank you."

The two men tipped their hats before settling back into their folding chairs.

Mia turned the corner and leaned against the wall, fighting the panic that threatened to overtake her. She counted the seconds, breathing deeply with each passing second. One. Two. Three. Four. She felt her anxiety lessen. Five. Six. Seven. Eight.

Each breath brought a sprinkling of calm. She looked up. Nine. Ten. As she released the last bit of air, she noticed a painting framed in ornate gold. It depicted a battle from the revolutionary war. The Battle of Breed's Hill, she thought. A place where the colonists stood their ground. Three times the soldiers battled, and three times they held their ground. The probability of victory had not been in their favor. She looked at the stained faces of the emaciated men. Smoke lingered around them, and their baggy uniforms appeared torn and bloodstained. But she could see a flicker of hope still in their eyes. What courage it must have taken to stand up against the well-funded English. She silently applauded them and then looked toward the banquet room, before pivoting her head toward the vault and re-centering her gaze on the painting.

She straightened her dress, raised her eyes, and headed toward the great hall.

CHAPTER 54

Mozart's *The Magic Flute* spilled from the six-piece orchestra and danced through the crowd of well-to-do executives, philanthropists, elected officials, and the likes of Nikki Santos. Mia surveyed the name plates on the tables, trying to ascertain where Rebekah had placed Nikki and the Bannister brothers.

She had three goals for the evening: transfer the remainder of the diamonds, survive her presentation duties, and avoid Nikki. As much as she dreaded having to speak at the event, she wanted a one-on-one conversation with Nikki even less. She searched the venue for Lionel or Rebekah when she felt someone lean in from behind her.

"Good evening, Mia." The scent of a floral perfume assaulted Mia. "Don't you look lovely?"

Mia turned to leave but Nikki sashayed and blocked the path. A quick, tit-for-tat conversation and then she'd move on, Mia thought to herself. "Well, teal seems to be your color. Your dress is beautiful and surprisingly modest, except for the slit that exposes your entire leg. And Jimmy Choos? I see you've gone all out for the occasion."

"Of course. They are diamond encrusted. Quite apropos, don't you think?" She twisted a thin ankle outward so Mia could see the sparkling stilettos. "Are you as excited as I am for tonight? It's going to be a lucrative event for everyone, you included."

"I don't want your money. What I want is for you to return Charlie. Now."

"All in good time. Don't fret. Your friend is being well taken care of and will be delivered to you soon."

"He had better not be hurt. Or I swear—"

"Now, now, this is no place for idle threats. And trust me, all this negative energy and stress is unnecessary. You'll find that this gets easier with time."

"Have you not been listening to me? There is no business between us, Nikki Santos. We are done."

"Sure." Nikki brushed off the comment with a laugh. "Your father said that once. He flew to Costa Rica and met with my mother. As I recall, my father was away on business. She warned him, and I watched as he nearly spat in the face of my mother. After he stormed out, my mother's anger grew until she reminded me of a volcano on the verge of eruption. She called your grandmother and told her she needed to talk some sense into him. Louisa knew your family could not escape this and I'm sure she tried to warn him, to persuade him to cooperate. When he did not agree, my mother took action. Unlike me, she is not a patient person. And as you are aware, the attempt to convince your parents went sideways."

"What are you talking about?"

"What am I talking about? The explosion, of course. The one that resulted in a deadly house fire. It was only supposed to be a message." Nikki looked off into the distance. "As I recall, a weekend getaway had been cancelled, and your parents were at home."

"What? What are you saying?"

"I'm saying they were warned. Your grandmother was warned. They were told something awful might happen and yet, they didn't listen. Fortunately, after the tragic fire, your grandmother proved to be woman enough to pick up the torch and carry on. It's too bad, really, that she couldn't convince her own son to just play along. And yet, here we are again. She apparently has forgotten everything she learned. I hope the lessons aren't lost on you, Mia."

"Are you saying the fire that killed my parents was because of you? The fire started because of, of…"

"Well, not me, per se. You see, my father, he's ruthless but has a bit more patience than my mother. She'd reached her limit. I believe I remember something about a slow gas leak and a timed detonator. Yes, that seems right." Mia lost all sense of facial control, and she felt like a dragon about to unleash its fire on its prey. "Whoa," Nikki said, responding to Mia's fiery gaze. "You look angry. You might need to take a breath, and as I said, it wasn't me. I was still quite young. Not yet calling the shots."

"And my grandmother knew? About the cause of the fire?"

Nikki shook her head as if amazed by the question. "She knew. And because she did nothing to convince your father," Nikki said thoughtfully, "I'd say she is partially responsible," "I do hope your grandmother wakes up. The two of you need to have a long talk, Mia dear."

The people, the music, and the lights around Mia seemed to be moving at the pace of a faucet drip. Blood drained from her face as she searched for something that made sense. Had her grandmother said something? Had she not been paying attention? Mia's thoughts returned to the morning of the funeral.

Dressed in a black silk dress and the cotton leggings her grandma had selected, Mia quietly descended the curved staircase of the brownstone. A thin layer of light illuminated the kitchen. Louisa stood in front of the window wearing a belted black dress, her hair neatly tucked into a bun. She did not turn as Mia stepped onto the landing.

"You have gone too far." Louisa's voice sounded like sandpaper rubbing on wood. "Recibí el mensaje. Si, I understand."

Mia swallowed hard and watched as her grandmother's neck turned deep red, and the tone of her voice turned icy cold.

"I am not going to discuss this with you today."

Louisa stood motionless. Saying nothing. The uneasiness of the moment extended to the landing. Mia counted her heartbeats. Finally, after thirty heartbeats, Louisa continued.

"I will meet you. Monday at noon."

Again, silence.

"I said I would cooperate." Louisa threw the phone across the counter. It spun wildly and crashed into the toaster.

Mia grabbed the edge of a nearby chair and replayed her grandmother's words. They ricocheted in her mind. *"You have gone too far."* Did Louisa know who started the fire? Had she known all along and let Mia carry the blame?

The people, music, and lights of the ballroom accelerated like parts of a carousel spinning around her. A passing server stopped to see if the ladies needed something. Nikki waved him on. "Did I hit a nerve, dear Mia? Still mourning the loss of your parents, or is it something more? About the fire perhaps?"

"Shut up." Mia's voice was fierce and quiet. "Don't talk about my family or that fire." Fumes rolled off Mia, and Nikki smirked. She seemed to enjoy Mia's anguish.

Lionel tapped on the microphone and the orchestra softened their melody. "Would everyone be so kind as to take their seats?" he politely requested. "We are ready to begin the program."

"I'll find you after the auction," Nikki said. "I'm sure the Bannister brothers will want to express their gratitude for your assistance. Enjoy the evening, Mia."

Nikki's assistant escorted her to her assigned table, leaving behind the smell of her perfume. A moment passed. As if pulled by magnets, guests filtered to their seats, everyone except Mia who found herself alone in the center of the room, unsure of what had just happened.

A strong arm encircled her waist and gently pulled her forward.

"Mia, may I escort you to our table?" Mia leaned against Sebastian, her eyes reflecting the nightmare of the fire and her years of guilt. "Are you okay?" His brow crinkled in concern.

They found their seats and he handed her a glass of water. "You're shaking. Mia, what happened?"

"Nikki Santos happened." Before she could say more, Lionel, dressed in a black-and-white-checked tuxedo, and velvet bowtie, enthusiastically greeted the crowd.

"Welcome to the Annual Hope for Tomorrow Gala and Auction."

⇒ ⦀ ⇐

"Please welcome to the stage Miss Mia Graham." The applause brought Mia out of her daze.

"You're up," Sebastian said. He stood and helped her to her feet. "Can you do this?"

Mia looked around the room, at the security duo standing thirty feet to her left, at the guests seated at her table, at Lionel who waited expectantly, and then at Sebastian.

"Please watch my handbag." She moved it toward him, and he placed his hand on it.

She swallowed as she walked and somehow mustered an academy-award-winning smile. Lionel kissed her on both checks and moved stage right.

The solid wood podium served as an anchor, and the tightness of her grip on its edges made the tips of her fingers tingle. After a few unsteady seconds, Mia settled into a pleasant cadence as she read her speech, thankful that Lionel had insisted on a teleprompter and practice run.

"And finally, I'd like to thank Lionel McMasters. Of course, his exceptional reputation as an art dealer and owner of the DaVinci Auction House precedes him, but not everyone is aware of the countless hours, time, effort, and personal investment he pours into our annual gala. His contribution is truly remarkable. He, and his wonderful staff," Mia pointed in their direction, "put on an event that is second to none." She smiled at Lionel and then looked to the audience. "Please join me in thanking Lionel and the entire staff at DaVinci Auction House." The audience stood, and Lionel and his team joined her stage center. Mia scanned the crowd. Her eyes landed on Nikki who was in a strange, huddled conversation with her assistant. Mia wondered what was distracting her and if it had to do with Charlie.

Once seated, she glanced toward Nikki's table and watched her retreat to the hallway. Mia reached for her water but decided to wait until her hand stopped shaking. Sebastian patted her arm. "You did a good job. Now take some breaths. This will all be over soon."

CHAPTER 55

"Miss Santos. A word?" Miguel whispered.

She shot him a look and mouthed a response. "Now?"

He nodded and escorted her away to the back hallway.

"What is this about?" she asked. "Is there a problem?"

Miguel straightened his jacket and squared his shoulders. "I've received word that your father has passed."

"What?" Her voice cracked and she covered her mouth with her hand. "No. That cannot be true." She walked to a settee a few feet away and allowed Miguel's announcement to chisel away at her strong exterior.

"No. No. No. Do not tell me this." Her face creased from the shock, and she looked to her assistant for more.

Miguel maintained his composure and stared intently into her eyes. "I am sorry, Miss Santos. Your father is gone."

"No." The word squeaked through her teeth, and she worked to stuff her emotion to the deepest recess of her being. She remained silent for several minutes, yet she could not stop her tears.

"When did this happen?" The question barely a whisper.

"Last night."

A few people wandered by chatting. She watched them idly going about their business. How could the world continue around her when hers had come to an abrupt stop?

Then, like a gust of unexpected wind, Miguel's response to her question reached her. She stood and stepped closer to him. "Last night? How am I just hearing of this? Why wasn't I informed?"

"I do not know. I have only just heard the news myself. From my grandmother. She assured me it is true."

Nikki's pulse quickened, and she could barely control the volume of her voice.

"Why didn't my mother call me?"

Nikki did not wait for a response. She staggered to the empty restroom and entered a stall, thankful for the full enclosure that ensured her a moment of privacy. Her chest ached as she held back her heartbreak. Her head ached as she held in her anger. Panic, fear, and anger surged against her like a tropical storm. Using the cold bathroom wall for support, she told herself that now was not the time to fall apart. She would. Later. And she would deal with her mother. But not now. Not tonight. Tonight, she must contain her emotions, bottle them up, and set them aside.

"Miss Santos? Can I get you anything?" Miguel's voice echoed through the empty women's restroom.

She looked up and tried to clear the thickness that filled her throat. "I'll be out in a moment."

She exited the stall and stood in front of the ornate mirror. The cold water spilled from the faucet and she splashed it through her hands then wetted her lips, and drank, allowing the liquid to moisten her dry mouth. After several minutes, Nikki wiped her eyes, touched up her makeup, and straightened her shoulders. Taking a deep breath, she headed back toward the banquet hall.

She had one task to complete and then she would head home. Back to Costa Rica. To say goodbye to her papa. And to find out how she would survive without him.

CHAPTER 56

A VIDEO PLAYED ON THE OVERSIZED SCREENS. The presentation documented many of the families and villages from around the world who benefited from the gala's proceeds. The program flew by in a blur, just as Sebastian had predicted. Mia picked at her food and nodded along with the conversation at her table. All the while, her thoughts ping-ponged from Charlie, to Louisa, to Nikki's words, and then to the vault and how she was going to get in, reach the chenets, and insert the remaining diamonds without detection.

The servers cleared the dinner plates and the room quieted as Lionel walked to the podium carrying a stunning, swirled crystal trophy and asked Mia to join him. She walked carefully to the stage, working to keep herself moving forward.

He presented Mia with the award, which she accepted on behalf of her grandmother. Lionel spoke of Louisa. About her kindness, her generosity, and strength. As Lionel lauded her grandmother, Mia wondered if the people in the audience knew Louisa as the kind woman Lionel described, or did they know about her grandmother's dark history?

The teleprompter moved to Lionel's last line, and Mia swallowed trying to moisten her throat. Lionel presented the trophy and she read through the scripted acceptance speech, relieved that this portion of the evening was finished. Lionel reclaimed the microphone. The auction would begin in fifteen minutes. He encouraged everyone to stretch their legs, mingle, and freshen their cocktails.

Mia glanced around the perimeter of the room as she returned to the table. No Pete. No Charlie. She leaned over to Sebastian.

"Sebastian. I need to get to the vault."

"Then, let's go."

They politely greeted people as they worked their way across the room, her two security guards twenty feet behind.

"Miss Graham." A hand grabbed her bare shoulder. She turned abruptly at the gesture.

Louisa's boss stood in front of her dressed in a standard black suit and tie. "Mr. St. Clair. You seem to be everywhere." He wore a serious scowl. "Is there something wrong?"

She watched him soften. "Nothing life threatening. I'm here about our investigation and would like a word with you now that the program is over." He glanced toward the stage. "Is there someplace we can visit privately?"

"I'm afraid I'll have to take a rain check, Mr. St. Clair. I still have a few work duties that can't wait."

"But, Miss Graham..." His face puffed up with indignation. He clearly was not used to being dismissed.

"It will have to wait," she said firmly. Every minute counted, and St. Clair had just stolen one of them. Without waiting for a response, she turned toward the hallway and ducked under the roped barricade.

Mia saw Rebekah and Angela halfway down the corridor deep in conversation and reviewing the first few auction items. Mia skirted past them unnoticed.

"Hi, Bernie," she said to the guard, trying to sound casual. "I'm back. Is the vault open?"

"Just opening now, Miss Graham. Just need to log you in."

It took all her energy to remain calm. As Bernie scanned her ID and logged her visit on his paperwork, Rebekah approached.

"Hi, Bernie. Mia. Angela went to grab the cart. We're ready to transfer the first set of items. Bernie, can you check us in?"

"Sure thing, Miss Richardson. Just as soon as I'm finished up with Miss Graham.

"Was there anything else you needed, Mia?" Rebekah asked.

Mia remained calm. "Just thought I'd come lend a hand."

"Oh, no need. Angela is here to help. You should go back and enjoy the evening."

"I don't mind."

"Well, I insist. Angela and I have this handled."

Her mind raced for options but came up empty. So she nodded her thanks and headed away from the vault. She'd find a way to get them to Nikki without jeopardizing Charlie's safety.

Her heartbeat reverberated in her eardrums with each step. She slipped into a hallway that led to the caterer's kitchen. A few strange looks greeted her. She moved faster and stepped through a side door that opened to a vacant courtyard. The crisp night air surrounded her as she made her way to an ornate, marble bench. She sat, holding her head, until her pulse slowed. She surveyed the space and found herself alone.

Glass walls surrounded the open-air courtyard. The door to the kitchen, where she had entered, had been skillfully hidden by landscaping, and most likely used as a shortcut to other areas of the venue. The main entrance, large glass sliders, were at the far end. Her phone buzzed in her bag. She reached in and her hand brushed the pill bottle.

"Hello?"

"Mia, where are you?" Sebastian said.

"I'm in the courtyard. East wing just past the kitchen."

"I've heard…" His words broke into unrecognizable sounds.

"Are you there?"

"I…talk…can…"

"I can't understand you, Sebastian. Bad connection." The line went dead. She waited for him to call back.

Her thoughts turned to what mattered most. Getting the rest of the diamonds to Nikki before she or the Bannister brothers realized the shortfall.

She texted Nikki.

Need to meet.

There's a small problem. It can be resolved.

Mia sat with her phone and the diamonds and waited. She heard Lionel introduce the auctioneer. Lionel read the description of the first item and listened as the rapid cadence of the auctioneer's voice echoed into her private atrium. She stood and paced while waiting for a reply from Nikki. Or perhaps a text from Pete. Or perhaps waiting for the night to be over. The auctioneer moved quickly through the lots and, from what she could hear, the items were bringing in a nice sum of money. She tried to smile knowing that would please Lionel and Louisa.

Goosebumps covered Mia's arms. She rubbed them to create friction, and wondered if her chill came from the cold air or the diamonds in her handbag or what she had learned from Nikki. After all these years, was it possible? Her parents were dead because of Gabriella Santos.

A tapping sound penetrated the background noise of the auction. She looked up, expecting to find a lost bird pecking away at the marble beside her. She scanned the room. Through the glass wall, she saw him. He stood looking at her. A black ring darkened his right eye, and a sling wrapped an arm, yet he smiled. She wiped her eyes to be sure it wasn't a dream. He made his way toward the entry doors. Charlie.

She walked the paved path to him, speeding up with each step. When they met, she wrapped her arms around him. With his free arm, he hugged her tightly. She loosened her grip when she heard him stifle a groan.

"I'm sorry. You're hurt. Do you need a doctor?" She pulled away.

"No, no, I'm going to be okay. Just a little sore."

"How did you get back? Did they let you go? Are you going to be okay?"

He smiled at the rapid-fire questions. "They didn't let me go, but I did leave a bit earlier than they had planned. I had some help," he said as he pointed to the window at Pete. "He's quite a guy, that one," Charlie said.

Pete smiled at Mia and gave a half salute. She mimicked the greeting. "He certainly is."

She turned back to Charlie and surveyed the damage to his face. "I'm sorry this all happened to you. It's all my fault."

"It's not your fault and I'm okay."

She searched his eyes.

"Really," he said pulling her chin up with his forefinger. "I'm okay."

Mia smiled and then looked back to the window. Pete was gone. Tears formed in her eyes.

"Mia?" Charlie said.

She looked at him and let herself connect with his inviting eyes. "I'm just relieved you are okay."

A tear rolled down her cheek, and with his free hand, his fingers absorbed the liquid. He tilted her chin up. "And I'm so glad to see you." His lips were soft and welcoming. She leaned into the embrace and felt relief. He pulled away for a moment.

And then they kissed again.

CHAPTER 57

Mia and Charlie found Sebastian and Pete near the back wall of the banquet hall. They stood at a high top and were taking four beverages from a waiter who stood with a round tray full of drinks and bite-sized desserts. Pete looked out of place, as did Charlie. Both were underdressed and dirty, not to mention the fact that Charlie looked like he'd come from a losing bout with a bear. Mia didn't care.

Pete handed Charlie and Mia a drink.

"Pete was telling us that the CPD have arrested the guys that were holding Charlie and they've issued an arrest warrant for the man who's responsible for the hit-and-run and the break-in," Sebastian said. "Here's to you, Pete, for getting Charlie back, and here's to you, Mia, for getting the transfer made. I know that wasn't easy." He raised his glass in a toast.

Mia hesitated.

"What is it? Mia?" He wore a concerned look on his face. "I haven't forgotten about Louisa and that the Santos family is still a possible problem. But trust me, Louisa will get better, and we'll get her home. Don't look so worried. Everything is going to be alright."

"I know. It's not that. I wasn't able to get back in the vault," she explained. "So, roughly half of the diamonds are in the chenet, and the other half is with me. I texted Nikki and told her I need to meet. But who knows, maybe the evil duo won't know how to count and think they have all the diamonds."

"Doubtful," Sebastian said.

They stood silent. Mia looked at them and assumed they were all mentally gnawing on the information and the looming danger the Bannister brothers presented if they didn't receive their merchandise as promised.

"Mia. There you are." It was Rebekah. "Sorry to interrupt."

"No problem. We were just visiting. Let me introduce you. Charlie Baker, Pete Haines. This is my associate, Rebekah Richardson. I believe you already know Sebastian?"

"Yes. Nice to see you all. Mia, can I steal you away for a minute? We've transferred all the auction pieces to the stage. In fact, I think Lionel is just about to auction off the last item."

"That's great. So how can I help?"

"I need the packing boxes from storage, but there's a moving cart in there. In fact, it's wedged in the closet, and I literally can't find a person who can help get it out."

"I'll give you a hand," Pete volunteered.

"Are you sure?" Rebekah asked.

"Yeah, no problem. Mia, you stay here with Sebastian and Charlie. I'll be right back."

Mia watched Pete head off with Rebekah until she heard the announcement from the stage.

"Ladies and gentlemen. It's time for our final item up for bid."

Mia looked at Charlie and Sebastian. "Here we go."

Lionel read the description of the chenets, building up their import with a growing bravado in his voice. "Who would like to start the bidding?"

The bids began low and quick. $4,000, $5,000, $7,500. Six people were actively bidding. As the price grew—$25,000, $40,000, $45,000—the competition landed between two people. Monica Stewart-Morgan, a stodgy woman and a well-known collector with old money and a tall, dapperly dressed gentleman with an antique walking cane who reminded her of the Planter's Peanut Man. Bidder number 673. Mia didn't recognize him. When the bid reached $75,000, Monica placed her paddle on her lap and passed on the next bid.

"Sold to 673," Lionel announced. Everyone applauded.

Mia watched the man stand and exit his row. The cane was purely ornamental. The man gave a nod to Jonathon Bannister, who lifted his glass just slightly in his direction.

It made sense. The Bannister brothers would want separation from the purchase, and so they used an intermediary, someone who would make the purchase, for a fee, while giving anonymity to the actual owners.

The man with the cane made his way to the partitioned meeting area to finalize the arrangements. After a few minutes, he emerged with a silver case, a bit larger than a bowling bag. He headed casually toward the two brothers and set the case on the floor. Mia watched as the elder Bannister brother slid an envelope across the table and the man slipped it into his breast pocket before ambling away, leaving the case behind. The two brothers shared a knowing smile and then headed toward a private meeting room, presumably to inspect the goods.

Mia's phone buzzed. It was Nikki.

Meet me on the balcony, west side, in 15 minutes.

It won't be long now, Mia thought. Then hopefully this chapter of her life would be over. She told Charlie and Sebastian that she needed to head to the balcony to meet Nikki.

"You two go ahead," Charlie said. "I'm going to stop in the men's room." Mia grabbed his free hand as he turned to go.

"I'll meet you out there," he said. "I'm fine. I just need a minute." He kissed her lightly on the lips before walking away.

CHAPTER 58

NIKKI MARKED THE TIME, her body tingling, waiting for the moment she could breathe freely again. The Bannister brothers were in the private viewing area. The DaVinci House had erected four small tents along the left side of the room, each with a table and chairs inside to allow clients to examine their purchases privately. She kept her eye on the third tent for the signal that her customers were happy.

She drummed her fingers on the table and nursed the last of her martini. The night had not gone perfectly. The raid on the chop shop was a concern, but she would deal with it, and Marco, later. And then there was the text from Mia. What could the newbie mean by a "*small problem*"? Regardless, as long as it didn't affect the outcome, it didn't matter, but it did remind Nikki that Mia would take some significant grooming. It had become apparent that Mia was green when it came to the family business.

She checked the time. Just minutes stood between her and the result she had worked hard to achieve. What was taking so long?

She took a deep breath to calm herself and scanned the room. Where the hell was Miguel? He'd been MIA since before dinner. She would need to reconsider his role in her organization if this continued. Someone tapped her on the shoulder.

"Would you like a fresh cocktail?" the server asked.

As Nikki exchanged her empty drink for a fresh one, she saw a shabbily dressed man walking toward the restrooms. He looked familiar, but it couldn't be. She stood and handed the cocktail back to the server.

Nikki recognized the solid build and handsome shape of his body, but his arm in a sling was new. He saw her, and they froze in place as if someone had hit a pause button. Her mind scrambled to catch up with reality. Charlie's face was bruised, but his expression was one of quiet satisfaction, like a thief who had just pulled off the perfect heist. He flashed a smile in her direction and entered the men's room.

She considered following him, to verify it was him, but she knew. It was Charlie Baker. How had he gotten away? The incompetence of her team made her angry, and she felt her blood pressure rising like water coming to a boil.

She wanted answers. She dialed Marco's number, but the call went to voicemail. Things were not going in her direction. She left him a message that he would not soon forget.

Nikki found herself in the back of the hall, scanning the crowd. Her legs felt anchored to the floor while waves of anxiety crashed at her from every side. A couple walked by and acknowledged her but did not stop. The music continued from the stage as the event began its descent to its final hour. Journalists took photos and interviewed a few of the dignitaries. Waiters carried round trays to the remaining guests. Near the stage, she saw a woman dressed in a flowy black gown and a silver shawl. Nikki recognized the sinewy profile, even from this distance. Her mother?

It couldn't be. Why would she be there? The idea of her mother coming to Chicago temporarily paralyzed her. Nikki's eyes bore into the woman as she walked toward her.

Her phone buzzed and she stopped.

Need to see you NOW. Back East doors. JB

The text from Jonathon Bannister made her tremble. Something was off. She looked to the front but did not see the woman. Perhaps she had imagined it. Then she looked for Marco or Antonio or Miguel. They were nowhere to be seen. She'd have to handle this storm alone. She took a deep breath to regain her composure and headed to the back doors to meet Jonathon. Her confidence grew with each step. She was a Santos after all, and she could handle any storm. But then she saw them. The brothers faced her, and fury emanated from their eyes.

CHAPTER 59

MIA STOOD ON THE BALCONY that overlooked the Chicago River. The sliver of the moon's light pierced through the thick clouds making the water look like TV static. The wind had taken its leave, and the cold air claimed ownership of the night. Restaurants across the river were brightly lit, all of the patrons inside, but the aroma of the cuisine met Mia where she stood. It smelled of fresh baked bread. Italian food.

Mia's eyes adjusted to the blackness of the evening, and she looked across the long patio. Twenty yards from her she saw the silhouette of a man, leaning against the balcony edge. Pete. She'd recognize him anywhere. He still looked like the boy she had met all those years ago, wearing jeans and a T-shirt under his bomber jacket.

"I'll be right back," she said to Sebastian.

Halfway there, he saw her. He turned and smiled. She felt his eyes photographing her.

"Has anyone told you that you clean up good?" he said.

"Who, me?"

They stood inches apart and met each other with a knowing smile.

"You look beautiful, but you're shivering. Take my jacket." He slipped his leather coat over her shoulders, and they turned toward the river, leaning their elbows on the concrete wall. Despite all that was going on, Pete still had the magical quality of a favorite blanket. She leaned against his shoulder.

"It's been quite a week, hasn't it, slugger?"

"You can say that."

They watched a tourist dinner cruise float down the river and then faced each other. "Can you tell me what happened? How you found Charlie?"

"I'll tell you about it sometime over wings and a beer. But for now, just know that he's safe. Let's focus on finishing this nasty business with Nikki Santos and then get you and Charlie home. And Louisa too."

"Will it really be over? After Nikki has the diamonds, will this be the end of it?"

"Let's take it one step at a time, okay? But yes, I think it will all be over soon." He studied her face. "There's something else. What's wrong?"

She dropped her shoulders and looked at the one person who would understand the gravity of her news. "I found out tonight, from Nikki, that I…I…" She paused.

"You what, Ellie?"

She swallowed. "The fire wasn't my fault. I didn't start the fire."

He absorbed her words and put his hands on her shoulders. His eyes searched hers as he waited for her to say more.

"Pete, I'm not responsible for the death of my parents." She gulped in a sob, and he held her tight.

"I never thought you were, Ellie. I always knew there had to be another explanation."

Someone approached and tapped Pete on the shoulder.

"Sorry to interrupt," Miguel said in a hushed tone. "Giving you a heads-up," he said, "it's going down. They're on their way." Then he scooted into the shadows and out of site.

"Was that's Nikki's assistant? How do you know each other?"

"Let's head back toward Sebastian," he said as they walked. "Yes, that's Nikki's assistant, Miguel Montoya. Remember, he'd reached out to me? At the time, I didn't know why. He's working undercover, and with his help, the feds have built a case against both the Santos organization and the Bannister brothers. They're planning an arrest tonight."

"Here? Now?"

Pete nodded. "Looks that way."

Mia stopped and turned toward Pete. "And what about Abeula? Is she in trouble? Or me?"

"He didn't say specifically, but I don't think so. Let's keep walking."

The sound of footsteps echoed against the tiled balcony. Pete and Mia turned. "What's going on here?" Charlie said sheepishly.

"Charlie, you doing okay?" Pete asked.

"I'm gonna be fine. Thanks, man," he said as they shook hands.

"I'm going to go see if Miguel needs any backup. Why don't you guys head back toward Sebastian."

"Mia, will you fill him in?"

She nodded. "Don't forget your jacket," she said and returned it to Pete.

"Okay, I'll check in later." Pete headed inside the museum.

"So, what's going on?" Charlie asked as they rejoined Sebastian.

"I'm waiting for Nikki. To give her the rest of the diamonds. But Pete just said the feds are here. I think they're going to make an arrest. And here I am with diamonds in my bag. I don't know what I should do. I need this whole thing to be over."

"Let's just play it out," Sebastian said. "Just for a few minutes."

Inside, the sound of the orchestra floated through the open doors and people milled casually about. Mia, Charlie, and Sebastian stood, silent in the cold, watching and waiting. Mia accepted Charlie's jacket, slipping her arms inside the openings, allowing the warmth to assuage her goosebumps. She inhaled his scent.

Her phone buzzed. Unknown number. She declined the call.

Her phone buzzed again. Mia recognized the number.

"Where are you?" Nikki's words shot through the phone like venom. Mia knew that Nikki had learned of the partial deposit of diamonds. Mia braced herself.

"Let me explain," Mia said as she spotted Nikki. She was at the far end of the balcony.

"Explain? How dare you double cross me." Nikki locked her sights on Mia. "You stay there. I am coming for the rest of the diamonds. You better have them."

Nikki marched toward them, the gemstones on her stilettos twinkling in the darkness. As Mia watched Nikki close the gap between them, she could see the Bannister brothers in the distance, their shapes highlighted by the yellow ballroom lights, the case with the chenets between them.

"I have them. And I'm willing to give them to you."

"Stay where you are," Nikki shouted.

Mia clenched her purse. Nikki stood within inches of Mia's face.

"Hand them over, you fool." The words dripped with venom. "You have nearly blown this entire deal."

Before Mia responded, a woman moved in beside Nikki.

"You are both fools. Too young and too stupid to handle such important business."

"Mother? It is you." The words pinched out of Nikki's mouth.

"What? You're surprised? I knew I couldn't leave this to you. Now Mia, give me the diamonds." Gabriella Santos's voice pierced the air and dared to be defied.

Mia recognized the woman in front of her from the photo at Louisa's. "You're…you're…," Mia stammered. "You are the person who killed my parents."

"It's good to see you too," Gabriella said in an icy tone. "The diamonds, Mia."

Mia's hand shook as she reached inside her clutch, her hand searching for the pill bottle but landing on the velvet bag instead. She clenched the bag and pulled it from her purse. "Is this what you want?" Mia shook the bag in the air. Giving her decision a nano-second of consideration, she popped the clasp off the bag, turned toward the balcony, and threw them toward the river. A guttural scream erupted from Nikki as the shimmery imitation diamonds fell to the water below, their glint catching the moonbeams before plummeting into the darkness. Nikki and her mother instinctively leaned over the edge reaching for the crystals. But they were gone.

Nikki turned and swung a clinched fist toward Mia. But Sebastian grabbed Nikki's arm before she made contact and Charlie pulled Mia a step back.

"What have you done?" The Santos matriarch looked between the two women. "I will fix this, but you two will pay."

Mia lunged toward the woman and landed a right hook to her jaw. Gabriella fell to the ground and Mia towered over her. "I don't work for you. Our family is done. Get away from me. Both of you."

From the ground, Gabriella laughed and said something that Mia couldn't make out.

A commotion erupted at the far end of the balcony. A dozen federal agents surrounded the Bannister brothers. Beams from flashlights lit the area, officers shouted commands, and guests of the gala headed for the exits. They all watched as the Bannisters were arrested. Mia watched Nikki's face turn pale in the moonlight. "They are getting what they deserve," Mia said.

Nikki turned to Mia, Sebastian and Charlie now flanking her, their stance daring Nikki to try anything. "Where is my mother?" Her head swerved left and then right. "Where did she go?" Nikki's words seethed like hot coals.

Gabriela Santos had vanished in the commotion.

"I need to get out of here," Nikki said. As she moved toward the exit, Miguel approached and took her by the arm.

"Miguel? Where the hell have you been?" Not waiting for an answer, she continued. "Come with me. We're leaving."

Miguel stepped in front of Nikki, blocking her path.

"Get out of my way." She attempted to skirt past him, but he held his ground. She pushed him and made it ten feet before he grabbed her. "Let go of me. I mean it, Miguel. Get your hands off me."

Miguel held her in place, and words spewed between them. Nikki slapped Miguel just before he grabbed her arm and twisted it behind her.

"Nikki Santos," he said with authority, "you are under arrest."

Miguel handcuffed Nikki who looked like a rabid animal. The reflection of the moon highlighted the explosion of anger on Nikki's face. Her fierce eyes locked on Mia.

Nikki writhed under Miguel's control. The chirp of Nikki's phone joined the mayhem.

"Let me go, Miguel. I need to answer that."

Miguel took the phone from her. "It's the Santoses' estate. Costa Rica," he said.

"Answer it," she demanded.

"No need. I know why they are calling."

"What do you mean you know why?"

"Your family's estate is being raided, as we speak. We have a warrant for your mother's arrest. The two of you can rot in a prison cell together, just like your family let my father rot in prison. But don't worry, he'll be out soon and I'm sure his cell will accommodate the two of you just fine." He slid the phone in his pocket and smiled. "Oh, and by the way, sorry to hear about the loss of your father."

The moment felt surreal. Nikki had transformed into a restrained dragon, her nostrils flared, and she thrashed around but could not escape Miguel's grasp. Nearly spent, Nikki re-lasered her death glare at Mia.

But Mia didn't care. Nikki was no longer a threat. Mia met her stare and smiled softly as Miguel took her away.

⸺ ⦀ ⸺

Inside the banquet hall, Lionel and St. Clair stood on the stage talking about the chenets, Mia guessed, as the members of the orchestra hurriedly packed their instruments. Sebastian, Charlie, and Mia headed to the coat-check room, which was now without its attendant. Pete joined them.

"I'd really like to get out of here," Mia said.

"I'll go get the car," Sebastian said. "I'll meet you at the side entrance in ten minutes."

She watched as Lionel answered questions, his arms moving in large, animated gestures. "At least he knew nothing about the diamonds. I'm sure they will be coming to me with questions too."

"According to Miguel, they have a solid case against Nikki," Pete said. "I don't think Lionel, or anyone else, will be implicated. Including you."

"I need to let Rebekah know I'm leaving," Mia said. "I wonder where she is?"

"I'll find her," Pete said. "You two go meet Sebastian. I'll call you later."

As Mia hugged Pete goodbye, her phone buzzed. Unknown caller.

"Are you going to answer it?" Charlie asked as they headed toward the elevator.

"I don't know who it is. And let's take the back stairs."

"Okay, but the call might be important."

They scampered down the stairwell and into the dark alleyway. On the fifth ring she answered.

"I'm calling for Mia Graham."

"Yes, who is this?" Mia asked as a tall woman in a torn black dress and silver shawl pushed past them nearly knocking her to the ground. Mia mouthed to Charlie. "Is that Gabriela Santos?" The woman headed toward the crowd of protesters at the end of the block, pulled her shawl over her hair, and disappeared.

"Miss Graham, this is Sophia Summers, your grandmother's nurse at Northwestern."

"Sophia. What is it? Is something wrong?"

"I'm afraid so. Can you come to the hospital? The doctor would like to see you."

CHAPTER 60

MIA PUSHED THE INTERCOM and waited for the ICU doors to open. Sebastian and Charlie kept pace as they rushed toward the desk.

"I need to see Dr. Cheung. Do you know where I can find him?" Mia looked frantically into the face of the nurse who sat behind the long counter and then at the two familiar faces who stood guard at Louisa's door. The guard she called Samson offered her a sympathetic smile. She hated those looks, and his frightened her.

"I'll page him. Just one moment."

Mia waited while the nurse punched in the doctor's number. Mia began to pace the length of the counter.

"What is taking so long?"

The phone on the desk rang. The nurse answered but said nothing into the receiver before hanging up. "The doctor is on his way. He'd like you to wait in the office at the end of the hall."

"Okay, but I want to see Louisa first."

Mia did not seek the permission of the nurse or of the guards as she entered Louisa's room.

Louisa lay sleeping, as before, but now the gray blanket covered her again. Mia had learned the language of the monitors and knew that Louisa's vitals were strong. So, what was the problem? Why the emergency meeting?

Mia, Charlie, and Sebastian entered the cramped office less than a minute before Dr. Cheung.

"Have a seat," Dr. Cheung said to Mia.

She reluctantly obliged. Charlie took the remaining chair and Sebastian stood behind her.

"What is going on?" Mia's terse request reminded her of the first time she'd met Dr. Cheung. This time, her frayed attitude did not affect him.

"There are signs that your grandmother's body is weakening. There is a marked decrease in liver, kidney, and heart function. Because of this, we believe it is time to bring her out of the coma."

"Okay, so why the hesitation?"

"There are a number of risks. But the main concern is whether or not she will be able to breathe on her own. When the anesthesiologist reverses the medication, we will remove the ventilator."

"What are you saying?"

"If your grandmother is unable to breath on her own, or does not wake up, do you want us to provide life support?"

"How long would she need it?"

"There is no way to know. Could be indefinitely."

"What? You mean she might never recover? Or breathe on her own?" She sorted through the information. "She would never want to live like that," she said softly. She looked at Dr. Cheung. "But surely, when she is out of the coma, she'll wake up, right?"

"She'll most likely remain unconscious for a short while. The question is whether or not, in her weakened state, her body will respond. Will she breathe on her own? There's no guarantee. Not at this point."

Mia worked to absorb what had been said. She clasped her hands and rested her head on them. With her eyes closed, she asked, "Would you just bottom line it for me?" She knew what he was saying, and she understood, but she needed to hear it again. She looked up and waited for his answer.

"Certainly." Dr. Cheung removed his black-framed glasses and leaned forward. "In my opinion, it is in your grandmother's best interest to remove her from the coma immediately. Your grandmother has a DNR on file, which means no life support. My question to you, since you have medical power of attorney, is, do you want to honor your grandmother's wishes? When the coma is reversed, are you willing to see if she is able to sustain life on her own?"

Mia looked at Sebastian and then at Charlie. She took deep breaths as if there was not enough oxygen in the room. "I'll be back in a minute." She left the room and began to walk around the ICU unit. She slowed when she heard voices from one of the rooms. "Alright, Cecilia," a man said. "Ready to go for a short walk?" As Mia passed the door, she looked in as an aid helped a blond-haired woman to her feet. The woman from the accident. It seemed so long ago. "You keep this up," the aid continued, "you'll be home in no time."

Mia returned to the doctor's office. The men stood and waited. Mia said nothing.

"Mia," Dr. Cheung said, "we need to remove Louisa from the coma. I've scheduled the reversal and the anesthesiologist is on his way. What have you decided?"

Mia met Dr. Cheung's eyes. "We will honor her wishes and hope and pray that she is strong enough to pull through." She looked at Sebastian who nodded and then at Charlie who came to her and wrapped her in his arms.

"Very well," Dr. Cheung said. "The nurse will bring you a form to sign. You can stay until we are ready for the procedure."

CHAPTER 61

Christmas Eve

I have always believed that second chances in life are rare. And, for some reason, I have been given a second chance.

For two days I remained unconscious and yet aware of the things going on around me. I could hear the fear in Mia's voice. "Abuela," she would say, "I need you to wake up. I love you, Abuela." I desperately wanted to come back to her, and somehow, I knew that the final choice was mine. I had to decide if I wanted to fight or drift away from this precious life I'd been given.

After waking, I struggled to regain my speech, my memory and, well, about everything else. Those first days are a blur, except for one thing. Every time I woke, I saw a familiar face. Mia, Sebastian, Pete, or Charlie. They anchored me and kept me in the here and now.

My life is different now. I feel like I've been transformed from a fast-moving cheetah into a three-toed sloth. And the change is a relief. The last twenty years of my life could be summed up by one word. Stress. And it had been brutal. The lies. The smuggling. The secrets. The constant looking over my shoulder. All while protecting Mia. I felt as if I'd been standing in the ocean and fighting against the undercurrent every waking moment.

The first chance I had, I called St. Clair and resigned my position. It was time to let someone else take the reins and play the political game. After that, I called my CEO at Graham Mining. He flew to Chicago, and we laid out the plans to sell my family's forty-nine-year-old company. The deal should be finalized this week, just in time for the new year. With the help of my skillful attorney, I cut a deal with the FBI, and informed them of the inner workings of the smuggling operation in exchange for immunity for me and Mia. Nikki is awaiting trial, and her mother, Gabriela, has found some rock to hide under, although I've been assured the authorities will eventually track her down.

It's cold here on the back porch, but it makes me feel alive. My wool blanket, mug of steaming tea, and Jasper keep me warm, and I am enjoying the crystal shimmer that the light snow brings to the back garden.

I hear the chime of the doorbell.

"Sebastian? Someone is at the door. Can you get it?"

"Got it," he answers.

Since leaving the hospital, Sebastian has become my very own superman. He's been quick to help me in my effort to fully regain my mobility. And he's a great companion and friend who has assisted me in tackling any obstacle that keeps me from living life to its fullest. I've found my very own superhero, but in truth, he's been that for a long time.

There's a commotion at the door.

"Louisa," Sebastian says, "Mia and Charlie are here."

"On my way." I set aside my tea and the blanket, and rock myself up to a standing position. Once I regain my balance, I can easily get around. I've come a long way.

"Grandma," Mia says, kissing me on the cheek. "Merry Christmas."

"Feliz Navidad, mi Mia. Charlie, how are you?" We hug.

"I'm good. Merry Christmas."

Charlie unloads a bag of presents and joins us by the fireplace. I look at Mia as she watches the flames. She glances at me, and we share a sad, knowing smile.

It's six thirty and Pete and Rebekah are here, gifts in hand. I've enjoyed getting to know Rebekah. She is delightful and perfect for Pete. Down to earth, smart, kind, and a die-hard Cubs fan.

"Just got off the phone with Mr. Kim," Sebastian says. "Malik will be here in forty-five minutes with our dinner. So, what's new with all of you?"

"I have some exciting news to share," Mia says.

We all give Mia our full attention.

"I've accepted Mr. Brisbane's job offer. I'll be working for Sotheby's in London. I start in February."

"That's amazing."

"Congratulations."

"That is amazing, Mia," Rebekah says. "I'm so happy for you, but you'll really be missed at the DaVinci House."

"Tell us what you'll be doing," I say.

"Well, it's a dream job. I will be Sotheby's European senior acquisitions and appraisal agent, which is a fancy way of saying

I get paid to travel all over Europe and evaluate some of the region's most amazing collections. It's a dream come true."

"Congratulations, Mia. You deserve this," Pete says.

"This calls for a toast," Sebastian says as he goes to retrieve a bottle of champagne.

"I'm happy for you, Ellie," Pete says, "but what about the home opener? Are you going to make it back? It's going to be the Cubs' year, you know."

"Yeah, you keep hoping. I'm not sure if I'll be able to make it back. I will if I can. But if I can't, maybe Rebekah can take my place?"

"Well, you gotta know that Rebekah is a tried-and-true Cubs fan. If you're not there, I doubt there will be a single person in the stadium cheering for the Sox."

"Yeah, right."

Sebastian returns with a tray of tall crystal glasses and a bottle of champagne.

Our Christmas Eve Chinese dinner arrives and does not disappoint. Clearly a non-traditional approach to the holiday but it seems to suit our tribe just fine. After dinner, everyone makes their way to the parlor for dessert, a delicious, homemade baklava provided by Ophelia Petrakis.

Mia and I are last out of the kitchen.

"Can you wait a minute, Grandma? I have something I'd like to give you."

She walks to her bag and pulls out a small white box with a plain ribbon tied around it.

"What's this?" I say as we sit on the couch.

I untie the string and pull off the lid. It's the journal. I look at her and we find words unnecessary. The worn notebook on my lap feels like a hundred-pound weight and represents nearly five decades of our family history. A history that nearly destroyed us.

"I didn't know what to do with it." Mia is staring hopefully into my eyes.

"Well, I do. We are done with this part of our lives, Bella." I walk to the grandfather clock and reach behind it. I open the back panel and find the latch that is hidden and push it. A small door opens, and I retrieve a second journal. Book One.

Mia watches me and says nothing, so I continue. "How would you feel about putting these, both of these, in the fire?" As we sit and watch them burn, the doorbell rings for the fourth time tonight. Sebastian answers and signs for a package. It is addressed to Mia. Inside is a single piece of folded stationery. A large *S* printed in calligraphy. The handwritten note reads,

Mia,

Feliz Navidad.
Hope to see you soon,

GS

The message causes a chill to run the course of my spine. Mia crumples the note in her palm and cringes before she adds the paper to the small blaze.

I encourage her to not let this ruin the evening, and we join the others in the parlor. The room is festive with Christmas decorations and a twelve-foot tree adorned with silver and red ornaments. Sebastian sits at the piano, softly playing "Silent Night,"

Rebekah is surveying the relics that adorn the shelves, and Charlie and Pete are enjoying Ophelia's baklava in the wingback chairs and talking sports.

"Louisa," Rebekah says, "would you mind if I took a closer look at this?" She points to the kaleidoscope. "I have always loved them."

"Of course." I smile at Mia. "I am fascinated with them as well."

Rebekah sits with us. "You know," I say, "a kaleidoscope is a lot like life. Always bursting with new possibilities and the promise of something extraordinary."

Rebekah holds the vessel to her eye and turns it. With each twist, it rattles. Rebekah raises an eyebrow as if to ask, 'What is that?'

"Just part of its charm," I say, and I smile at Mia. "Would you like to hear how we came to purchase the kaleidoscope? One summer," I begin, "Mia and I took a trip a most wonderful trip to Italy. It's one of my favorite memories."

CHAPTER 62

SEPTEMBER 12 – NINE MONTHS LATER

The bell on the clock tower chimes one time as Mia leaves the Library of Birmingham, England. The trip to the library's archives had provided everything she needed to complete her report on a collection of ancient art objects, mostly small items that were linked to ancient religion.

A black Mercedes pulls to the front of the building and a driver opens Mia's door. A vanilla-scented coffee and a copy of *Time* magazine wait inside. She looks forward to catching up on news from home during the two-hour trip to her London flat.

As the driver maneuvers his way out of the city and into the English countryside, Mia relaxes in the comfort of the spacious back seat and picks up the magazine. The headline read:

SMUGGLING RING VERDICT
NIKKI SANTOS CONVICTED

The photo of Nikki, dressed in an orange jumpsuit, filled the front page. A wave of relief filters through Mia. Nikki, with no makeup or jewelry, still looked beautiful, but now she wore a torment in her eyes and permanent worry lines on her forehead.

Gabriella is still at large, the article confirms. Goosebumps appear on Mia's arm as she thinks about the Christmas package she'd received. Mia let out a long breath and focuses on the hope that the matriarch can't remain hidden from authorities forever. For now, just knowing that Nikki sits behind bars provides a small amount of peace.

It's the anniversary of her parents' deaths, and for the first time, Mia realizes, she is entering the day without her longtime companions—torment, regret, and guilt. Those three had become as familiar as the smell of chamomile tea.

A reminder on her calendar flashes a notification. She checks her watch and dials the number.

"Hola, Mia." The strong voice of her grandmother drifts through the phone.

Mia smiles. "*Buenos Dias, mi Abuela. Como esta?*"

"We are doing well. It's a beautiful Chicago day. Sebastian and I are just leaving the cemetery. How are you, *mi Mia*?"

"Focusing on the future, *mi Abuela*. Focusing on the future."

ACKNOWLEDGMENTS

WRITING A BOOK IS LIKE RUNNING A MARATHON. You don't just get up one day, head to the race, and run. It requires a combination of training, encouragement, and support to cross the finish line.

Training — To the authors who willingly share their expertise on the craft of writing, I am grateful, and I have hungrily devoured your teaching. Special thanks to DiAnn Mills, Jerry Jenkins, and Bill and Lara Bernhardt, for your guidance these past few years.

Encouragement —To each of you who have cheered me on, thank you. Special thanks to my parents, my husband, my children and grandchildren, my extended family, and amazing circle of friends. Your encouragement has kept me running the race.

Support — Thanks to my amazing beta readers. Your insightful feedback challenged me and helped to create a better end product. Thanks to Parker Hathaway for guiding me through the publishing process and connecting me with great talent in editing and graphic design. And a huge thank you to Kristen Chavez, April Jackson, and Vanessa media. I could not have done this without you. You are simply the best.

And to the reader — I am beyond grateful to you. I hope you have enjoyed *Kaleidoscope of Secrets.* Cheers to you, my friends.

Born and raised in Missouri, Sandy Clements writes novels that take readers on a suspenseful journey, leaving them inspired, and ready for the next adventure. Sandy is a lifelong KC Chiefs fan, enjoys travel, and reading a good book. She resides in Missouri with her husband. *Kaleidoscope of Secrets* is her debut novel.

For book club discussion questions, or more information about books by Sandy Clements, visit her website at: **www.sandyclements.com**.